SURPRISE PARTY

SURPRISE PARTY

William Katz

McGRAW-HILL BOOK COMPANY

New York St. Louis San Francisco
Toronto Hamburg Mexico

1 2 3 4 5 6 7 8 9 D O C D O C 8 7 6 5 4

ISBN 0-07-033371-8

LIBRARY OF CONGRESS CATALOGING IN PUBLICATION DATA

Katz, William, 1940-
Surprise Party
I. Title.
PS3561.A777D4 1984 813'.54 84-814
ISBN 0-07-033371-8

Book design by Roberta Rezk

SURPRISE PARTY

Prologue

He looked down at his sixth victim, proud of his work. She lay there, as the others had, utterly still, life taken from her by a combination of two weapons. Her hair, in that bright, wonderful color, was spread out over the grass. She'd be discovered soon, he realized, and the authorities would know that he'd succeeded again. And they would prepare for his next insult.

He had to do it one more time. That was the compact. That was the act of faith. He knew who his victim would be, he knew everything about her. She wouldn't suspect, any more than the others suspected, nor would she resist. She too would play her role as if rehearsed by some gifted director. It would happen on schedule. All his victims died on schedule.

And it would be very easy.

Spencer Cross-Wade looked down at the picture of the sixth victim, baffled. What was the key? What was the formula? What was the motive? Why had this monster eluded him and every other detective on the case? He knew the killer would strike again, and once again Cross-Wade would have to walk up two flights to his superiors and report another dead woman and another fruitless day for the New York Police Department. He was determined that this not happen. It was becoming a passion, an obsession in a career marked by a cool reserve more appropriate for Scotland Yard.

But it *was* a passion.

He *had* to find him.

1

New York, November 198–

They sat opposite each other at breakfast in their spacious five-room apartment overlooking Central Park West. Samantha was thirty-five, with blue eyes and auburn hair that she wore long and loose, and she was incredibly happy. Her eight-month-old marriage to Marty was sublime, and the thought that anything could convulse it, that any horror could shatter it, was inconceivable. Some marriages were made to last, and she believed passionately that this was one of them.

"I'm still bowled over," Marty said.

Samantha smiled, knowing what he meant. "By the party?"

"Yeah."

"Marty, honey, it's weeks away."

"Hey, I've never had my wife throw me a fortieth birthday party before. Let me enjoy it. You making up the list?"

"Sure. I want everyone who means anything to you."

"That's a pretty big bunch."

"I'll get to them early," Samantha said. "I'll bet you don't have a single turn-down."

"Except Mel Pierce. He spends December in Aspen."

"So, he'll send a wire." Samantha leaned forward, across the white tablecloth, closer to Marty's eyes, which, as usual, remained fixed intently on her. "Marty," she asked, "are you absolutely sure about the date?"

"Sure am."

"December fifth?"

"That's my birthday, isn't it?"

"A Thursday."

Marty sighed. "Sam, we went over this. It means a lot to me to have the party right on my birthday. Thursday, December fifth." Then he lowered those eyes, and fell silent for a few moments. Maybe thinking of the little speech he'd make at his own party, Samantha thought, or some friends from the past he wished he could locate. Samantha gazed at him, momentarily contemplated how her life had changed, and realized once again how lucky she was.

A year before, Samantha Reardon had been a second-string copywriter in a small advertising agency, barely keeping up with the rent on what she liked to describe as a "junior studio" in a crumbling section of Manhattan. The men she'd met were mostly combat veterans of screwed up marriages—dazed, weary males with war stories to tell, yearning for someone to listen, someone to take their side against bitchy wives, conniving divorce lawyers, or dive-bombing in-laws. Samantha had put in too many evenings as a professional ear, listening and nodding, sometimes sharing the agony of close male friends whose marriages-made-in-heaven had descended to Civil Court, Part B, Matrimonial. No, that wasn't going to happen to her. She desperately wanted to find someone, a man to love her, one she could love. But she wasn't going to settle for any of the walking wounded. She'd wait, as she'd already waited, for the right man, not just the convenient man.

But she'd tired of waiting, tired of searching, for some ideal who was always just around the bend.

Then, at a party launching an eat-all-you-want diet book, she met Martin Everett Shaw. Marty. Mart. M.E.

Samantha had grown up on Long Island, her father a lawyer for an airline, her mother a high-school English teacher. She had an instinct for elegance and style, and Marty Shaw had both, as well as some more basic animal magnetism. It wasn't simply his imposing height—he had the build of a fullback—or the unerring talent he had for matching the right shirt with the right suit. It was, rather, his indefinable air of being in charge. Marty could walk across a room, make the floorboards rattle, and make it clear that he was getting to the other side no matter what, or who, was in the way. His voice was firm and resonant, and he never raised it. He radiated power. Samantha felt it, reveled in it. She'd imagined he got up at six in the morning to prepare for the day, and time proved her right. She'd imagined he'd work until eleven at night if need be, and time proved her right again.

"Got a big lunch today?" she asked him as he finished his breakfast.

"I don't think so," he replied, placing the napkin neatly back on the table. "But something usually comes up at the last minute. If I'm free I'll wander around a bookstore. There's a new book on corporations I want to pick up."

"Home on time?"

"You jest. I tell you, sweet, when you run your own business you own everything but your time. You ought to see the stack of paperwork."

"Can't someone else...?"

"No. I've got to be my own man."

It was the kind of thing Samantha's own father might have said. In fact, Marty reminded her of her father, which may have been the magic ingredient.

And yet, Marty filled a need that Samantha had felt since childhood. Her home had been cold. Her parents had led independent lives, with little to say to each other, and even less to her. She'd been an only child, but with none of the special attention lavished on her that only children often receive. She'd idolized her father, but only from a distance, and when he died she felt she'd never known him.

Marty gave her the attention and recognition she craved. Even in expensive restaurants he focused on *her*, on what she was saying, as if the exquisite meal were only incidental. With her parents, Samantha had felt like an ornament, the required child in the American home. Marty made her feel wanted, for just being Samantha.

She identified with him, perhaps because she had lost a parent while in her teens, and their similar experiences created an even deeper emotional bond between them. It seemed hard for her to believe that this strong, achieving man had no family at all. She recalled the shock of sympathy she'd felt when he told her how he'd lost both parents in his teens, how he'd worked his way through Northwestern selling magazine subscriptions, how other family members had abandoned and ignored him, how he wished he had a brother or sister. Samantha could imagine him going from town to town after college, getting small jobs in public relations departments of stores and little companies, finally putting some cash together to come to New York and launch his own firm.

Now he had a family, or at least a wife. Now he had someone to talk to, someone who cared about him. Samantha had always imagined herself married to a man with a large family, making visits with him to his old home, having the kind of relationships she'd never had. She abandoned that dream for Marty, and she did so gladly.

There was only one thing that seemed curious about him —those eyes, which sometimes appeared to shift defensively. They were guarded, watchful eyes, and Samantha wondered why. Maybe it was the reality of business competition. Maybe it was Marty's tough early life, his sense of aloneness, a sense that made Samantha want to take care of him.

Her energies now were directed toward his party. Samantha had to tell Marty about it because he often went out of town, and she wanted to be sure that the guest of honor would actually be there. But she kept the one great secret. She was sure he'd never suspect. It would highlight the evening, give him an occasion he'd always remember, and make the event what she really wanted it to be—a *true* surprise party.

Marty glanced at his watch, got up and kissed Samantha with a kind of concentrated affection rare for a successful and harassed executive. "I'm off," he said.

He disappeared out the door, and Samantha soon heard the elevator come up, open, close, then descend again.

She walked across the deep white carpet to the living room window, then gazed down at the winding paths and roadways of Central Park. The last autumn leaves were falling, and she followed one as it floated toward a man of about twenty, his hands stuffed in jacket pockets, walking toward Fifth Avenue. The view of the park and the skyline downtown was sweeping and magnificent, but Samantha knew it wasn't the scenery that gave her, for the first time in her life, such complete peace. She saw Marty rush out the front of the building, then turn and wave up to her. That was it. That was the factor. That was the cake and the frosting as well.

She gazed around her apartment. They'd designed it in modern—lots of whites, some metal, indirect track lighting throughout. It was a contrast to the brooding presence of the half-century-old building, formal with its gray stone facade, more comfortable in an era when doormen wore white gloves and the upper crust arrived in open touring cars. Samantha grabbed a phone, quickly tapping out a familiar number.

"Lynne? Sam. Marty just left. Want to sneak over?"

Lynne was coming. She'd been entrusted with Sam's secret, and it would be a productive day. By this time, Samantha knew, Marty was in a taxi and five or six blocks downtown, heading for his office.

He had entrusted *his* secret to no one.

Lynne Gould was one of those women of endless energy who seemed to get twenty-six hours into every day. She worked for a legion of charities, ran an art gallery, and took care of two young children, all while keeping her short, blond hair absolutely in place. She does it with mirrors, Samantha thought. I'm doing it poorly, Lynne thought. Neither was right. Lynne occupied the apartment across the hall, and had become Samantha's best friend since the Shaws moved in just after their marriage. Samantha was five-three, so Lynne, at five-seven, seemed to tower over her. It would have been intimidating, except Lynne exuded a simple warmth that put the world at ease.

Lynne charged in a few minutes after Samantha called, pencil and pad in hand. "I'm ready," she announced. "I expect to spend the rest of the morning delving into Marty's sordid past."

But Samantha served some coffee first. "You have no idea how much Marty is looking forward to this," she said. "He keeps mentioning it. Even this morning..."

"I'll bet he's never had a party before, at least not as an adult," Lynne replied.

"Since he has no family, you're probably right."

"I'll have to have one for Charles," Lynne said, "if I can get him home long enough to cut the cake."

"I'll do some missionary work," Samantha replied. "I'm sure he'll get the same kick that Marty's getting." Then a slightly troubled look came across Samantha's face. "You're sure this is a good idea?" she asked, looking for encouragement.

"You kidding?" Lynne shot back. "It's sterling. I mean, going back to the beginning of Marty's life, contacting his teachers and professors and all those types, and having them send messages for his birthday. My God, if anyone did that for me, I'd kiss 'em, or more."

"I just hope it doesn't bring up any bad memories."

"Come on, Sam. You know the way Marty talks about his early days. Tough, sure. But he feels nostalgia, like all of us. Look, you're right on target. You're doing *This Is Your Life* for dear old Martin Shaw."

Lynne had volunteered to call the information operators in the places where Marty had lived, worked, or gone to school, to track down the numbers of Marty's old contacts and give them to Samantha. Samantha would actually call the people. Lynne would be saving Samantha considerable time, but, more important, she'd be moral support, a buddy to be with during the party planning.

It wasn't long before Samantha was seated at a small black writing table in the hallway, reaching for her Trimline phone, pressing the 312 area code and a phone number, and waiting, as the clicks brought her closer to her first encounter with Marty's past, the roots he talked about so much.

Her heart began to beat faster. Yes, Lynne was right. This *was* a super scheme, a spectacular love feast. Inevitably, her mind flashed back to Marty's tales of his pranks at Northwestern University's Medill School of Journalism, where, he never tired of telling her, he learned the craft that eventually would make him a public-relations wizard. She remembered him describing how he and a friend from an advertising class had fanned out through Evanston, going door-to-door soliciting orders for gift-wrapped cans of elbow grease. They had gotten, so Marty claimed, twenty-three orders when the dean found out and ordered them to apologize. Their apologies had been so touching, Marty related, that six people reordered.

Samantha's phone connection was completed.

"Medill," an operator said.

"Yes," Samantha answered, "I wonder if someone could help me with a special request."

"Yes, ma'am?" the female voice asked.

"I'd like to get some information about a former student."

"Are you an employer?"

"No, a wife. Well, what I mean is, I'm married to someone from your class of '66. I'm having a birthday party for him and I want to collect old stories, maybe remembrances by professors. That sort of thing."

"That *is* an unusual request."

"I know," Samantha replied, with an embarrassed little laugh. "Look, if it's a bother..."

"Not at all. Give me his name and I'll get out the yearbook. Do you have a copy?"

"No, Marty misplaced it before we were married. His name is Martin Everett Shaw, and he graduated with honors."

"Shore? S-h-o-r-e?"

"No, S-h-a-w."

"I'll check."

There was a long pause. Samantha and Lynne smiled at each other, now that the delightful plot was under way. Samantha cupped her hand over the receiver. "She's looking," she whispered to Lynne. She heard the woman moving around at the other end of the line. Oh, Marty was going to love hearing from those Medill people. Samantha could see the glow on his face already.

The voice came back on the line. "Ma'am, you sure of the class?"

"Yes. Why?"

"There's no Martin Shaw listed."

"That's impossible. Marty always talks about the class of '66."

"Wait a second. Did he get an M.A. or B.A.?"

"Bachelor's."

"Sorry. I had the wrong list. They've got these things all confused here. One moment please."

Samantha waited, winking at Lynne over the delay and tapping a silver Cross ballpoint pen with her right hand.

"Ma'am?"

"Yes."

"He's not on the baccalaureate list either."

"There's obviously some mistake," Samantha said.

"Well, I've checked the yearbook and our own official list of graduates. No Martin Shaw. Is it possible you're confusing us with some other journalism school, like Columbia?"

Samantha felt a little irritation. "I know where my husband went to school," she replied. Then she realized she was being rude to someone trying to help. "I'm sorry. Maybe you've got him listed in the wrong year."

"I've checked our master list of alumni, ma'am," the voice replied stoically. "And I've just punched up the bursar's records on my terminal. That would show his financial payments. No Martin Shaw. There's a David Shaw in '66, but I see he's British. Maybe he was registered under a different name. Has he changed his name?"

"No. He's always been a Shaw."

"I don't know what more we can do," the voice said with a sigh.

Samantha searched her mind for a way out of the confusion. "Marty was feature editor of the newspaper," she recalled. "Even if the other lists have dropped him—somehow—his byline would be there."

"I'll check the bound volumes." The voice was getting annoyed.

"I know I'm asking a lot," Samantha said.

"It's all right. By the way, does your husband get alumni mail?"

Samantha thought for a moment. "I haven't seen any. But he's moved quite a bit and..."

"Our graduates are journalists. They often move, and we follow them." Now the voice was abrupt, delivering a message. But Samantha didn't catch on. She heard the woman leafing through pages...many pages.

"No," the answer finally came. "I've checked six issues of the paper from '66. Someone else was feature editor."

"Impossible."

The voice let out a long, impatient breath. "Ma'am, may I speak frankly?"

Samantha was startled by the question. "Of course."

"This happens all the time, ma'am."

"What do you mean?"

"Maybe you'd better ask your husband." There was a touch of sympathy now.

"Why?"

"Mrs. Shaw, it's obvious that your husband never attended this school, and I *hope* he isn't using our name to secure employment. If we found out, we would instantly notify..."

"Thank you very much." Samantha hung up, actually growled at the phone, then pushed her pen aside. "Would you believe that?" she asked Lynne. "Would you believe they can't find Marty's name? An honor graduate? A journalism school? Can you believe the incompetence?"

"Yes," Lynne replied. "It's those damn computers. They probably lost his name from one of those little discs. I bet all she did was punch some button. No name, no deal."

"But she looked through books."

"That's what she said. Sam, it's an old story with these college computers. They got all my brother's grades wrong. We'll straighten it out."

"I know that," Samantha answered, trying to shrug off the incident. But inside she was going through a mixture of anger and denial. Not for a second did she believe that Marty had lied about his background. That wasn't Marty, and she knew him inside out. She also knew what she'd do next. She'd call the dean, not some flunkie in the office. She'd get the information she wanted.

But when she called, she was told the dean was at a meeting. She'd have to call back.

"You want to make some other calls?" Lynne asked. "I've got the number for the Elkhart town hall."

"I want to nail down the college stuff first, before calling his home town," Samantha replied. "Let's talk war plans."

"Sure."

Samantha reached into her table drawer and took out a copy of *New York Magazine*. She turned to an ad near the rear and handed the magazine to Lynne. "There's a guy here who videotapes birthday parties."

"That's a great idea."

"You think anyone would mind?"

"If they mind," Lynne said, "they can turn away from the camera. We take movies. I think this is better. It's got sound and everything."

"I'll give him a call," Samantha said, jotting down a note. "If Marty knew what this cost, he'd lynch me."

"Sam," Lynne rebutted, "men never lynch when the cash is spent on *them*. If we spend it on *us*, the rope comes out. That's a word of wisdom. My brother told me. He's a divorce lawyer."

Samantha and Lynne talked on, getting to the menu. Marty was meat and potatoes, so the menu would be...meat and potatoes, but served elegantly and romantically. Samantha made a few additions to a guest list that was already too large, a tribute to the many friends Marty had made in New York. She wanted a live band too. Now *that* was expensive, but Marty liked Broadway music, so Samantha phoned a little group from the Juilliard School that entertained at parties, playing anything from classics to pops.

"Why don't you try that dean again?" Lynne asked after an hour.

Samantha reached for the phone, then stopped. She wanted to call that dean. Of course she did. She wanted to get the whole Medill business taken care of. But she also looked into Lynne's eyes, and what she saw made her a little uneasy. There was anticipation in those best friend's eyes, and curiosity. Maybe there was too much curiosity. Was it possible that Lynne thought Marty hadn't attended...? No, Lynne wasn't that way. She was too loyal. But, somehow, Samantha almost wished that Lynne wasn't there for the call. Sure, it was a gigantic mix-up, but it was an *embarrassing* mix-up as well, and even among friends these things could get awkward. After all, what if the dean couldn't find Marty's name either? What would Lynne think? What would Lynne say to her husband?

"I don't feel like calling now," Samantha said abruptly. "I'll call later."

She needed some ammunition for that second call, and she knew where to get it: from Marty himself. She was sure there was no problem.

2

The only thing Marty worried about was seeing someone he knew. Why was Martin Everett Shaw getting off a subway in Queens at lunchtime on a business day? Of course, Marty would have a quick explanation. Marty Shaw *always* came up with the right words. But this was one day he didn't want to be noticed.

He walked down the packed street in Forest Hills, the cold wind hitting him in the face. He hated days like this. His mind became a blur of images, memories fueling a growing rage. He noticed a red light just as he was stepping off a curb. He quickly stepped back. He tried to clear his mind, but knew from habit that he couldn't, that this episode would have to run its course. And each time one of these things erupted inside him, he felt tremendous guilt, but the need finally to set things right had begun to grow, to overwhelm him.

He saw Granville's Hardware Store, one of the larger shops on the Boulevard. He had not phoned ahead. He didn't want to call attention to himself, to have someone remember his call later. Marty didn't know if Granville's carried what he wanted, but he assumed a store its size would. It was urgent. There were things he had to have. Automatically he straightened his striped silk tie and ran his right hand through his hair. Look right. Look normal. Look confident. Don't seem anxious. You're only buying things a lot of people buy. Pay by cash. No credit cards. No name on the receipt.

Granville's was one of those hardware stores where a person had to squeeze down each narrow, dark aisle, between hooks bulging with light sockets, bags of screws, and gaudy numerals for front doors. Marty moved slowly down an aisle, noticing that he was one of the few customers. But there were enough others for him not to feel conspicuous. He feigned a look of confusion, drawing a tired salesman with a narrow mustache.

"Lookin' for something?"

"Uh, yes," Marty replied. "I need one of those sockets that you screw in, the kind that takes a bulb."

"Look, I got a million sockets in here. You want one with a pull chain?"

"Yes, that's the kind."

"Right here."

The salesman was slightly hunched and had a strong scent of low-grade tobacco. Marty followed him down the aisle to the electrical-supply section. The salesman pulled a socket from its hook. "This is what you want. Anything else?"

"Uh, let me think," Marty answered.

"Think all you like."

The light socket was a ploy. Marty always bought extra items to hide the ones he really wanted. "I need a Roberts tackhammer," he finally said, fearful that he may have sounded too anxious.

"A what?" the salesman snapped, throwing Marty a look reserved for men who didn't know hardware.

"A Roberts. Tackhammer."

The salesman grunted and shook his head. "I never seen

a guy who wanted a brand of hammer. A hammer's a hammer. Look, I got Stanley, I got Skil, I got...what the hell's the name of it? But Roberts? I ain't seen that one in..."

"But you've heard of it." There was an unintended intensity in Marty's large, green eyes.

"Sure I heard of it."

"Where could I get one?"

"You gotta have *that* kind? Look, fella, the Stanley is better. You read *Consumer's*? It lasts..."

"I want the Roberts."

The salesman threw up his hands in surrender. "Just helpin'. Try Becker. He's two blocks down. He's got Roberts. Somethin' else?"

"A bicycle chain."

"That I got."

"I want one with a red rubber coating over the links." The salesman took a deep, disgusted breath. "How 'bout flowers on it?"

Marty ignored him.

"Gotta be red?" the salesman asked.

Marty thought back. Yes, it had to be red. "Red," he answered, his voice now its usual assertive self.

"I got one."

The salesman led Marty to the toy and game department and picked out a bicycle chain covered in red rubber. Marty took it from him, curling his strong fingers over the links as if caressing it. It was heavy. It *had* to be heavy. He wound it around his right hand like a snake, then let it hang down. But he quickly realized he was focusing too much attention on it. "I'll take this," he said. "That's all."

He left the store with the light socket and chain in a brown paper bag, and walked toward Becker's. As he walked, he slipped the bag into his leather attaché case. "This is for you," he whispered, hardly moving his lips, as if talking to someone close by.

But still, nothing showed on the outside. Marty Shaw was

just another businessman walking down the street. Not even Samantha had an inkling of the turmoil stirring inside the man she thought ideal.

He glanced at his Rolex Submariner watch. It was 1:46. He was due at his office for an appointment at three. It was important to be on time, important to avoid questions. He walked faster. He found Becker's, a store slightly larger than Granville's. Marty walked in, feeling awkward about having been in a competing store, and fearing that he'd be asked to show the contents of his attaché case before leaving. After all, a sign posted at the entrance said, "We reserve the right to inspect all packages." Hiram Becker, tall and elderly, walked over to him.

"Need help?"

"Yes," Marty replied. "I need a tackhammer, a Roberts."

"I carry Roberts."

"It has a light handle and the head is painted black."

"Insist on that model?"

"It's a gift for my son. It matches his other tools."

"I'll look. I'm a franchised dealer. Authorized."

Marty felt the tension well up inside him. What a waste of time if Becker didn't have that hammer.

Becker disappeared into his rear storeroom, then came back carrying the Roberts hammer, sealed in a plastic enclosure glued to a piece of cardboard. "Here, I got it," he said. "Last one."

Relieved, Marty followed Becker down a dusty aisle, paid the $3.98 plus tax and quickly left the store. No one asked him to open his case.

He walked down Queens Boulevard, heading for a subway that would take him back to Manhattan. He knew there were other things to do before December fifth, but they could wait. The trains were no problem. The right set could be picked up in bits and pieces around town. Samantha would accept the explanations about new things being brought into the apartment. Samantha was always so understanding. She was perfect.

Marty boarded the subway, sitting next to an alcoholic old woman in an overheated car for most of the ride. He gripped his case tightly, but, finally realizing his knuckles were turning white, transferred the case to the floor between his feet. As the train rattled towards his stop, Rockefeller Center, his eyes shifted around, exhibiting the wary defensiveness that Samantha so often noticed. He didn't want anyone making a try for that expensive-looking case. Too much had been invested in what was inside.

When the train arrived, he walked up the station steps past shoppers heading toward Fifth Avenue for early Christmas buying.

Shaw Enterprises had four offices on the twelfth floor of 1290 Avenue of the Americas, a modern stone and metal building whose only distinction was having a Sam Goody record store in the lobby. Marty's offices were the artistic reverse of the neat, functional styling of his apartment. Here everything was in lavish, curving French design, more like a museum than a business office. The windows were outlined with heavy drapes, and the prints on the wall were mounted in gold-leaf, ornate frames. He had reasons for the choices, he'd told Samantha, but he never discussed what they were.

Even before he entered, Marty's heavy tread tipped the staff that he had returned. He smiled as he opened the large oak door. Be positive, he kept telling himself. Only the positive get along.

"Afternoon, everyone. Calls?"

Lois Carroll, his twenty-year-old secretary, instantly handed Marty four pink sheets as he stopped at her desk. He gently put his case on the floor and flipped through them.

"What did CBS want?"

"Warner Wolf needs an interview with the girl who's trying out for the new football team," Lois answered. "Since we represent the team...."

"Let's hold off on that," Marty said. "I'll call Warner and offer him something else. I don't like that image for the team." He turned to another call sheet. "*Newsweek*?"

"Just to say they don't want the story of Rohr-Tech's water-softening process."

"Hell with them. The world's most quoted newsweekly doesn't know pure water when they drink it. I guess this one from Princess Fashions is about our billing."

"Naturally."

Marty ignored it and turned to the last sheet. "What'd Samantha want?"

"Just for you to call back. She was a little..."

"A little what?"

"Tense."

"Sick?"

"No, just not your usual laid-back Samantha."

"My home number please."

Marty rushed into his twenty-by-thirteen office, its light brown walls lined with framed copies of stories he'd placed in magazines and newspapers. As he sat at his desk, Lois made the call. She made it quickly, feeling the pressure of Marty's concern. Everyone in the office knew how Marty protected Samantha, how he watched out for her, how he worried about her in the big city. He would constantly ask Lois's advice on gifts to buy Samantha, and where to get them. It was an old-style devotion, Lois thought, rare for those in the crazed media world. She wished *she* had a husband like Marty Shaw.

"I have Samantha," she said over the intercom.

Marty picked up. "Sam?"

"Sweet, I called before but you'd just gone out."

"Is something wrong?"

"Oh no. Not at all."

"Sam, you sound a little shaky." Samantha couldn't hide her continued annoyance over the Northwestern flap. "I'm fine, Marty."

"You sure? You usually don't call at midday."

"No, really. You sound like my mother. I'm just a little tired. I actually called because I was getting things together for the great gala. There's a guy who videotapes these things. I think it's terrific, unless you're against it."

"Why should I be against it? How much?"

"That's a private matter, Mr. Shaw."

"Forge on."

"I have to arrange it early. Otherwise, I wouldn't bother you at work."

"Sam, you never bother me."

"Oh, that's so, so good to hear. Say, Martin Everett Shaw, I had another bright idea: framing your college diploma and having it up for the party. You've never done that and..."

"Sam, you know I don't believe in that stuff."

"Yeah, but I do. Marty, I'm proud of you. I want the world to know."

"Can I exercise my veto?" Marty asked, a slight touch of embarrassed laughter in his voice.

Samantha hesitated. "Well, as president of Shaw Enterprises, I guess you have the power. But Marty, you should at least preserve the diploma. Don't ignore those things. I'll take care of it. Where is it?"

There was a long, painful pause. "You know," Marty answered, "I don't even remember where it is."

A chill shot through Samantha's body. That wasn't the reply she wanted. She'd never doubted Marty. She wasn't ready to doubt him, emotionally or rationally. "Think, genius," she told him, trying powerfully to hide her heightened concern.

"Gee, I..."

"Try." In a way, Samantha was almost begging, almost praying that this good man hadn't faked his educational background, as, she knew, so many others had.

Marty snapped his fingers. "Sure," he recalled. "With all that moving I shunted some old documents around. You know that pile of papers in the file drawer of my desk?"

"It's not stuffed in there, is it?" Samantha asked, scoldingly.

"Guilty. My sincere apologies to the Medill School of Journalism, Lawrence S. Krieger, dean and general bore." Marty smiled broadly, exposing an oversized and not entirely straight set of teeth.

"I'll rescue it," Samantha sighed. "Look, you're busy. I'll let you go."

"I'm home by seven."

"Bye, love."

They hung up. Marty was a bit baffled. Why had Samantha called him about the videotape instead of waiting until he got home? Did she *really* think those camera guys would be busy on a Thursday night in December? And who cared about a sheepskin? Sam was usually so casual, so much the opposite of urgency. Maybe it was the challenge of throwing a big party for the first time.

Marty forgot about it.

Samantha rushed to Marty's desk and rummaged through the papers. Soon she found the large blue folder with the raised seal of Northwestern University. Quickly, but with a reverence mirrored in the gentle touch of her hands, she opened the folder and slid out a piece of stiff parchment protected by tissue paper. She could feel the relief overcoming her. Of *course* that lady at the school had been wrong. Here was undeniable concrete proof. Samantha examined the diploma carefully, feeling closer to Marty's past simply by holding it.

MARTIN EVERETT SHAW
Bachelor of Arts with Honors
June 16, 1966

She slipped the diploma back in its folder and put it in a fireproof cabinet for safekeeping. Now she felt guilty for having asked Marty about the document. She'd never need such reassurance again, she told herself. Never again.

She sat down to do some more party planning, then placed her right hand on her stomach. Samantha tried to restrain her hope that December fifth would bring, not only a great party, but an announcement of even greater joy. How Marty wanted it! There were some signs that it might happen. She'd made an appointment with her doctor. Now she hoped, and prayed.

Martin Everett Shaw slowly dialed the combination on his office wall safe. The dial locked at 18 and he swung open the armored door, which was at eye level. Aside from a brown envelope, the safe was empty. Marty carefully placed the tackhammer and bicycle chain inside, pushing both items toward the back. He recalled how he had put the last hammer and chain inside the year before, and how he had hidden the previous ones in the bottom of an old photographic case.

He gazed at the brown envelope, his eyes and body motionless, as if it contained some holy artifact. He reached in and took it out, placing it on his cluttered desk. Then he walked to the door and locked it, and closed the curtain on the one large picture window. He was alone, completely at one with himself, isolated from a world that he saw differently from others. He walked back to his desk, sat, and opened the envelope. Inside was a set of newspaper clippings, bound with a rubber band, some yellowed, some more recent. They were from all over the country.

Marty snapped on his intercom. "No calls, please," he said. He picked one clipping near the top of the pack. He had read it many times before, but he particularly liked its tone and style. And, through his public-relations work, he knew the reporter. He read the story again, savoring each word:

"Connecticut State Police were baffled today by the discovery, in a patch of grass just off Route I-95 near Greenwich, of a..."

3

Samantha once again put off her second call to Northwestern. Yes, she had the "ammunition" that she needed in the form of Marty's diploma, but she was still offended by the response to her first call, and her very human reaction was to find other things to do. She arranged for the videotaping, walked up to Gartner's Hardware on West 72nd Street to buy a new toaster, and went to the Ansonia post office to get a roll of one hundred stamps. Her plans for the party were big, and getting bigger.

She alternately repressed and exulted in her schedule for the next day. When morning came she saw Marty off to work and hopped into a cab. She'd kept her appointment a secret from him. Why get him excited? Why build up hope that might turn out to be false? But her heart pounded as the cab headed east into Central Park and beyond, then south—past Bloomingdale's and Alexander's, and on further. Samantha finally saw the stark white buildings ahead, buildings that, she knew, would play an overwhelming part in her life, and Marty's.

University Hospital, on First Avenue in the thirties, is the more elegant half of the NYU—Bellevue Medical Center. When the cab pulled into its circular driveway, Samantha paid the driver and walked into one of the white towers she had seen from the distance.

"Dr. Fromer?" she asked a uniformed guard inside the revolving door. She knew he had moved his office.

"Five sixteen," the rotund guard replied.

Samantha took the elevator. Now the pounding heart was joined by a tension in her throat and stomach. She identified herself to Fromer's nurse and waited more than forty-five minutes before her examination.

Harold Fromer was approaching fifty, heavy and tired, with a drooping chin and thinning hair. And yet he was quiet and attentive, and a thoroughly reliable physician. He spoke in an offhand manner, but was particularly careful not to patronize his generally much younger patients.

After his examination and tests, he ushered Samantha into his small, institutionally decorated office, which Samantha thought looked more like the hideaway of a corporate treasurer than a place where medical confidences were exchanged.

"What do you want me to say?" Fromer asked as he collapsed his frame behind the laminated desk. He said it with a smile. He'd been Samantha's doctor for twelve years.

"Tell me that we'd better start thinking about college," Samantha replied.

"Start thinking."

"You sure?"

Fromer shrugged. "The lab technician flipped a coin, and came up with the answer. That's the best we can do."

Strange, but Samantha felt remarkably calm. She didn't jump up, or laugh, or cry. Rather, a kind of spiritual serenity came over her. Perhaps it was because she had been anticipating Fromer's diagnosis. Perhaps it was because she knew this would bring Marty and her even closer together, or perhaps it was because the thought of bringing up a child would remind Marty of his own unhappy childhood. He'd want to give this baby everything he never had.

"Well," she asked, her face finally breaking out in a glow, "what do I do?"

"Well, you celebrate," Fromer replied. "Aren't you happy?"

"Of course I'm happy."

"Does your husband want a baby, too?"

"Sure. He participated. He was a volunteer."

Fromer laughed awkwardly. He always laughed awkwardly. He thought laughing made a man less manly. "I see no reason why you shouldn't have a normal pregnancy," he said. Then he carefully explained all that Samantha had to know, and the changes she would experience.

"I'm guessing I'm in my second month," she said.

"You're about right. When we start using the ultrasound to examine you I can be more precise. Would you want to know the sex of the baby beforehand?"

"No."

"Really?" Fromer's eyes widened. Samantha was in a decided minority. "You'd only have to choose one name. You could get ready..."

Samantha shrugged. "We're a little old-fashioned. I think we'd like to do things the way people used to do them."

"I see." Fromer frowned a bit, then tapped a pencil on his desk. Samantha watched the pencil as Fromer manipulated it with his pudgy hands. He seemed concerned.

"Are you holding something back?" he asked.

Samantha stiffened slightly. "What do you mean?"

"You were a little more tense than usual during the examination. When you brought up your husband I could detect a little...unease. This is a time for you to be relaxed, not under stress. If there's a problem..."

"Problem?"

"I mean, in the marriage."

"Not at all." Samantha was slightly offended, but knew that Fromer meant well.

"Okay, but should there be, you should consider counseling. Some people with... marital difficulties... have a baby because they think it'll make the marriage better. It doesn't. Just a little doctorly advice."

"I'm having a big party for Marty," Samantha said. "It's on my mind. Maybe that's why I seem a little less bouncy."

"Right," Fromer replied. "Just stay calm. The first three months are a bit touchy." Fromer actually came out from behind his desk and kissed Samantha on the cheek, something he saw as an obstetrical prerogative. "Congratulations," he said. "You'll be fine."

"Thank you. When do you want to see me again?"

"A month. Then every month after that."

Samantha started to get up, then fidgeted a little with her Coach leather bag. "Uh, we haven't even mentioned..."

"Cost."

"Yeah." Samantha *was* old-fashioned—she hated to discuss money with a doctor.

"Everything is in this booklet," Fromer replied. "If there's a question, just ask me. You... have insurance?"

"Blue Cross. Major medical."

"You're home. Go give your husband the news."

They chatted for a few more moments about nothing in particular, then Fromer escorted Samantha out a side door that led to the noisy, bustling main corridor.

As she rode down in the elevator, the serenity that Samantha felt in Fromer's office began to melt away, and she sensed her insides filling with an unbridled joy. She started smiling, not even realizing it, drawing curious glances from doctors and patients. Instinctively she placed her hand in front of her stomach as other passengers boarded and the crush became greater.

"Pregnant?" a doctor next to her asked.

Now she was deathly embarrassed, feeling ever so uncool. "Oh, no," she replied. It was stupid. It was the last time she'd ever deny it. When she left the building and got into a cab her first words were, "I'm pregnant. Drive slowly." The driver smiled condescendingly, then actually followed her instructions.

Lynne was waiting outside their apartment building on Central Park West. Her instinct gave her all the information she needed.

"It's a go," she said as Samantha stepped out of the cab, into a light, windy drizzle.

"It's a go," Samantha confirmed.

"I knew it. I can tell by the texture of people's skin."

"Come on."

"Doctors have their ways, I have mine." Lynne let out a laugh, grabbed Samantha's arm, and steered her into the building. The doorman, no gloves, opened the door, oblivious to their excitement.

Their heels clicked as they walked through the lobby, almost entirely marble and lit by a huge crystal chandelier that reminded comers and goers of the building's great days. "You have to make a big dinner," Lynne said, insistently pushing the elevator button.

"Why?"

"Why? Why, she asks. When you get pregnant, you make a big dinner to tell your husband. Didn't you ever see it in the movies? It's the American way."

"I'm not telling Marty."

"You're not... You're putting me on."

"I thought about it in the cab," Samantha said. "I'm telling him at the party. I'm announcing it. I want everyone to see his face."

"He'll faint."

"No. He may cry a little."

Lynne began warming to the idea. "Well, you'll have those videotape guys. Boy, what a moment to remember. Yeah, it's a great idea. Tell him at the party. I told Charlie at my mother's house, after a fight."

"I just want to see Marty's face," Samantha said, more to herself than to Lynne. "Just that face."

They went back to Samantha's apartment, which was freezing because Samantha had forgotten to turn up the heat before leaving. She snapped on the thermostat and kept her coat on. "Want to lie down?" Lynne asked. "It's another tradition."

"I want to work," Samantha replied.

"Hero mother. Boy, I can just see you having that baby without help. Yeah, you're the type. Hey, I collected more numbers for you. You ever call Northwestern back?"

"No, I'll save that," Samantha said. She turned around to gaze into Lynne's eyes, looking for the curiosity she'd seen earlier. She found it.

"Okay," Lynne answered, whipping a pad from her handbag. "Here's the number for George Braden Elementary School, Elkhart, Indiana. Marty's first alma mater."

Samantha beamed, feeling herself back in the rhythm of party planning. She sat down at her small table, jotting some notes on what she would ask the people at Braden. She knew she had to be careful. Universities might be used to recalling their alumni, but it wasn't an elementary school specialty. She dialed.

"Braden," answered the dry Midwestern female voice.

"Yes, hello," Samantha said, a little nervous, "I'm calling from New York."

"New York City?"

"Yes. It's about my husband. He was a student at Braden."

"Oh dear, that must have been a few years ago."

"Yes, it was in the late forties and early fifties."

"Do you need a school certificate, ma'am?"

"No," Samantha replied, "this is actually an odd request. I'm having a fortieth birthday party for him..."

"How nice."

"...and I wanted to collect the remembrances of old friends and teachers. Is there a way I can get the names of his teachers, and his principal?"

"Well... I guess so. Some of the teachers might be..."

"Deceased."

"Yes. But the principal is the same."

"Really?"

"Mr. Cotrell took over in his twenties back then. He's still here."

"And the teachers?"

"Those records would be in the district warehouse. We only keep them five years."

"Could someone look? I mean, I'd be happy to pay." Samantha smiled over at Lynne, feeling once more that she was getting close to Marty's past.

"I could have someone check, ma'am. There's a ten dollar search fee. Oh, would you like to speak with Mr. Cotrell in the meantime? He's in his office."

Samantha hesitated. School principals had always intimidated her. The principal was the person you never spoke to unless asked. But this was special, and Samantha overcame her girlhood fears. "Yes," she said, "I'd love that."

"Your name, ma'am?"

"Samantha Shaw. My husband is Martin Everett Shaw."

"One moment."

Samantha heard clicks on the line, and cupped her hand over the receiver. "She's connecting me to the principal," she told Lynne. "He was there with Marty." She heard a phone being picked up.

"Lou Cotrell, Mrs. Shaw," came the cheerful, singsongy voice, a testament to the notion that principals and pediatricians sometimes take on the personalities of their charges. "I remember your husband well."

"You do?" Samantha asked excitedly.

"Shaw was a hell raiser. Always the devil."

"That's Marty."

"Thin little boy."

"No, heavy."

"Well, they change. You're feeding him too well."

"Probably."

"Surprised to hear Martin's in New York. He was one of those real outdoors types. Sorry he never came back to visit us. I'd like to see him."

"I'll make a note of that," Samantha said. "I'll insist that he go back. Both of us, in fact."

"Just grand. Now, my assistant tells me you'd like some remembrances."

"Yes."

"I'll dig 'em up. I'll give you some myself. Tell you what, do you have one of those cassette machines?"

"Yes, we do."

"I'll make a little tape for you."

"Wonderful!"

"You just give me the address. And you tell Martin that the old schoolyard is just waitin' for him to dig it up again."

"Thank you, Mr. Cotrell."

"Lou. We're all adults now."

"Thank you, Lou."

"Thank *you* for thinking of us, Mrs. Shaw."

They both laughed. Samantha gave Cotrell her address, and added the phone number in case he had some last-minute thoughts. She also cautioned him that this was a surprise and asked that the tape be sent on a Monday so it would arrive midweek, when Marty wasn't home. Every detail had to be covered, Samantha realized. Then she felt compelled, because of her deep feelings for Marty, to add something.

"Mr. Cotrell, do you remember anything about Marty's parents—warm stories, anecdotes, that kind of thing?"

"I remember them as nice people."

"Well, unfortunately, they died rather young. Both while Marty was in his teens."

"That's so sad," Cotrell said.

"It was tough for Marty, but he worked his way through Northwestern."

"That's Martin's spirit."

"Yes, it is. Thank you again, Mr. Cotrell. Lou."

They hung up. "Well, that was terrific!" Samantha told Lynne.

"I got the drift," Lynne replied. "Now you're cookin'."

"I'd better have our tape machine checked," Samantha reminded herself. "It was jamming last week. I don't want a December fifth disaster with Mr. Cotrell's extravaganza."

"I got a guy for that. I'll send him." Then Lynne looked at the Mickey Mouse watch she'd gotten at Disneyland. "Hey, gotta dash," she said. "Big art shindig downtown. Rich bores and all."

As was Lynne's style, she was gone in seconds, with no long goodbyes. Now Samantha was alone, feeling extremely good about herself, about Marty, about life. She'd had a completely successful day.

She took out Dr. Fromer's pamphlet and started reading. It was straightforward, describing the techniques Fromer would use to check the pregnancy, pointing out that the mother would feel the baby move about the fifth month, and warning against smoking and drugs. But there was a particularly impassioned section about the dangers of having the baby away from the hospital. Fromer was a fanatic about this, listing all the emergency equipment the hospital had that would not be available to a woman who delivered, say, at home. Samantha took note. She'd go to the hospital.

She was reading the section on the hospital's nursery—it had a large viewing window for relatives to observe the little princes and princesses—when the phone rang. Samantha assumed it was Marty, and picked up.

It wasn't Marty.

"Mrs. Shaw?"

She knew the voice instantly. "Mr. Cotrell, Lou, how nice of you to call back so soon. Did you dig up something about my husband?"

"Well, that's what I called about."

"Let me get a pad and pencil to take it all down."

"That won't be necessary, Mrs. Shaw. I'm afraid...oh, this *is* embarrassing."

"Embarrassing?"

"Well, let me put it this way. You know, it's awfully easy to get mixed up when you've known so many children."

"Of course."

"And my memory...I guess I'm the absent-minded professor. When you called I had a youngster in mind, and I remembered him as Martin Shaw. But...well, the name wasn't Martin, it was Melvin. Mel Shaw."

"You don't remember my husband?"

"You said his parents were dead, rest 'em. This youngster's mother is alive, and still living here. That's what jolted my memory."

Samantha sensed how mortified Cotrell was, and felt for him. "Lou," she said, "it's okay. How could you possibly remember all your students? Look, I do appreciate your calling. We'll have the school records, and maybe some teachers will remember..."

"That's the other problem, Mrs. Shaw."

"I beg your pardon?"

"I sent over for the records. They don't show a Martin Shaw."

"What?"

"Surprised me too. Now, occasionally a pupil's record for one year is lost. But *all* his are missing."

The Northwestern call flashed violently through Samantha's mind, but she repressed it. The world was full of mistakes. She'd simply run into two in a row. "Martin went to Braden," she said, almost too firmly. "He talks about it."

"I understand."

"Well, what can we do?"

"I really don't know, Mrs. Shaw. Without the records we're kind of lost. All I can think of is that they were requested before and were taken out and left somewhere."

"That must be it," Samantha replied, grasping for any straw.

"But that doesn't explain the pictures."

"Pictures?"

"Class pictures. Every class gets its picture taken every year. I had them check the pictures. No Martin."

"He could've been absent," Samantha retorted.

"Six years in a row?"

There was a long silence, the kind of silence Samantha had experienced during the Northwestern call. She finally broke it. "Lou," she asked, a little defensively, "what does this mean?"

Cotrell laughed, but it was an uneasy, not entirely friendly laugh. "Well," he said, "maybe we've got a mistake here."

"Please explain that, Lou."

"Must I?"

A chill shot up Samantha's spine. "I would...appreciate it."

"Well, all right, here goes. You know, sometimes a kid comes from a poor family, and when he grows up he's embarrassed about it. So he...improves on his background." Another uneasy laugh.

"I see," Samantha said quietly.

"It's hardly the worst thing, Mrs. Shaw. There are some outlying areas around Elkhart...modest areas...and maybe Martin thought Elkhart sounded better."

"I can't believe that," Samantha whispered.

"If there's anything more I can do, please call," Cotrell continued. "Goodbye now."

Samantha hung up the phone, stunned. She was relieved only that Lynne wasn't there to see her embarrassment. But no, she thought. This couldn't be. Marty couldn't be hiding his past from her. He'd spoken about Braden too often, in great detail. People who have something to hide avoid subjects altogether. Her own grandfather had an alcohol problem, so he never discussed drinking. And the Northwestern thing had worked itself out when she found Marty's diploma. No, this was just another case of poor recordkeeping. It was understandable. Old records and pictures got lost, and Cotrell simply had to cover for his school. After a few minutes, Samantha began feeling good again, convinced that this flap, like the first, would end happily.

She did feel, though, that some of the fun, the zip, had

been taken out of the party planning by these foul-ups. She hungered for the first call to someone who remembered Marty, knew a lot about him, and hadn't lost a chunk of his past.

For Marty, it was another lunch hour of shopping. This time he was in Brooklyn, on 13th Avenue, which was crammed with mothers, baby carriages, assorted pickpockets, and sidewalk hawkers selling guaranteed genuine solid gold Omega watches for $29.95. It was an avenue of small, independent shops, a throwback to the era of the little guy and the closely knit neighborhood. It wasn't stylish—it was a kind of organized chaos—and Marty felt like an alien. But that was the point, as it had been in Queens. No one was likely to recognize him here.

He walked down the packed avenue, and again there were the cold winds. Again the bitter memories erupted inside him. Words shot through his mind, words that he associated with cold winds.

"You only care about him, not me!" she'd screamed. *I'm just garbage. I just clean up and wipe their mouths! You bring 'em toys! What am I doin' with you?"*

"Come on, it's his birthday. It only comes once a year, Alice."

"You're a bum! Go play with your trains!"

"I'm not a bum. I need a break."

"Other men don't need no breaks!"

The words reverberated in his brain, and Marty knew they'd be there as long as he lived. He looked around at the addresses now, trying to find Walson's, a well known toy and hobby store. In this case he had had to call ahead because he needed a number of specific items. Walson's had most of them. No store ever had everything. It wasn't like the old days. He finally found Walson's between a luncheonette and a dry cleaner, in the middle of a block with no fewer than three bakeries. He was immediately impressed with the place.

A good hobby shop had model planes and trains jammed end to end. It had kits that were impossible to find and back issues of such magazines as *Model Railroading*. It had concave-chested, thick-spectacled salesmen in their early twenties who could tell you every engine that Lionel Trains had ever manufactured, and the year it came out. Finally, it had customers who liked to hang around on Saturdays and debate the esoterica of the world of models. Walson's had it all.

"Need help?" asked a young salesman with an enthusiasm that said "Let me tell you everything I know."

"I called," Marty replied. "I spoke to Steve." Salesmen in hobby shops never have last names.

"I'm Steve." Yes, he had glasses, the concave chest, and the required plaid shirt. "You wanted the diesel switcher."

"Yes."

"Over here."

Steve led Marty to a dusty section at the back where used electric trains were sold. Marty recognized the orange and blue Lionel boxes from the early fifties. He thought it amazing that people kept those old boxes and returned them when they sold their trains, sometimes a generation later.

"Here we go," Steve said. He pulled out an orange and blue box. Inside was a black, square-shaped locomotive with the Santa Fe insignia on its side. "Santa Fe," Steve said. "That's the one you wanted, right?"

"Yes, exactly," Marty replied, holding the engine in his hand and caressing it.

"We also have Chesapeake and Ohio."

"No, this is the one."

"We can put any emblem on there. We have this artist..."

"No, I want Santa Fe."

"Fine. It's in good shape."

"How much?"

"One twenty."

"I'll take it."

"Okay. You know about the magne-traction?"

"Yes. I had one of these."

"It's a magnet that holds the engine to the tracks."

"Yes," Marty repeated, "I know. I had one." Steve was already driving him crazy, but he refused to show annoyance. Annoyed people were remembered.

"You wanted a milk car, I think," Steve said.

"That's right."

"I've got it, but only with five milk cans. It works, though."

"If it works, I want it."

"Dented platform, too."

"I'll still take it."

"You have the automatic track? It only works when it's on the auto track."

"I'll need one," Marty replied. Now his mind came alive again with memories: how he pressed the little red button attached to the auto track, how the man shot out of the milk car and delivered the silver cans to the platform, how the mechanism buzzed. And he remembered the voice. *"Are you happy, Frankie? Is this what you wanted?"* It was such a kind voice, a good voice. *"Frankie, this is for you."* Marty seemed to be in another world.

"You okay, mister?" Steve asked.

"Oh, sure," Marty replied. "Just tired."

"Yeah. All this Christmas shopping. Mostly new stuff, though. You givin' these antiques for Christmas? Great gift."

"No, it's for me. I'm a hobbyist. I've always liked Lionel trains, but the old ones were better."

"That's for sure," Steve said. "That's why we can get these prices."

"Okay," Marty continued, pressing on, "I need the old work train caboose. The gray one."

"Have it."

"Automatic boxcar."

"Yup."

"On the phone you said you didn't know if you had the cattle car."

"I looked," Steve answered. "Don't have it. They go out faster than they come in. I can't promise anything on that one."

Marty requested a few more items and made a mental note of what he still had to get. Steve wrapped the package and Marty paid in cash—$371.86. There were no signatures to trace.

Marty felt a special thrill holding the trains as he walked down 13th Avenue, heading for a subway. He'd loved his trains, even though he'd had them only a few days. He wondered—he knew it was a fantasy—whether these were *the* trains, the very ones he'd been given. Someone could have sold them to Walson's. He knew it was a distant long shot, but it was possible.

Since he'd told Steve the trains were for himself he couldn't ask that they be gift-wrapped. Yet they had to be. He wanted his office staff to think they were simply Christmas gifts for business associates. He didn't want anyone seeing the store name. So he went into a card shop, bought some wrapping paper and tape, sat down at a bus-stop bench, and wrapped the trains himself.

"You're a bum. Go play with your trains!"

The words came back to Marty once more. He knew the trains would trigger them again. It had happened the year before, and the year before that.

"Not in front of the children, Alice!"

Had it really all been because of the trains? No, Marty knew it had been much more. Again, he fought to blot it out, especially as he walked down into the subway station, where three teenagers with threatening faces eyed him and his Christmas packages. Marty looked away, felt his heart palpitate, and got to the token window as quickly as possible.

"Merry Christmas," one of the kids said sarcastically. Then the three just walked away. They preferred old men who couldn't fight back.

Marty saw a nun with a tin cup sitting beside a turnstile,

collecting money for orphaned children. He felt for orphans, and dropped a dollar in the cup.

"Bless you," the nun said.

"Thank you, Sister," Marty replied.

The chain, the hammer, the trains. Marty was getting closer, December fifth was getting closer. Soon, he knew, he would have that strange feeling, that compulsion, and he knew he wouldn't be able to resist.

4

Methodically, Samantha continued tracking Marty's past. She still put off the second call to Northwestern—the Lou Cotrell disaster hadn't encouraged a call that could be awkward—but she pursued his early life in Elkhart. She called the junior high school, but the assistant principal refused to cooperate in any way. Samantha would have to send a letter, notarized, explaining her request. Student records were private, the administrator explained, in a lecturing, pedantic voice that would have intimidated any student, teacher, or parent.

So Samantha called the high school. The atmosphere there was much warmer.

But there was no record of a Martin Shaw.

He was not among the list of graduates.

Samantha felt panic begin to well up inside her, but she quickly contained it. She recalled Cotrell's wondering whether records had been requested, then not returned. *All* of Marty's records might have been requested sometime, then not put back. And as for the class pictures, the originals of those might have been pulled, and never refiled. There could be many explanations.

So Samantha called Elkhart City Hall, requesting a birth record. "No, ma'am," came the gruff, bureaucratic voice at the other end, "we don't show a Shaw, Martin, ever been born here."

"Could his birth have been unregistered?" Samantha asked, a touch of desperation in her voice.

"Possible," came the reply, "but a thousand to one shot. I mean, that was modern times. *Everyone* got registered."

Now Samantha's incipient panic began to grow. No birth certificate. No school records. No trace of Marty in Elkhart. The word "registered" stuck in her mind, and she called the Elkhart office that stored old draft records. No Martin Shaw. He'd never been registered. Planning for Marty's fortieth birthday party was becoming a horror, an excursion into a past that might not exist. Yet Samantha refused to believe that. There had to be *some* explanation.

She could turn to no one for help. It was all too embarrassing. How do you tell a friend that you can't find your husband's past? How do you tell her that your husband might have something to hide? You don't. You don't face the stares, or Lynne's penetrating look of curiosity. Only Marty could provide the answers, Samantha knew, and he would. No, she wouldn't confront him directly. To reveal that she'd been probing his past would blow the main surprise of his party. She would extract information indirectly. She'd be subtle. He'd never know.

But first Samantha realized there was one call she had to make. Awkward or not, she had to call Northwestern and get that issue nailed down. It could be some anchor, some positive note. After all, Marty *did* have his diploma. That was solid proof.

She steeled herself. Every call was difficult now, each bringing the fear of rebuff or insult. She looked up the number, reached the school, and asked for the dean of students, Sanford Beale. It took more than four minutes to track Beale down—he was arguing with a student in the hall—and another six before he'd come to the phone. Samantha, sitting at her little table, tapped the phone nervously with her fingers, waiting.

"Beale," came the drab, uninterested voice.

"Dean Beale, my name is Samantha Shaw."

"Yes, I know all about you," Beale said, with no warmth at all. "The lady who took your call told me. What more can I do?"

"Well, first off, I have some good news," Samantha replied. "I don't know what happened to your records, but Marty does have his diploma. It's right here."

"Oh, really?" Beale asked. The coldness in his voice shook Samantha.

"Yes," she replied. "He had filed it away."

"Madam, it's a fake."

There was dead silence. What could Samantha say to that? What could anyone say? "How do you know all the way out there?" she asked, fighting to control her frustration.

"It's because I *am* out here that I know," Beale said. "Your husband never went to Northwestern. It's as simple as that."

"But how do you *know*?"

"Because people don't pass through here without a trace, that's how I know. If he uses the fake diploma, we'll take action. You may have been told that already. Now if you'll excuse me..."

A fantasy shot through Samantha's mind. "What if Marty was involved in secret government work and they wanted traces of him at Northwestern removed...for whatever reason?"

"Someone here would still remember him," Beale replied. "Besides, if he wanted to hide his Northwestern past, he wouldn't leave a diploma lying around."

It was true.

"You might have a little talk with him," Beale went on, sounding human for the first time. "Or you might just drop it. The forgery could be a misjudgment from your husband's past. If he doesn't use it, you might not want to risk..."

Beale didn't finish. He didn't have to spell it out. A confrontation over a fake past could easily destroy a marriage.

The conversation ended on that sour note. Instinctively, Samantha rushed to examine Marty's "diploma" once more. It looked genuine enough, but of course she knew how easy it would be to manufacture a forgery. She was unaware how her hands were shaking until she tried to read the fine print under the words *Northwestern University*. Yes, this was a full-blown crisis, the first in the marriage, and it was especially severe. Now even the party itself was fading in importance. Never had Samantha expected to confront Marty's past this way. Never had she expected to question him.

He'd be home in a few hours. Samantha had to plan her actions, plan each nuance of conversation. She felt the strain. She felt it in her head, and now even in her stomach. She feared for her baby on the very day she'd learned it existed.

Marty came home, hungry and tired as usual. He'd had an afternoon of nonstop meetings with clients, and one client had worn him thin by insisting that a story about his wife's exercise plan be placed in the science section of the *New York Times*. Marty had explained that the *Times* was a tough order for any public-relations man, that the paper insisted on real news. The client then had suggested paying for the story. Marty had to explain that the paper couldn't be bribed. "They can all be bribed," the client insisted. "I want Ruthie in the paper." He'd then stomped out. Marty had to drop the account, although it was a big loss for the firm.

He noticed nothing unusual about Samantha when he walked in. She was dressed in the same gray skirt and blue top she'd worn during the day, her hair was combed back, she looked serene. She had the ability to hide worries, and, on this remarkable day, to hide the news about the baby. But, when Marty's eyes were elsewhere, she did stare at him more than she usually did. She wondered what the real story was, how the riddle would be solved. Those eyes, those suspicious eyes—were they hinting at something in his background? Samantha feared the answer. She was still in the stage of denial. This man was good. This man was pure. It would all work out.

"You look exhausted," she said.

"Exhausted, yes. Maybe beaten."

Samantha frowned. "You don't usually talk that way."

Marty slipped off his coat and jacket, and started on his red-striped silk tie. "I don't usually have Jesse James for a client either." As he slumped into a black leather Barcelona chair and unceremoniously put his feet up on a Parsons table, he told Sam the story of his bribery bent client. "You should have heard this idiot," he declared. "The guy wanted me to take five thousand in cash—all hundreds—to a *Times* editor to place a story about his overweight wife and her homemade exercises. And he was offended when I wouldn't do it."

"Did you suggest another plan?" Samantha asked, bringing Marty a box of chocolates.

"Negative. He wasn't the type. I had to kiss him goodbye."

"Good for you."

"Not good for the bank account."

"Still, good for you. People like that aren't worth the aggravation. They're crooks."

Marty looked at Samantha, somewhat amused. "Look, sweet, most of them are crooks. God knows what they do on their taxes. But this guy advertised it. I think his wife has the money. I can usually spot that."

"You did the right thing," Samantha said. "Hey, forget that creep. How about some sirloin?"

Instantly, Marty seemed to relax. "Now that's greatness," he answered. Then his eyes lit up. "By the way, I saw a note on your table. Didn't you have an appointment with Dr. Fromer today?"

Samantha thought fast. "Yes. Just the annual Pap smear."

"Is it okay?"

"It takes a few days for results. But I'm healthy."

"You sure are," Marty replied, standing up and putting his arms around Samantha, and Samantha *knew* there was love in those words. "You'll live to be a hundred...and I want to be there."

"You will," Samantha said softly.

"Why don't we eat?" He eased himself away and went to wash while Samantha finished the dinner.

Dinner at the Shaws' was always by candlelight, on a table near the living room window, and always with a white tablecloth. It was the kind of elegance both Marty and Samantha liked. To them, it symbolized that their marriage deserved the best, that it was special, that every evening was an event, that the marriage wouldn't be allowed to deteriorate into overcooked hot dogs on a stained kitchen table.

As they sat down they instinctively gazed out the window at the city lights fully ablaze. They never tired of the sight. The skyline simply whispered romance. This was a dream, Samantha had always thought, one that she desperately wanted to continue.

And yet, she went over her strategy in her mind. She had to get information out of Marty. "Something funny happened today," she related.

"Oh?"

"I was walking near Fromer's office and a guy stopped me for directions. He was about your age. Guess where he came from?"

"Mars."

"Close. Elkhart."

Marty brightened. "Elkart, Indiana?"

Samantha shot him her "what else?" look.

"Maybe I know him," Marty said.

"You might. We got to talking. He went to Braden."

"Name?"

"Wilson. Fred."

Samantha watched and listened carefully. Would Marty respond to a complete fake?

"Doesn' t sound familiar," he said.

"He was a year behind you. He said he *thought* he knew your name."

"It was a long time ago. There were other Shaws in Elkhart. I don't know the guy."

"He went to high school there too. He said he played football."

"Maybe. I still don't know him."

"Did Elkhart have a good team?"

Marty shrugged. "Fair."

Samantha tightened, but tried once again to hide it. She'd done her homework and called an Elkhart paper. For three of Marty's four high-school years the team had been undefeated.

"Only fair?"

Now, suddenly, Marty stared at Samantha intently. Suspicion was in his eyes. "Why?" he asked abruptly.

"Just wondering," Samantha replied, feeling her heart skip a beat. "The way this guy was talking, you'd think they were the New York Jets."

Marty started eating again. "I didn't follow football much," he said. "With all my family problems."

There was an awkward silence. Samantha felt a little ashamed. She'd forgotten.

"Come to think of it, though," Marty continued, now sounding more cheerful, "I remember they had an undefeated streak that went on for years."

For Samantha, there was instant relief. He knew. He remembered. "That's what he told me," she said. "You two would probably enjoy talking."

At that moment Samantha saw a subtle fear in Marty's eyes. He stopped eating, then caught himself and resumed. "You didn't give him our number, did you?"

"No."

Marty looked relieved. "Never give the number," he said. "You just never know." Then he looked at Samantha, almost sadly. "I sometimes have these nightmares about you, about something happening to you."

"Marty, nothing's going to happen to me."

"No, no, of course not. But you've got to be careful. I've seen so much in my life. Terrible things done to people."

He reached out and grasped Samantha's hand, almost too tightly, as if wanting never to let go. "Just be careful," he implored her. "You're my whole world."

"I'll watch out for both of us," Samantha replied. They were like that for almost a minute, just looking into each other's eyes, hardly moving, the feeling expressed through the grasp of hands. Marty needed her, Samantha knew. It was a very good feeling, even with the questions about his background.

Finally, slowly, they returned to dinner. Marty zeroed in on the main course, as Samantha knew he would.

"Great steak," he commented. "Where'd you get it?"

"D'Agostino's. On sale."

"Regular coupon clipper."

"Guess who taught me."

"Yeah," Marty responded devilishly. "Old Marty Shaw knows how to save a buck. Dumping clients is one good method." He laughed at himself.

Samantha changed the subject, still probing. "You know," she said, "I want to tell you this before I forget. I was watching that news channel today..."

"CNN?"

"I think so. They had this reporter on who was blasting journalism schools. He mentioned yours and Columbia, and another one."

"Probably Missouri."

"Yeah. He said they produced mechanics. Kind of made me angry."

Marty shrugged. "That line's been around for a long time."

"Did Medill help you?"

"Sure. I learned a lot, and made contacts."

"That guy said you could learn the same things on the job."

"You could say that about any field," Marty declared. "A medical student could probably learn the same thing from a practicing doctor as in med school." Marty had no idea that the TV interview Samantha was discussing had never occurred.

"What did you take at Medill?" she asked.

Marty leaned back in his chair. "Oh, let's see. There was newswriting, reporting, copy editing, photography."

"Does the journalism school have its own building?"

"Oh, sure."

"I'm surprised they never send you anything. They must have an alumni group."

"Yeah, but I didn't keep them up to date on my address." Then Marty looked directly into Samantha's eyes. "Boy, you're really going into my past tonight."

Samantha felt the ice, but feigned nonchalance. "Hey, I love you. Your past interests me."

"Well, I don't think it's such a hot past."

Samantha knew not to press the subject too far, fearing Marty might begin to suspect something. But she wanted to get in one more shot, one more probe, and she did it playfully. "Okay, I'll stay off your history," she said, "but I still intend to frame your birth certificate someday."

"If you can find it," Marty mumbled. But he didn't seem disturbed by the mention of the certificate.

They finished dinner and discussed the party. Marty approved some new guests, but was clearly preoccupied. Samantha assumed it was because of the lost client. Actually, Marty was fighting memories again, memories of an electric train going round on tracks laid temporarily on a living room floor. He didn't know what had triggered this episode, but a truck horn outside sounded remarkably like the diesel horn on his old train set. That's all it took for him to float into a different world, a world struggling to dominate him.

For Samantha, Marty's being preoccupied was a rarity—such was the attention he normally paid her—but it did happen. It almost always involved the office. But she was less concerned about that now than with the results of her discreet probes. She suddenly realized that she had learned very little. So Marty knew about Elkhart High's football record. So what? Any man faking his past could've familiarized himself with local sports legends. The same held true for his knowledge of Medill's curriculum. Easy to learn. Samantha hadn't had the chance to ask anything so detailed that only the genuine article would know. With Marty's sensitivity about his past, she sensed she never would.

She did, though, cook up one more scheme that night, although realizing that it might antagonize Marty. It was a go-for-broke shot, something that might crack the logjam and expose at least part of the truth. As Marty was getting ready for bed, Samantha entered the room. Intentionally, she looked apprehensive.

"What's wrong?" Marty asked.

"You really want to know?"

"Yes." Marty stopped undressing. He looked concerned. "Did something happen?"

"No, but something may be about to."

Marty was all curiosity.

"All right, here goes," Samantha said. "You were a little touchy about your past tonight."

Marty stiffened slightly, then laughed. "Not really."

"Oh yes," Samantha insisted. "You got testy. Maybe I should've understood. At any rate, I wanted to get you this really great birthday gift."

"Sam, the party's my gift."

"Besides that. Something for you. For us."

"You're terrific."

"Listen on. I thought it would be super if I got you...got us...some plane tickets."

"A vacation?"

"Kind of." She shrugged innocently. "I thought we could go to the Midwest. You could return to Elkhart, visit your old home, then hop over to Northwestern. I know you had it tough, love, but every man wants to go home again." She turned away, playing it to the hilt. "Maybe it's not such a hot idea."

There was a pause. "When would you like to go?" Marty asked quietly.

"After the party. Christmastime. It's cold, but festive."

"Let's do it!"

"You mean it? Elkhart? Northwestern?"

"Absolutely. It's a great time to go. Business is sluggish. And I'd love to."

A thrill began forming in Samantha's heart.

"Hey," Marty went on, "I'll take you to the same places I took my old dates."

"The combat zones, eh?"

"Look, I knew the best spots. I'll show you my room at Northwestern. It had a view of Lake Michigan that... well, I'll just show you."

"I want to see the house you lived in."

"Little white place, clapboard, with two chimneys. That was the odd thing," Marty said. "Everyone knew the Shaw house by that."

A new optimism was beginning to come over Samantha. By agreeing to the trip, Marty was hardly evading his past. He seemed, in fact, to be suddenly enthusiastic about it. Samantha couldn't figure out why. Maybe her suggestion of the trip just stirred some deep, sentimental feelings that Marty himself never knew were there. Whatever the reason, Samantha was sure of one thing: A man hiding his past would never agree to this trip. No, she still couldn't explain all the lost records and confusion she'd encountered at Northwestern and in Elkhart. Maybe Marty had been the victim of a string of negligent administrators. Or maybe records had been removed by order of some court, for reasons Samantha couldn't conceive.

"I'll get the tickets," she said.

"Try United," Marty replied. "Why don't we fly into O'Hare in Chicago and start with Northwestern? We can rent a car and drive to Elkhart. I used to do it all the time."

"Any good restaurants in Evanston?"

"Sure. And they'll remember me. There was a guy at the journalism school who wanted to be a food critic. He changed later and opened his own restaurant. I'd get a kick seeing him again."

Samantha was in heaven. *This* was what she'd wanted to hear.

Then Marty did what he'd done only once before, just after she'd agreed to marry him: He did a little Irish jig around the bedroom. He stopped. His eyes widened, like those of a little boy.

"I'm ordering out for ice cream," he announced. "That new place that delivers twenty-four hours. Chocolate chip okay?"

Samantha laughed at him, but she loved the scene. "Okay," she replied.

Marty made the call.

He was sanguine.

He knew that trip to the Midwest would never happen.

5

"So it's still there, with the two chimneys. That's wonderful. And, look, thank you for the name of the family that lives there now. We'll be contacting them."

Samantha put down the phone, thoroughly pleased, and turned to Lynne. "That's the kind of phone call I like. Makes my day."

"The house is just the way Marty described it?" Lynne asked.

"Exactly. That's what the police captain said. He doesn't think there've been any additions. I'll write the people who live there. Maybe they'll let us in so Marty can see his old room."

Lynne was stretched out on Samantha's white couch. "I've got an idea," she said, yawning. "If you pay for it maybe they'll send pictures for you to show at the party."

"I'll ask them," Samantha replied. She was rolling now. The call to the police precinct in Marty's old neighborhood in Elkhart had been reassuring. The captain confirmed every description Marty had ever given of the area. And Samantha had made another successful call too. Recalling that Marty had a passport, she called the State Department and learned he had used his birth certificate as proof of citizenship. It had been issued in Elkhart. Elkhart City Hall, Samantha reasoned, had given her the wrong information.

Her full confidence in Marty restored by his own words the night before and by these calls, Samantha still had to tackle her main objective: getting people who'd known Marty to share their recollections. No one in the precinct remembered him, but none had been in the neighborhood more than fifteen years. Samantha decided against calling Northwestern again, primarily because the school was connected with Marty's career. If she was seen as a pest, it might get out to some well-placed graduate who was in a position to hurt Marty.

"He talks so much about the Army," Samantha said to Lynne. "You know, he enlisted."

"I can believe it," Lynne replied, taking an apple from a basket of fruit on a glass table. "Marty's gung-ho. My Charlie would've just surrendered and left it at that."

"They wanted him to be an officer, but he refused," Samantha went on. "He liked the enlisted guys. So here he was in some office, a private with a journalism degree."

"Probably had more education than the big shots," Lynne said.

"Sure. He told me they treated him almost as an equal. One major told him he was embarrassed because he didn't even have a college degree."

"He ever tell you the names of his Army buddies?"

Samantha reflected for a moment. "There was a Corporal Bose. That was his best friend. Richard Bose. Marty's lost contact with him. Too bad."

Lynne bit into her apple and got up. "Create a miracle," she said. "Call Washington and find out where Bose lives now. Maybe they'll know."

Without even responding, Samantha went to the phone. She'd been thinking of tracking down Marty's Army chums, and Lynne gave her the push to do it immediately. She got the number for the Defense Department and called. Within seconds she was phone-to-phone with the military bureaucracy. By her own count she was transferred nine times before reaching a personnel sergeant who had some idea that men had served in the military prior to the week before.

"Sergeant Mulligan."

"Sergeant," Samantha replied, already exhausted by her trip through the defense establishment, "my name is Samantha Shaw."

"Yes, ma'am. How may I help you, ma'am?" Mulligan's voice gave the impression that he was literally sitting at attention as he responded to her.

"My husband, Martin Shaw, was in the Army back in the sixties, after college."

"In Nam, ma'am?"

"I beg your pardon?"

"Was he in Vietnam, Mrs. Shaw?"

"Only for a short time. He was mostly at Fort Polk."

"I was stationed there. This about veterans' rights, ma'am?"

"No, Sergeant. It's nothing that important. My husband was a volunteer."

"RA."

"I'm... sorry. Again I don't..."

"Regular Army, ma'am. He joined up."

"Yes, he did. He had some close friends. I'm trying to find one of them."

"And you want us to give an address if we got it."

"That's right."

"No big hassle, Mrs. Shaw. We get action requests like that all the time. There are always reunions, stuff like that."

"Well, I appreciate this." Samantha threw one of Marty's mock salutes to Lynne, who loved it. Lynne was already putting on her coat to leave for still another obligation, but she gestured that she'd be back soon.

"If you'd give me the name of the serviceman, ma'am," Mulligan requested.

"Bose. Richard Bose."

"Army?"

"Oh yes."

"Service jackets are in St. Louis, ma'am, but we're computerizing. I'll see if Bose is in the computer bank."

"Thank you."

Samantha could hear Mulligan tapping something on a computer keyboard. Then she heard her own door close as Lynne left. Everything fell silent as Mulligan worked. All Samantha could think of, over and over, was the party and her upcoming trip with Marty.

"Ma'am?"

"Yes?"

"I don't get a Richard Bose on my terminal, but that's not unusual. I could cross-reference it by punching up your husband. I'll get his unit designations. Was Bose in one of his units?"

"I think so," Samantha recalled. "You know, I hate to take up your time like this, Sergeant. I'm sure you have more important things to do."

"Not really, ma'am. By the way, do *you* know your husband's unit designations?"

"No, I'm afraid not."

"I guess you wouldn't know his service number either." Samantha's eyes lit up as she swung around in her chair. "Now *that* I know. I once memorized it as a joke. It's RA38567194."

"I'll punch it up."

Again Samantha waited, this time going down her list of people to contact after she'd located Bose. Marty had worked for a small paper in California, and she thought they'd have stories about him from his reporting days, before he got into public relations. They'd be next.

Mulligan soon came back on the line. "That number came

up, ma'am. Shaw, Martin." Then there was a pause. Samantha thought nothing of it. "His service history," Mulligan went on, but there was a distinct change in his tone. He was quieter, less flamboyant. "It's all in front of me, ma'am."

Samantha noticed the change. "Is something wrong?" she asked.

"I'm...I'm sorry, ma'am."

"Sorry? About what?"

"About your husband, ma'am."

"What about my husband?"

Mulligan hesitated. He thought Samantha's behavior strange. "I'm sorry he was killed in Vietnam, Mrs. Shaw."

It was as if someone had hit Samantha between the eyes with a hammer. For a few moments she almost blacked out. She said nothing, but simply removed the receiver from her ear and stared into it, almost believing she could see Mulligan's face. It had all been so wonderful just hours before, when Marty had agreed to the trip west. Now everything was in ruins once again. She had heard words she would not believe. They were too bizarre, too sick. Marty was alive. He was flesh and blood. But who was dead?

The conference room was filling with smoke, sucked upward by the vents that Marty had insisted on. He sat at the head of a long teakwood table, presiding over a strategy session with an important new client—an airline whose passenger business was falling off rapidly. Marty and a much younger woman were the only people from his firm. The airline was, naturally, represented by eight executives, including two lawyers, an accountant, and a psychologist retained to show the executives how to relate to their passengers. Marty had a bunch of looseleaf presentation books in front of him, had his tie pulled slightly down, and looked like a man ready for combat. It was an act. He knew these clients liked their public relations people to look as if kilowatts of creative energy were ready to spring forth and engulf the competition. It was the image of an image-maker and Marty knew how to turn it on.

"Your problem," he told the gathering, "is that no one sees your airline as having an outstanding trait. You're Mr. Average."

The airline president was a trim man of forty-eight, suntanned and healthy, a former pilot. "What is your solution?" he asked in a clipped, almost military manner.

"We've got to identify things that make you outstanding," Marty replied.

The room erupted in laughter. Marty looked around at each person from the airline. He was not laughing. "That bad, eh?"

"Look," the president answered, "we're not Delta or Lufthansa. That's why we need you."

"I think that's the source of the problem," Marty countered. "You're too modest. You've got a fine record, but you only see the shadow of the big guys. Now, instead of me talking, I want you to tell me what you're proud of in your operation. I mean it."

Marty leaned back in his chair and gestured toward the president, who began to speak, first haltingly, then rapidly, about the technical talent he'd been able to attract. But as he spoke, Marty's mind started to drift. It had happened fairly often, but now was happening every day. This had been the pattern in other years as well. As December fifth approached, his mind simply couldn't stick to business. Now words came back. He heard the voices again.

"Afraid the kids'll find out about you? The way you lose jobs?"

"Maybe they'll find out about you! Where'd you spend the night, Alice?"

"You callin' me a slut? You callin' me that?"

Marty barely heard the airline executives drone on. He felt the sweat oozing from his forehead. It was a horror show, an internal storm that contradicted the picture of his being in complete control.

"Call me a slut! I dare you! Use the word!"

"Frankie," the gentle voice had said, *"maybe you'd better go to your room."*

And now Marty heard a question darting across the table. "Wouldn't *that* be something for the airline to emphasize, Marty?"

Thank God he'd heard the question, he thought. None of them around the table suspected what was going on inside him. But he hadn't heard the sentences that had gone before. Fake it. Fake it good.

Marty cleared his throat. "I think it has to be weighed against other factors," he said. "The public has a saturation point. Not all things can be treated equally."

"But we *could* emphasize it," said an airline V.P.

"I don't think we should commit to it now," Marty replied. "I'd like to do some testing."

"I'll buy that," the president said.

They all nodded. They knew Marty was sharp.

"I'd like to hear more," he said.

The accountant started expounding on how the airline had saved money by printing its menus in Taiwan, and Marty's mind again began to travel. An image formed in his brain: the trains set up and running, their clickety-click filling the house. As the accountant rattled off a list of figures, Marty took out a pen. The executives thought he was making notes for them. But he was composing a letter.

Dear Dad,

It's that time again. Just like last year and all the years before. I know you worry about me, and what's going to happen to me. But you shouldn't. I'll be fine. The important thing is to remember you the right way. I hope you're proud of me. I hope you'll be proud of me on the fifth.

Your loving son,

Frankie

The accountant stopped. "Did you get all that?" he asked Marty.

"Oh sure," Marty replied. "I jotted down everything I had to." He slipped the letter into a folder.

"I see," Samantha answered, as she looked down at her hands, now trembling slightly. "I'm sorry I took up your time." She hung up the phone.

So, Marty hadn't worked at the *San Diego Union*, although he'd told her stories of how he'd covered the police and the courts. They'd never heard of him. They didn't even have an application on file from a Martin Shaw. And none of the editors could recall the stories he claimed to have covered. Samantha phoned the *Des Moines Register*—Marty had told her he'd worked there too—and got the same reply. Now she was no longer willing to believe that all the people she'd contacted were incompetents with faulty records.

She was thunderstruck by the fact that there'd been a Martin Shaw in the Army and that her husband had used his service number. Obviously Marty had found out about the dead soldier and taken his number because he needed some kind of verifiable military reference. But why? And why was he so willing to travel back and retrace a past that, it was becoming clear, was in the shadows?

Was national security involved? Was Marty a kind of James Bond who had to hide his tracks? She rejected that, returning to her belief that a man trying to cover something would never agree to a "nostalgic" trip.

But maybe it wasn't a nostalgic trip. Maybe Marty had learned about specific areas of the country as part of some cover story. Samantha was beginning to feel overwhelmed by the questions, frightened by other possibilities. Maybe there was something mentally wrong with Marty, something that made him lie. Maybe he'd had an accident and injured his brain. Maybe he just imagined things.

But if he were "normal" and there were something unusual in his past, why had he not confided it to the woman he'd married?

Samantha couldn't handle this herself. She was beginning to accept that. But to whom could she turn to for advice? Lynne? She was a bit too close, and a bit too curious. A friend of Marty's? That would humiliate him behind his back. What if there were an entirely proper explanation for the mystery? What if it were medical, or psychiatric?

She certainly wasn't ready to confront Marty directly and risk the marriage.

Samantha Shaw knew of no wife who'd faced what she now faced—being married to a wonderful man whose past seemed not to exist.

Finally she made a decision to act. She decided there was only one person to call for counsel. Yes, he was a friend of Marty's, but a friend so special, so loyal, that, in Samantha's mind, no damage would be done. Tom Edwards was, after all, Marty's best pal, his alter ego, someone he spoke to each day. Tom and Marty seemed to think and feel alike. Tom was a few years younger, but it never appeared to matter.

Tom was a real-estate agent for one of the major brokers in Manhattan, occupying a glass cubicle on East 56th Street that was decorated with floor plans, pictures of apartment buildings and news clippings warning of new rent increases. Like Marty, Tom was well-built, but he had a quieter, softer personality, with none of Marty's commanding flair. They understood each other, Samantha thought, on a more emotional, subliminal level. Tom had a kindness that Marty needed, she reasoned, after spending his days with the sharks of business.

"Tom Edwards," Tom answered in his matter-of-fact, I'm-just-a-nice-guy style.

"Tom, Samantha."

"Hey, Sam. What an honor. You never call me. You looking for a new pad or something?"

Samantha laughed. "No, Thomas, I'm looking for *you*."

"For me? What'd I do?"

"Nothing illegal. I just need some help."

"Something bad happen?"

"Not at all. Oh, I'm not getting you at a rough time, am I?"

"No, it's a slow day. In fact, I'm gonna call old Mart later just to chat." Tom ran his hand through his longish, prematurely gray hair. "Now shoot. How can I help you?"

"You know the bash I'm having for Marty?"

"Of course."

"Keep this under your hat." Then Samantha stopped, frozen for a moment.

"Yeah?" Tom asked.

But Samantha remained silent. She couldn't do what she had planned—reveal everything that had happened, even to Tom. She wasn't as emotionally ready for that as she'd thought. No, she'd hedge. She'd ease into it. She'd start by some probing around. "Tommy," she finally continued, "I'm adding a surprise. I'm trying to find Marty's old friends and teachers, and have them give remembrances."

"Fantastic."

"So...you know any?"

"Gee," Tom replied, "old friends and teachers."

"Righto, Thomas, that's what I said."

"Let me think." Tom pondered for a few moments. "Harold Tyler."

"Tom, Marty knows Harold now."

"But don't they go way back?"

"Yeah, but I want people he's lost touch with."

"Oh, I get the picture. Well, let's see. There's...no, he knows him now too."

"Teachers from Northwestern," Samantha suggested, probing to see how Tom would react, "or people from Elkhart."

"Sam, I just don't know any," Tom finally admitted. "You know, Marty and I have only been buddies about five years. We never talk about the old times. I know that sounds strange, but it's true. His only friends I know are the ones you know, with maybe a couple of exceptions."

"Tom, you're not telling me that Marty never *mentioned* anyone, are you?"

Tom laughed, a bit nervously. "Well, maybe some old girl-friends."

"Okay, fair enough. Let's have the names."

"Sam," Tom explained, "all I have is first names...and certain characteristics. That's the way guys talk."

"So I'm batting zero," Samantha said, slightly disappointed in Tom.

"Well, I could give you names of Marty's current friends—the ones you don't know, I mean."

"We'll get to that. I really need the old crew."

"There's no other way you can get names?"

"How? I don't want to tip Marty. And he doesn't have many...links to his past."

"Well, it wasn't the hottest upbringing."

Samantha decided to try a slightly different tack. "You were in the Army, weren't you, Tom?"

"Yeah."

"Surprising you two don't trade war stories."

"Maybe. But look, why don't you concentrate on the here and now. Come to think of it, going back into Marty's past may not be that fantastic after all. Memories have strange effects."

"You really think so?"

"Well, who knows? But think it over. Marty has loads of friends now. They're the ones who matter."

"I'll think," Samantha promised. "Hey, you're working. I'd better buzz off."

"If you need help on the party, just whistle."

They hung up. Samantha had learned nothing. But Tom's lack of information did confirm one idea—that Marty's past was no open book. How, after all, does a man not discuss his early years with his best friend? That was unnatural, abnormal. The conversation with Tom simply increased Samantha's anxieties.

Samantha pushed on. She tried to invent some way to bring up Marty's past without provoking him. After all, he'd chided her the last time she'd probed. So, after dinner that night, as they relaxed watching an old Humphrey Bogart movie, she gracefully broached the subject. During a commercial she turned to Marty, who was slumped in an easy chair.

"You know, it just occured to me, we've got the guest list complete...except for people who have to be tracked down."

Marty was baffled. "Tracked down?"

"Well, I mean, you might want some people you've lost contact with. Tell me now because it takes time to get addresses. I wouldn't want the invitations to be late."

"There's nobody," Marty replied, hardly taking his eyes off the Coca-Cola ad.

"Sure?"

"Very. I know who I want."

"Not even Bose, from the Army? You've talked about him."

"Sam, that was years ago. It was a totally different time."

"But if you liked him..."

"Who knows if I'd like him now. Maybe he's got a pushy wife. Maybe he's a junkie. I don't like dredging people up."

"Okay. Case closed."

Then Marty turned to Samantha, smiling gently. "I appreciate the thought," he said. "I really do."

That made Samantha feel good, but it wasn't the "good" that she was used to feeling. Marty's words couldn't completely soothe her now, not with all those questions hanging over her head.

And then Marty did something that Samantha thought strange. He got up in the middle of the film—something he'd never done—and started walking out of the room. "You interested in the movie?" he asked.

"Not really," Samantha replied.

"Come with me."

Samantha followed Marty into their bedroom. He stood at one end for a few moments and surveyed the room, his eyes moving gradually from left to right, then back again.

"What's this about?" Samantha asked.

"I want to rearrange the room," Marty replied.

"Why? It's fine the way it is."

"Fine isn't great." There was a mildly contemptuous tone to Marty's voice that Samantha had not heard before. It bothered her, but she tried not to show it. "What'd you have in mind?" she asked.

"Something I saw in an architecture magazine. I liked it."

"You have the magazine?"

"No, I threw it away."

Why would he throw away a magazine that he wanted to use as a model? Samantha asked the question only of herself. She sensed Marty was in no mood to be challenged. "Let me show you something," he said. He took a package out of his attaché case and unwrapped it, revealing a gold-colored picture frame, gaudy and cheap-looking, made for a five-by-seven picture. "I bought this," he went on. "I think it should go here." He placed the frame over their bed.

"Well..." Samantha began to reply, utterly repelled by the frame.

"What's wrong?"

"You sure you want it there?"

"Yes," Marty answered. "You disagree?"

Samantha was becoming increasingly exasperated. "Marty," she said, "we've always bought things together."

"You don't like it," he said, seemingly deflated.

"Oh, I do. It's lovely. But if we're redecorating, I have some ideas."

Marty rushed over to Samantha and embraced her. "Hey," he said, suddenly the old Marty, "this is a partnership. Maybe I got a little excited. I want you in on *everything*. But,

Sam, this is a great layout. It means a lot to me. Let's at least try it."

"Sure," Samantha agreed. How could she resist when Marty spoke so reasonably? Besides, she had more important worries than his sudden interest in interior decorating.

Without a word, Marty started rearranging the room, refusing help from Samantha. He had a determined, almost passionate look on his face, as if his deepest feelings were involved. She couldn't understand it.

Marty nailed the picture frame exactly where he'd wanted to. It looked awful, but he seemed to take a special pride in it. He moved the bed around so the headboard was against the radiator, something Samantha knew was absolutely wrong. She was sure Marty knew it too. And surely he knew that the bureau shouldn't be blocking a window. But when he was finished, it was. And what logic he saw in rolling up the area rugs and storing them was beyond Samantha. It was also beyond her that any architecture magazine would feature such an arrangement, or even allow it in its pages.

"There," he said after the job was done, the beads of sweat running down his brow, "I happen to like that."

Samantha said nothing.

"What about you?" Marty finally asked.

"Well," she replied, "it has its merits."

"I know it's unusual," Marty went on, "and our room isn't exactly the right shape. But let's give it a chance. If you decide you don't like it, I'll change it back."

"Fine," Samantha agreed. It was curious, very, very curious. She walked out of the room to make some notes for the party.

Martin Shaw slowly approached the bed, then lay down. He grabbed Samantha's pillow and clutched it to his chest, as one would a stuffed animal. He looked up. His lips began to form words. "Frankie wants a kiss," he whispered.

6

The shop was on West 15th Street, near the Hudson River. The area was crammed with warehouses and importers, and Samantha's cab could barely squeeze by the trailer trucks that filled the street, picking up and delivering. Her ears were assaulted by what seemed like one long honking diesel horn. It was the symphony of West 15th. People in the neighborhood were used to it.

The sign outside said SIMON'S FRAMING AND LAMINATING and when she walked in Samantha could feel the sawdust in the air. The front of the store was divided from the rear by a simple partition, in front of which was a metal desk and chair. No one was at the desk, so Samantha had to ring a little rusted bell for service. It wasn't regal, but if Simon had the answer to one critical question, nothing else mattered.

Howard Simon was a man in miniature—about five-three, well into his eighties, with a narrow face that made him look elflike. He came out from behind the partition in his usual outfit, blue coveralls over a white shirt and red tie. He had virtually no hair. When he saw Samantha he immediately smiled, almost deferentially. Most of Simon's framing business came from big department stores, shipped to his little shop by impersonal messengers, and getting a flesh-and-blood customer, especially an attractive one, was something of an event.

"May I help you?" Simon asked, bowing slightly in the old tradition.

"Yes," Samantha replied, feeling instant trust in the man, "I have a diploma."

"You want it framed?"

"I don't know."

"You don't know?" Simon asked, throwing his hands up in mock, but gentle surprise. "Maybe I can help you decide."

"It's for a... business associate," Samantha went on. "But I have a question about it. I don't know if it's genuine. It might be a mistake or something."

Samantha was at her most awkward, and Simon could see right through her. The problem had come up before. "May I see it?" he asked.

Samantha had the diploma in an oversized handbag. She reached in. "This is in confidence, isn't it?"

"Who would I tell?" Simon replied.

Samantha slowly took the diploma out and handed it to Simon. "Northwestern," he said. "A fine university." He turned the diploma over and examined its back, running his hand along the surface. "Too bad this person never went there."

Samantha's whole body tightened. "What do you mean?" she asked, challenging Simon.

"The document is a fake," Simon replied with a shrug. "I've seen many, many diplomas from this school. They're all engraved. You can feel the letters through the back. This is printed. A very cheap job. The gentleman probably had it made up in one of those places that does things like this."

"You're... sure?" Samantha asked.

"Sixty years in business, madam."

"Thank you," Samantha whispered. Simon could see her

eyes well up with tears. There was something about physical evidence that was so definitive, so final. Now there could be no doubt about Marty's Northwestern years. They had never happened.

Without another word, Samantha left the shop and took a cab back home. It was the saddest ride she'd ever had. She really didn't want to go home to face Lynne's incessant cheerfulness and Marty's...she still didn't know what to call it. He'd lied to her about Northwestern, and, she was beginning to understand, about many other things. He *wasn't* the Marty Shaw she thought she knew. He was someone else, and the marriage wasn't the dream she'd assumed it to be. It was becoming a nightmare.

She fought to remain in control, not to panic, not to go to pieces. If there was one thing the cold years before Marty had taught her, it was the futility of despair. And the defense mechanism that psychiatrists call denial was still working inside her. Even as she rode up Central Park West she began thinking that she must have overlooked the one logical, honorable, explanation for all she'd discovered, the one solution that would let her retain her love and respect for Marty. Until —unless—she found it, her feelings, her fears, her hopes would remain in conflict with each other.

As she re-entered her apartment she made one firm decision: She needed professional help. If there was something wrong with Marty, she couldn't diagnose it herself. A psychiatrist would probably be her best bet, and she knew exactly whom she wanted. She'd heard him lecture at the New School when she'd taken a psychology course there. He seemed articulate and learned, yet warm. His subject had been the stresses in men's lives. As soon as she took off her coat, Samantha grabbed the phone and made an urgent appointment with Kenneth S. Levine, M.D.

Levine was affiliated with New York Hospital, but had a small, private office in a townhouse on East 66th Street. Samantha had the taxi drop her at the end of the block. She still had an uneasy feeling about psychiatrists—her parents had never approved of them—and even felt a bit embarrassed. Slipping on a pair of dark glasses, she climbed the white steps to Levine's office.

Up close, Levine seemed older than Samantha had remembered him. He was in his late fifties, with totally gray hair and deep-set eyes. He *looked* like a psychiatrist, Samantha thought, which partially accounted for the faith patients had in him. His office was done in reddish wood paneling, with indirect lighting. It was easy on the eyes, designed to make anxious people relax. Levine sat in an oversized orthopedic chair behind his cluttered desk as he discussed Marty's case with Samantha.

"I don't understand it," Samantha told him. "Marty's an honest man. People in business respect him. But so many things he told me turned out not to be true. And yet he wants to make that trip."

"Does he have a tendency to exaggerate?" Levine asked.

"No."

"But he's in public relations. Exaggeration is part of his job."

"Oh, sure. But he doesn't take it home."

"Does he seem to feel the need to impress you?"

"No more than anyone else. He doesn't brag. He doesn't claim abilities he doesn't have."

"I see." Levine made notes on a yellow pad as he went along. "Have you noticed any lapses of memory?"

Samantha thought for a moment. "Marty can be forgetful," she conceded.

"How forgetful?"

"I don't understand."

"Does he forget obvious things, like the names of relatives?"

"Oh, no. He'll just forget to pay a bill or buy batteries for his Walkman."

"Has he changed since you married him?"

"Not really."

"Any medical problems?"

"No."

"Brushes with the law?"

"What?"

"It's important that I know," Levine explained.

"None that he's told me about," Samantha answered. Then she laughed ironically. "Of course, what does *that* prove?"

"Does Marty see a psychiatrist?"

"No, unless he's hiding it."

"What I'm trying to get at," Levine said, "is anything that might be disturbing Marty, something that may be warping his judgment. Sometimes people lie—about their past, for example—out of desperation. They may need to invent a second identity."

"I understand," Samantha replied. "But I can't think of anything that could be disturbing him. He seems quite content."

"And it's always been this way?"

"For as long as I've known him."

"This may be a difficult question, Mrs. Shaw, but does he ever use expressions like, 'I'd like to kill myself'?"

"No. Never."

"Good. By the way, have you discussed the fake diploma with him?"

"No."

"Well don't. Men can react to a challenge like that in very strange ways."

The discussion lasted almost two hours. At the end, Samantha was exhausted and Levine had filled forty-two pages with notes. He reviewed some of them before passing judgment. "Mrs. Shaw," he said, "you've described a perfectly normal man...except for his false past and this odd redecorating of the room. I told you earlier that it might be impossible for me to assess this without seeing Marty. All you've said reinforces that. I'd have to talk with him to be of any help."

"But Doctor Levine, you asked me not to challenge him."

Levine sighed. "That's right. You couldn't confront him with your real concerns. We'd have to find a way to get him in here."

"Like what?"

"Well, you could suggest to him that he seems under stress ...from work, I mean. You could urge him to see a doctor for *your* sake."

Samantha weighed the idea, then shook her head negatively. "He wouldn't buy it," she said. "Marty's one of those professional I-can-handle-it types."

"All right. Well, Mrs. Shaw, the bottom line is, no Marty, no answers."

It was another dead end. Samantha couldn't devise a way to get Marty to a psychiatrist, and she now wondered whether Levine could actually help. What if Marty were just a deceitful man with no mental problems? What could Levine do with that?

A discouraged Samantha left Levine's office. She didn't take a cab home, preferring to walk through Central Park in the chill breeze, trying to collect her thoughts, to figure a way out of her dilemma. The park was empty, almost desolate, and it made Samantha feel even more alone. She'd tried Tom Edwards and Kenneth Levine. She'd even tried Marty with her amateurish probes. She'd seen no progress. Now she almost wished she'd never thought of the party or of finding people from Marty's past. Ignorance *is* sometimes bliss, she thought to herself. What would have been wrong with not knowing that Marty's past was a fake? She would have had a happy marriage, a peaceful existence. Now what did she have? "Little Miss Curiosity," she mumbled, almost with contempt. She was, in a way, blaming herself. It was natural.

A few days later Samantha spoke with a psychologist, then, the next day, with another psychiatrist. Both echoed what Levine had said—that without Marty's presence, they could offer no help. Samantha gave up on shrinks.

But there was one question Levine had asked that kept

going through her mind. It frightened her, but it wouldn't go away. He'd asked whether Marty had had brushes with the law. It was a possibility, Samantha knew, one that could explain why he'd falsified his past.

She decided to see a lawyer.

But which one? She would never go to the family attorney, for that would be too embarrassing. Besides, he was really Marty's lawyer from the time before their marriage. She needed a criminal lawyer, someone who might have handled problems like the one she now faced. So Samantha Shaw left her apartment one Thursday, in the middle of a November snowfall, and took a cab to the Newspaper Division of the New York Public Library. There she went through back issues of newspapers seeking the name of a lawyer with a winning record. For if Marty were in trouble, she'd want him to win. No matter what he'd done, no matter what he'd told her, she'd still want him to win. What she needed was a modern Clarence Darrow. And she thought she'd found him in the person of L. Douglas Grimes.

Grimes had two offices, an opulent set-up on Wall Street and a stylishly shabby affair in a West Manhattan brownstone. Samantha, the lady with a personal problem, was seen in the brownstone. The office was tiny, with white Kentile floor and chipped wooden desk, a perfect setting for the downtrodden, and those who imagined they were. But behind the desk were sixteen awards from civic groups, citing Grimes as certifiably wonderful. That was clout.

He was average looking and slightly paunchy, but his common looks, rolled-up sleeves, mussed hair, worn shoes, creased and wide-suspendered pants all worked to his advantage with the "underprivileged" side of his practice. He was one of "us" rather than one of "them."

He listened to what Samantha said, those practiced eyes staring her down, and she did spill out everything. When she finished he waited a full minute before commenting. He removed his rimless glasses, leaned back, and placed his hands flatly on his head, signaling that he was thinking carefully. Then, looking her over once more, he tried to detect, from his twenty years' experience, whether she was lying. He guessed she wasn't.

"You have one of the most difficult problems I've ever encountered," he said. "I don't know how you take it."

"I love him," Samantha replied. "That's how."

Grimes laughed nervously. "You'd make a good defense witness. Very sympathetic. But I'm amazed you haven't confronted him."

"I can't. What if he has good reasons for all this? Sometimes I think I'd be better off if I'd never known."

"I understand." Grimes eased out of his rolling chair and anchored himself to the edge of the desk. "But you don't mean that. You want the truth precisely *because* you love him. You sense he may be in danger. After all, you did come to me."

Samantha conceded that Grimes was right. She was prepared to forgive almost anything, including a past littered with shame, but she had to know. "Do you think he may have a legal problem?" she asked.

"Impossible to say," Grimes replied. "You'd need a private investigator to follow Marty and trace his roots. That's expensive and he might come up empty-handed. And Marty might catch on. Some of these private eyes are no geniuses."

"Have you seen other cases like this?"

Grimes laughed the laugh of experience. "Oh, many, many, many. Hiding the past to cover something is common. Ex-cons do it all the time. So do bankrupts. And, you know, you've got the draft dodgers, tax evaders, the alcoholics, guys who skip out on child support..."

Samantha winced. Grimes caught it. "I knew you'd pop at that last one," he said. "Women do."

Samantha shook her head in an exaggerated no. "Marty wouldn't do that. He..."

"It's something you may have to face," Grimes countered.

Samantha sighed, then took a deep breath. Stay calm, she told herself. Don't hate Grimes because he's saying hateful things. He's *trying* to help.

"What are the chances of the...child support thing?" she asked.

Grimes shrugged. "Again, impossible to say. Look, don't jump to conclusions. There are plenty of other possibilities. I mean, Marty might have done something heroic."

Samantha warmed. "Like?"

"He could've caught a criminal." Now Grimes started to pace, lawyerlike, creating a theory that he knew would please his client. "Maybe he's afraid of retaliation and had to establish a new identity for self-protection. The government has a program that does that, you know."

"Could I find out?"

"Probably not. Clearly, he's not using his real name. Who would we ask? What could they go on?"

"What if I went to the police?"

Grimes chewed on that one, strolling briefly over to straighten an award from the Citizens Union. Any answer he gave could be trouble. "It depends on the real truth about Marty," he replied. "You could send him to jail if he's running and the cops find out. If he has a mental problem, amnesia or something, you could be helping him. Chances are, going to the cops wouldn't have any effect. They've got hotter cases to worry about."

Samantha knew she was batting zero. Theories, more theories, still more theories, all billable to her. She felt herself coming to an obvious conclusion—one she would fight—that Marty had to be confronted directly.

"Do you have any legal advice?" she finally asked Grimes.

"Sure. If your husband does anything suspicious, don't get involved. You could be charged as an accomplice, even if you claimed you didn't know. If he does something odd, call me."

"What's 'odd'?"

"Anything that smacks of sudden material gain. If he

wants a vacation that he can't afford, don't go. He may be using dirty money. If he brings you a gift that busts the budget, tell him you'd be embarrassed to accept it, and buzz me." Grimes approached Samantha, gazing directly into her fearful eyes. "If you discover a weapon in the house, call me *instantly.* Unexplained phone charges...I want to know. You'll sense if something's wrong. Wives always do. You're the best private eyes."

On that note, they parted. Samantha returned by cab to the apartment building. She had no idea what to do next.

When she arrived she said her usual, friendly hello to Al, the ancient doorman, who'd been there thirty-five years and held the door with the style of a man who took pride in his work. "Oh, oh, Mrs. Shaw," he called as Samantha was halfway to the elevator, "there's a package."

"For me?"

"I think it's for Mr. Shaw."

Al took Samantha to the package room and gave her a small parcel wrapped in plain brown paper. It was clearly addressed to Marty, but had no return address. Samantha stared at it, felt around it, and suddenly she was scared. But why be scared? It was only a package. She knew why. A plain parcel, no return address, and Grimes warning about weapons and odd things. "Thanks, Al," she said mechanically, then rushed to the elevator.

When she got to her apartment, Samantha placed the package on a kitchen table. She stood and looked at it, perhaps for two minutes. She'd never opened Marty's mail before. Her father had said that mail, even after decades of marriage, was personal. She thought of spy movies, where they open packages, then reseal them so no one would know. Could she do that? No, it wasn't in her nature. Yes, she *had* to. Suspicion, worry, fright, were gripping her. Her normal instincts fell away.

She carefully opened the package.

There was a box inside. It, too, was plain. As Samantha

placed her fingers on it, ready to remove the lid, she hesitated. What was in there? A gun? A pack of money? Explosives?

She lifted the lid.

She looked down.

She felt nothing, for there was nothing to feel. Inside the box was a book, with a note. It was an early birthday present from one of Marty's friends, someone who couldn't make the party. The book: *A History of the American Press*, by a professor at Medill. Irony, Samantha thought. Just irony.

She rewrapped the package. It was better than new. Minutes later the phone rang. It was Grimes. Samantha's heart raced. Had he come up with something? Had he made calls and gotten some information? It *had* to be progress. Why else would he call?

"I was thinking about your case," Grimes said. For Samantha, instant disappointment. "You know," Grimes continued, "you may get nowhere no matter what you do."

"I realize that," Samantha said.

"And this is tearing you apart. I was wondering whether you've considered eliminating the problem at its source."

Eliminating? Samantha sat down as nerves overcame her. Grimes's language was more suitable for an underworld hit than a family crisis. "What do you mean?" she asked quietly.

"Divorce."

"No."

"Well, all right. You're the client. But 'no' can't be forever. You've got to think about it. This can devour you."

Samantha wasn't really angry at Grimes's suggestion. Maybe she was even thankful. Yes, there *could* be a divorce if things got worse. Her heart might say no, but her mind could say maybe. Of course, she refused to take it *that* seriously. It would all work out. Even after Grimes's call she told herself that. The nightmare would end. Marty would come through.

But, maybe...

She was wracked with doubts. She had no plan. She was numb. She threw herself back into planning a party for a man she didn't know, if only to escape the darkness.

Four days after Samantha saw Grimes, Marty brought home the electric trains. Samantha was nonplussed. A grown man with choo-choo trains? In a city apartment? Without kids? But Marty explained it.

"I never had trains," he said boyishly. "They're great. A lot of men have them. Sam, there are clubs all over the world."

She wasn't convinced.

"Look, I'll build a small layout, the kind you can take apart and put in the closet. You'll love it."

What a temptation to tell Marty about the baby. But Samantha held it in. There were too many doubts. "I guess it'll be all right," she said.

"It's very relaxing for me," Marty went on, as if appealing to Samantha's devotion. Then he explained how he bought only used trains because he preferred the older models.

"You never buy anything used," Samantha protested.

"This is different. You have to understand the hobby. The old Lionel stuff—it's terrific."

It was odd, but not odd enough to trigger a phone call to L. Douglas Grimes. And Samantha saw nothing to link the trains to the mystery of Marty's past. Maybe he *did* just want a hobby. What was the big deal? Okay, no crisis. Peace. Let him have his toys if he needed them. Samantha was prepared to let the trains chug by as just the eccentricity of a hard-working man.

Tom Edwards came over and helped Marty set them up in the living room. They ran the trains for a time, then Tom went home, allowing Marty to run them alone. Samantha studied him from a hallway, watching the intensity in his face, the fascination in his eyes.

"I've never seen you happier," she said, walking into the living room.

He didn't answer. He didn't even acknowledge her presence. All right, men got wrapped up in things. Football. The Series. It happened. She forced herself not to take offense.

"Can I run them?" she asked.

Marty looked up at her. It was such a lighthearted question, yet he looked so grim. "You sure you want to?"

"Yeah."

But Frankie wouldn't have allowed it, would he? Marty knew that Frankie wouldn't, but he also knew he had to avoid suspicion. "Sure," he said. "Run them. I'll make an engineer of you yet. But only do it a few minutes." He winked at her. "We kids gotta play before homework."

Samantha sat on the floor beside Marty. He gently placed her right hand on the throttle of the bulky Lionel transformer, the control center of the set. She felt ridiculous, and the whole set-up looked ridiculous as well. Marty asked her to press the button that sounded the diesel horn. She did. God, what if the neighbors heard? What if *Lynne* heard?

She was giving the long, black throttle back to Marty when she noticed that some locomotive grease had smeared on the white rug. It upset her. How could Marty have done it? He was always so careful about what he owned, about keeping everything in good order. What was so important about these trains that would allow him to sacrifice a good rug, without so much as a comment? Maybe the trains were more than a hobby. Maybe they meant something to Marty that he just didn't want to reveal. But Samantha had no way of finding out.

For the next few days she tried to organize some kind of strategy for dealing with the mystery of Marty. "Police" kept going through her mind. She recited all the arguments against going, but instinct told her that it might be her only way out. Who could tell? Who knew anything for sure? Samantha's life was becoming a series of guesses and hunches.

Lynne came over to help with invitations and arrangements. "Have you ever been to the Twentieth Precinct?" Samantha asked her.

Lynne was surprised by the question. "Why?" she asked.

"I was bothered outside this morning."

"The guy with the lumberjack shirt?"

"Uh...no. He didn't have a lumberjack shirt. He had a black leather jacket and a green sweater underneath. I thought of filing a complaint, but I've never been in a police station."

"It's not sin city," Lynne laughed. "I've been there." Then she sensed how serious Samantha was. "Hey, did this dude really do something?"

"Oh no, just some comments. I think he was drunk. But he kind of scared me."

"Look, they're very nice there. If you want to go, I'll go with you."

"Let me think about it," Samantha said.

7

One man was waiting for Samantha Shaw to decide to come to the police, but neither he nor she knew it.

Spencer Cross-Wade glanced up at his calendar at New York's main police headquarters and felt a surge of disgust, coupled with the intense frustration he had felt since taking on the case. Only three weeks remained until December fifth. Three weeks to piece together a horrendous puzzle. Three weeks to prevent another tragedy. Three weeks to cap a career approaching its end. He had circled the date with a black Magic Marker, and the blackness itself seemed to capture the moment. What chance was there? What lightning bolt had to strike? He wanted to solve the mysteries, but now he saw no realistic chance.

Small, balding, pushing sixty, Spencer Cross-Wade was more Scotland Yard than New York Police Department. His father had been with the Yard, and his grandfather before him. But Spencer had come to America while in the Royal Navy during World War II, married an American and stayed. She died in 1955. They had no children. He never remarried. He lived alone in a small Brooklyn apartment overlooking the East River, seemingly content with his memories, with his recollections of England, and with plans to travel once he retired in a few months.

His detective's office was simple—a steel desk, gray walls, some visitors' chairs and, for cheerfulness, an assortment of flowers that he kept replacing. "A man should have a garden," he was fond of telling associates with the familiar twinkle in his eye. It was very British, very much a part of his quiet campaign to bring a bit of British gentility to the gruff New York department.

His intercom buzzed. He reached over, pressed the red button, and heard Sally, the homicide bureau's receptionist.

"Sir, Detective Loggins to see you."

"Ah," Cross-Wade replied. "I've been expecting. Let me fetch him."

Arthur Loggins was waiting in the reception area, sitting on a metal guest chair, reading over the sports pages of the *New York Post.*

"Arthur," Cross-Wade exclaimed, refusing to use the more familiar "Arty," by which Loggins had been known for all of his forty-two years. "Come in. I need you."

Loggins, heavy-set, awkward, plodding, dull-looking, but with a detective's eye for detail and subtlety, followed Cross-Wade back to his office.

"Sorry I'm late, sir," Loggins said in a maddening monotone, "but I had to finish a case."

"Always finish," Cross-Wade admonished. "A policeman must always finish. I admire that. In the Yard an inspector takes the case from start to end. Never excuse yourself for finishing—not around here."

"Yes, sir," Loggins replied, not having expected such an avalanche of police wisdom. He hurried along as Cross-Wade disappeared into his office, leaving him still walking down the hall. He finally entered and sat down.

"Do you have a green thumb?" Cross-Wade asked.

"No, sir," Loggins replied. "The little woman, she does

some putterin' around the house. Petunias and stuff. Me? I watch football."

"I see. Gardening gives a man a sense of creating," Cross-Wade asserted. "But, I suppose there's merit in watching twenty-two grown men push each other down." He winked. He always wanted to make sure his men knew when he was kidding. "Now," he said, "you've been transferred to my command for a single case. This is not to be discussed outside this area, and not with the press. Am I clear?"

"Yes, sir," Loggins replied, impressed that he would be called for something so hush-hush.

"We don't want it discussed because we don't want a public panic. Nothing like Son of Sam. That was a rodeo. You've been selected because you're a dogged investigator, a detail man. And God knows, I need details."

"Thank you for the nice words," Loggins said.

Cross-Wade squirmed out of his desk chair, got up and tapped the circled December fifth on his calendar. "That's the key to the whole blitz," he told Loggins. "That date is our target and our nightmare. If it passes without an arrest, a woman will die. I hope you regard that as serious."

"Very, Mr. Cross-Wade. I just got off a murder case."

"This is multiple murder," Cross-Wade continued. "It seems that each December fifth, for the last six years, a woman has been murdered in the same way somewhere in North America. All have been struck on the head with a blunt instrument, then choked with a chain-like device."

"Did the victims have anything in common?" Loggins asked.

"Yes," Cross-Wade replied. "Each had long, free-falling auburn hair."

"Nothing else?"

"Nothing that we can tell."

"Witnesses, sir?"

"There were some scattered witnesses from a few of the killings. They saw a large man in the vicinity of the murders, but none could give a clear physical description. The departments involved tried hypnosis, lie detection, all the usual that we and the Yard would use. Nothing developed."

"You said North America, sir. I wonder..."

"I was getting to that, Arthur. The last three killings occurred in or near New York, which is why we're on the case. We fully expect another woman to die December fifth."

"No suspects?"

"Not one. But we do know something about the killer. The date itself seems to be the key to the puzzle, so, I've had my staff check each December fifth for fifty years." Cross-Wade reached into his desk drawer and pulled out a green folder. "The results are quite remarkable. They're here for you to read." He handed the file to Loggins.

"I also had our psychologists look at the case. A question, Arthur. Have you ever heard of the term 'anniversary excitement schizophrenia'?"

"No, sir."

"Well, you'll be hearing it a lot. I call it 'calendar schizophrenia.' It's all in the folder. Read what's there, then report back to me."

Loggins left the office. Cross-Wade stared ahead, knowing that the assignment of still another man, no matter how capable, would probably bring him no closer to his target. To know the probable motive, to know the date of the next killing, to know the physical characteristics of the victim, yet not to know the identity of the killer—that was the greatest frustration of his police career.

Samantha blundered.

It was serious, in some ways inexcusable.

She'd forgotten that all the calls she'd made checking Marty's past would appear on the phone bill. The bill came on a Saturday, Marty was home, and, as Samantha's fortune would have it, it was he who went down to the lobby to get the mail.

He noticed immediately. The calls to Northwestern, to Elkhart, to Washington. What the hell was she doing? Why was she calling these places? Marty stood against a marble wall in the mailroom, just staring at the bill, as if it were some Chinese puzzle. Did Samantha suspect something? Had she been tipped?

He couldn't ask her about those calls. The question itself would be suspicious. He simply paid the bill without showing it to her, hoping she'd never notice that a phone bill was missing.

But he was apprehensive, and he wasn't used to it. He'd always been in exquisite control, never felt any real risk of detection. But now Samantha was making these calls, and this was something he *couldn't* control. It was the most important year of all, and something might be screwed up.

He went on another secret mission the next Monday—to Wall Street, not to a brokerage firm or a bank, but to one of the biggest greeting-card stores in Manhattan. The store thrived on the Wall Street trade, the owner calculating that the striped-suit crowd was always sending cards to customers and potentials. Since each "target" required a card on holidays, birthdays, and anniversaries, the shop could boom year 'round. The owner took home six figures and lived in Greenwich, Connecticut.

Marty eyed an older saleswoman in a polka-dot dress and knew in his gut that this was a lady who'd memorized the entire stock.

"Help you?" she asked.

"Yes," Marty replied. "I need cards for special customers. Specific cards."

"We probably have them."

Marty took a list from his inside jacket pocket. "I need a birthday card for a boy, with a horse on the front."

"Plenty of horse cards," the woman said. She wore glasses on a chain around her neck and put them on, anticipating the search.

"A brown horse if you can."

The woman was unperturbed. "We have brown."

"And I need an anniversary card with a picture of a sailboat."

"Any particular anniversary?"

"No, a general card."

"That won't be difficult. Sailboats are always popular. In fact, I have one where the sail is actually made of fabric. Canvas, I think. Would you like to see that? It's three dollars."

"A plain one will do," Marty replied. "I also need a Christmas card showing Joseph and Mary at prayer."

"Standard," the woman said.

"And a retirement card with a farmer."

The woman paused. "Well," she said, "farmers aren't too big around here. Would something with flowers do?"

"No."

Marty realized he'd been too abrupt. "I mean, I'm sure it would be nice, but the man who's retiring just bought this farm and..."

"What about a landscape, with cattle grazing?"

Was that adequate? Did it meet the needs of the ritual, and would it have satisfied Uncle Ned? "Yes, I'll take that one," Marty answered, hoping the card would meet the test. He then went through six more requests on his list. The woman satisfied him, or came incredibly close, on each one, the first time Marty recalled that happening with just one visit to one store.

He took the cards back to his office and quietly locked the door. Now he made out each one, signing them, "Love, Frankie." One went to Jim and Greta Carman, another to Uncle Fred and Aunt Mil. Some were for relatives, others for friends. He addressed the cards, but left the state and zip codes off. They'd wind up in the dead letter box, he knew, but that was fine. It was ritual, all ritual, all important.

The next day he took a cab to 116th Street and Broadway —Columbia University. This wasn't ritual. This was real life. He'd never be recognized here. None of the midtown bunch had reason to be up at Columbia, and he melted in well with the diverse crowd that circulated through the neighborhood.

He crossed Broadway to Radius, a travel agency. It was on the second floor of an old sandstone building, above a camera shop, and had the usual airline posters in the window advertising cut-rate flights to Spain, Puerto Rico, Brazil, and Peru. No doubt about the population trends on the West Side, Marty thought.

He walked the two short flights of wooden stairs, edging around a derelict clearly stoned on drugs. The door to Radius was ajar, unusual in a neighborhood where double locks were standard issue. Inside, Radius was the traditional agency—rows of desks piled with papers, timetables, phone messages, and letters. Ann Sherman, a tall Columbia graduate student in Chinese history who booked travel part-time, spotted Marty. "Help you?" she asked, gesturing for him to come to her desk.

"Yeah," Marty answered. Don't act the executive, he told himself. Not in this neighborhood. Just be a guy looking for a trip. "I'd like to buy a ticket to Rome," he said.

"Sure," Ann replied, as Marty sat down in her guest chair. She reached for a thick black book containing the international airline schedules and turned to Rome. "Is this a round trip?" she asked.

"Yes." It wasn't, but a one-way ticket to Rome might raise suspicions.

"For yourself?"

"Yes. One person."

"Okay, and when would you like to go?"

"December sixth, in the morning." The date sent an unaccustomed chill up Marty's spine.

"Has to be morning?" Ann asked.

"Yes, I've got a tight schedule."

"And you'll be returning...?"

"December eighteenth."

"Too bad you can't stay for Christmas. Christmas in Rome is great."

"I know," Marty answered, "but I just can't do it this year."

"If you could return two days later," Ann said, keeping her finger on one line of the book, "I could get you a lower fare."

"How much lower?"

"Oh, about two hundred dollars."

"Well, I don't think so. I'd lose business days here."

"Okay. You want nonstop, of course."

"Sure."

"Alitalia leaves at nine-twenty in the morning and arrives in Rome about eleven-thirty at night."

"That's fine."

"Will you be needing a hotel?"

"No, I'm staying privately."

"Okay. Let's check your return." She found an acceptable return trip and started taking ticket information. "Your name, sir?"

"Steele," Marty replied. "Elliot Steele." And he had a fake passport to prove it. Indeed, in his safe he had a complete set of Elliot Steele ID papers, acquired from the same San Francisco counterfeiter who, eighteen years earlier, had made up all the documents he'd needed to become Martin Everett Shaw.

He gave Ann an answering service as his phone number. He'd engaged it, under the Steele name, just for December.

The tension was too much for Samantha.

She was pacing the living room, pondering her next move in penetrating Marty's past, when she suddenly felt dizzy. Nothing much, she thought. Maybe morning sickness. But then something seemed to squeeze her nostrils together. She gasped for breath, felt herself on the verge of panic. Stay in control, she exhorted herself. She stumbled to the phone and called Lynne.

"Lynne... I'm choking." She collapsed.

It took six precious minutes for a handyman to let Lynne in. Samantha was unconscious, but breathing. An ambulance lurched up to the building's entrance twelve minutes later.

Two paramedics charged in with medical bags, an oxygen tank, and a box of instruments.

"What happened?" one snapped at Lynne.

"I don't know," she answered, almost intimidated. "She was choking."

Samantha's color—good. Her breathing—relatively normal. There were no signs of choking. The second paramedic whipped out his stethoscope and checked her heart. Normal.

"History of heart disease?" he asked Lynne.

"None that I know of. I'm just a friend."

They brought Samantha around with smelling salts and massage. She opened her eyes, looked about fearfully, finally focusing on Lynne. "I'm sorry," she said.

"You're sorry? I'm glad you're alive."

"I guess I just lost my breath." Instinctively, she felt her stomach. "I just hope..."

"Let's go to the hospital," Lynne said.

"No," Samantha answered, and she was firm. Lynne was stunned, but Samantha wouldn't budge. "I'll just rest," she said. She wanted no hospital, and she *didn't* want Marty told. "I'd worry him," she explained, and he'd inevitably find out about the baby. She retained the old warm feelings through all the hurt and mystery. "It was just a fainting spell," she reasoned. "Maybe something I ate."

She did agree to see Dr. Fromer, who took her immediately. He examined her, then sat her down in a tiny office adjoining his medical room. Lynne waited outside, respecting Samantha's privacy.

"Look," Fromer said, "I don't see any medical problem. There's no complication with the pregnancy." He could see the relief cross Samantha's face. "But come clean with me. Did you do anything to bring on this fainting?"

"No," Samantha insisted.

"Drinking?"

"No. You know that."

"No other substances? You know what I mean."

"I wouldn't *touch* that stuff!"

"Of course," Fromer said, with a warm smile. "Not in normal times. But times change. When you were here before I said you seemed under stress. That seems worse now."

Samantha shrugged. Oh, how she wanted to pour it out, yet keep her secret. "Maybe it's having the baby," she said.

"I don't think so." He'd seen too many women with personal problems to be fooled. "I'll repeat what I said before. You should consider counseling if there's a personal problem. Another episode like this *could* affect the baby. I've got to be blunt about that."

Samantha looked at him, and for a few moments said nothing. Suddenly she realized that the crisis might affect the health—the life—of someone other than herself. It was simply something she hadn't confronted before. "Thank you," she said softly. "I really want this baby."

8

"Jesus Christ a-mighty," Loggins said as he walked into Cross-Wade's office carrying a stack of background material on the calendar schizophrenic case. "This is horrible."

"Yes," Cross-Wade replied, "and nothing new has come in. Have you theories, Arthur?"

"No, sir. We're dealin' with a loose cannon. Any clues would come from the past murders."

"Precisely."

"And there's not much."

"I've been weighing a change in strategy," Cross-Wade revealed. "Up to now I've resisted going public. The circus would be disgusting. But if we issued a public alert to women with long auburn hair—there're thousands of them—maybe we could frighten the killer. Or maybe one of these women would see something suspicious in a man she knows."

Loggins shrugged. He didn't think much of the idea.

"On the other hand," Cross-Wade went on, "if the killer strikes, we look impotent. It would encourage him, maybe even others. A public alert is a dare." Cross-Wade was coming to agree with Loggins. "No," he concluded, "I think I'll hold off."

December fifth was seventeen days away.

Samantha rested for only a day after her fainting spell. She'd come to a crushing conclusion: she had to reach out to close friends to solve the mystery of Marty's past. Nothing else was likely to work. The baby inside spurred her on. What if her questions about Marty weren't resolved by the delivery date? What if she were wheeled into that delivery room not really knowing who her husband was, and what was going on in his mind? What if the truth had some tragic impact on the child?

So she went to a few of Marty's social friends, revealing only part of the problem, telling them she'd had trouble finding small things in Marty's past. All she got were shrugs, hints that she'd probably misunderstood Marty's comments about his past, and the distinct impression that no one wanted to get too close to someone else's family puzzle.

Inevitably, she thought of Tom Edwards. She'd called him before, of course, but she'd hedged, not revealing how serious her problem was. She was still reluctant to tell all to Tom. After all *that* could damage his deep friendship with Marty. But if there were one person who could help, it was Tom Edwards. No one knew more about Marty, the way he ticked, what he thought. Samantha called him and asked him to lunch. It was about Marty, she said, and it was important.

"Is he sick?" Tom asked urgently.

"Possibly," Samantha replied. Be as dramatic as you can, she told herself. Jolt Tom. Get him in the right frame of mind.

"When do you need me?" Tom responded.

They agreed to meet at a small Chinese restaurant near Tom's office. He knew the manager and secured a booth toward the rear, out of the flight path of dashing waiters.

Tom took one look at Samantha and saw trouble. There was a vacant look in her eyes. A flame had gone out. The mellowness, which usually seemed to cover her like a curtain, was replaced by a tightness that made Tom sense the worst. He didn't wait to offer Samantha a drink, didn't even go through the amenities.

"Sam, what's wrong?" he asked. "I want it straight."

"I'm not sure," she answered, still zipped into her winter coat, thawing out from the cold.

"Is Marty dying?"

"No, nothing like that."

"You said he might be sick."

Samantha hesitated. All right, this may be melodramatic, she thought, continuing the tack she had used when calling Tom, but it was all right, it reflected the way she felt. "Another kind of sick," she said. "Tom, before I tell you, you've got to answer some questions."

"Shoot." He waved away a waiter who'd stopped.

"Where did Marty go to college?"

He looked at her as if she were putting him on. "Why, Northwestern. *You* knew that."

"I thought I knew."

"Come again."

"Where did he go to high school?"

Tom threw her another odd look. "Elkhart, Indiana."

"How do you know?"

"What do you mean, how do I know?"

"Tom, please!"

"He told me, Sam."

"Elementary school?"

"Elkhart again."

"What service was he in?"

"Army."

"You *sure*?"

"Of *course* I'm sure. Sam, you called me a few weeks ago and asked for Marty's old friends. Is this about that?"

"Are you *absolutely* sure, Tom?"

"Yes!"

"How?"

"The same thing as before. He told me."

"Tom, is there anything about Marty's past that you know directly?"

"Directly?"

"Without him telling you."

"No."

"I see."

"Sam, what is this about? You've got to tell me."

Samantha looked around the dimly lit restaurant, as if any of the anonymous people were actually interested. She leaned forward, almost spilling a glass of water, making sure that Tom would hear every word over the clatter and din. "Tom," she said, a sudden calm coming over her as her personal purging began, "I went back to find people for the party. I called Northwestern, Elkhart, the Army."

"That's great."

"No it isn't. None of it is true, Tom. Marty never went to Northwestern or the Elkhart schools."

Tom was flabbergasted, his eyes almost closing in skepticism. "Come on."

"I checked and doublechecked. There *was* a Martin Shaw in the Army...but he was killed."

Tom simply stared at Samantha, at first saying nothing, not really knowing how to respond. "I don't believe it" was all he could say.

"Neither did I," Samantha replied. "Tom, I took Marty's diploma to be checked. It's a fake."

Tom took a deep, troubled breath, showing a kind of tension rare for him. "Let's order," he said, buying time to think it over. They ordered some simple dishes, the talk with the waiter reducing the electricity a few volts. Then Tom got to the core of the matter.

"Now," he asked, "is it possible you're overlooking something?"

"Like what?"

"Maybe Marty's diploma is a duplicate. People lose their originals and get copies."

"Tom, there's no *record* of Marty at Northwestern...or anywhere else. Elkhart had no record of any school pictures in any year. Marty doesn't seem to have a past."

"Sam, you sound like a Hollywood movie."

"They couldn't write one like this, Tom."

"You've checked everything?"

"Everything."

Tom leaned back, finally accepting what Samantha was telling him. "Now I know," he said, "why you thought Marty might be sick. You meant mentally sick."

"Yes," Samantha replied softly.

There was a long, almost ominous pause, but then, incredibly, a wide grin came to Tom's face, a grin that seemed totally out of place.

"You *know* something," Samantha said, hoping, hoping so hard, that Tom *did* have the answer.

"No, I really don't," he replied, deflating her. "I'm smiling because I'm sure this'll all be cleared up. Sam, Marty's a straight guy."

"God, I know that," Samantha answered, "more than anyone else."

"If he had to tell you some tales about his past, he must've had a reason. If I know Marty, it was a *damned good* reason."

Samantha felt the urge to tell Tom about the baby, how it was increasing the pressure on her to resolve her doubts about Marty. But even Marty didn't know about the child. No, it would be wrong, utterly wrong, to have another man know first. But there was something else she *had* to get out.

"Tom, did Marty ever mention any legal trouble?"

"Why, is he having a problem?"

"That's what I'm trying to find out."

Tom shrugged. "No, he never mentioned anything to me."

"Do you think he might have...a past? You know what I mean?"

"Marty? Boy, I'd sure doubt it. But look, hell, who knows?

Maybe he made a mistake once—you know, when he was a young guy."

"We could find out," Samantha said. "We could go to the FBI and people like that."

"Hey," Tom cautioned her, "if Marty did something wrong, what makes you think he didn't change his name?"

"Yes." Lawyer Grimes had said the same thing.

"And something else," Tom continued, "we talked about sickness. Maybe Marty has amnesia, or something psychological."

"Could *you* find out?"

"Me?" Tom was incredulous.

"Tom, I've tried everything." There was a rare, pleading look in Samantha's eyes. "I've even seen a lawyer."

"But you haven't talked to Marty."

"God, no."

Tom looked sternly at Samantha, ready to give what he thought was a dose of common sense. "You still love him, Sam?" he asked.

"Of course."

"Would you love him even if he had something sour in his past?"

"I really think I would."

"Then you've got two choices—either forget the whole thing...or confront him directly."

The first course came just then, wonton soup for Samantha, egg drop for Tom, spare ribs for both. But Samantha just couldn't eat. "Tom, what would *you* do?" she asked.

"I don't know," Tom replied as he picked up a soup spoon. "I'm not married, and I'm not a woman...obviously. But..." He hesitated. Samantha sensed that he was not quite ready to commit himself.

"Please tell me," she asked.

"Maybe you'd better not confront him. That could wreck the marriage."

"Tom, I've just *got* to know."

Tom nodded with the special warmth that was his. "I know what's inside you," he said softly.

They suddenly fell silent. Samantha was learning nothing, even from Marty's closest friend; the advice she was getting sounded logical but brought her no closer to a solution. She felt, in a way, that Tom was protecting Marty, as some of Marty's other friends had. Maybe he felt that probing Marty's past was an improper intrusion for a wife. And maybe it was. Maybe there were things she *shouldn't* know. Didn't *she* have secrets, embarrassments, things she'd rather not have Marty discover? Her father had told her that in every closet was at least part of a skeleton.

But she wanted to try one more stab with Tom. "Tom," she said, "I asked if *you* could find out. You danced around it. Could you?"

"Sam," Tom replied, "I wouldn't even know how. I mean, how do you go into a man's past?"

He was right, of course. Just as Grimes had said, this was a job for a private investigator. Samantha was starting to feel a bit foolish. She'd guessed wrong. Tom really didn't know that much about Marty. Now his attitude toward Marty would surely be affected, and his attitude toward her as well. All she'd done, she feared, was reduce herself in Tom's estimation. He did finally volunteer to probe Marty gently about his past, and maybe to do some independent checking. Other than that, the lunch with Tom resulted in nothing.

Yet, Samantha would not relent. Maybe still other friends knew more, or were willing to say more. She called two additional friends of Marty's, explaining the "problem" while assuring each that it was probably just a mix-up. They were cooperative and sympathetic, but could supply no useful information. The pattern of their answers added up to the same refrain Samantha had heard before—that it would all work out, that Marty must have his reasons, that he may have been involved in Government work, that he might be hiding something he has a right to hide. And what does it matter, if he's such a good husband?

Samantha hit a dead end.
December fifth was thirteen days away.

Marty was still concerned. Yes, the plans were made. Almost everything was set. But what about those phone calls? What was this woman up to? Were the calls continuing, and, if so, what did they reveal?

It was four in the afternoon when a bonded messenger arrived at Marty's office with a sealed note. He knew who it was from by the envelope, and was surprised. He immediately closed the door and took it to his desk. Carefully, he tore it open and read a handwritten letter. It was a note he'd feared might someday come. He stared at the big, printed warning at the bottom, scrawled in an angry handwriting that seared across the page. "Wifey knows," it said. "Wifey knows you have no past."

He shredded the letter.

9

Marty didn't panic. He never panicked. Yes, Samantha knew more than he wanted her to know, but she didn't know what he had planned. She couldn't know. She couldn't suspect. So she'd have some questions. That was hardly a dent in so beautiful a plan, so perfect a ritual. His apprehension—now confirmed by the sealed note—turned to an iron resolve. He could handle it—until December fifth.

"I've never tasted such great chicken," Marty exulted to Samantha as he was eating dinner that night. "My lady, you have that special touch."

Samantha hadn't seen Marty this buoyant since the electric trains. He seemed less fatigued. "I'm going to supervise all the cooking for the party," she said.

"No way," he answered. "You may be Supercreature in the kitchen, but you're a guest at my party. That's the only way to do it."

"Marty, I said *supervise*. I won't touch a pot."

"Come on, I know you. Look, those professionals know what they're doing."

"I'm crushed."

Marty laughed. "All right, supervise. But at least come out and say hello. Is that a deal?"

"It's a deal."

Marty smiled with that large, rugged face that had magnetized Samantha from the first moment. Yet it couldn't be the same for her now. The questions were racing through her mind. How do I probe him? How do I find out? When do I confront him, if ever?

"There's very little more to do for the bash," she said. "All I have to do is select the cake and arrange for flowers. You won't *mind* flowers, will you?"

"Me? No. Why?"

"Well, I thought that men sometimes..."

"I like flowers. I'm a sentimental guy," Marty said, prompting Samantha to wonder what he was really sentimental about.

"Did you see today's RSVPs?" she asked.

"No."

"Paul, Keith Harris, Fred and Maryann, Seymour Rose. All coming. Read Fred's little note. You'll get a kick. Uh, Hank Burnham from NBC can't make it."

"Oh, I'm sorry. Hank's a good guy. We were at Fort Polk at the same time... but we didn't know each other."

Good God, Samantha thought, how could he do it? How could he keep up that fiction? Or didn't he know it was fiction?

"He's going to Indiana to help cover a football game," she explained. "Oh, by the way, he's sending you a collector's item from a Super Bowl game."

Marty's eyes caught fire. "Yeah? What?"

"He didn't say. It's a secret."

"That's real nice." He looked at his watch. "Say, how about a movie?"

"Tonight?"

"Unless I have to date you months ahead."

Samantha wasn't up to it. Her head was in too much turmoil, and entertainment was the last thing on her priority list. "Could I beg off?" she asked softly.

"You're not feeling well," Marty said. Samantha thought she saw worry crossing his face.

"No, just tired."

"Okay. Can't blame a fellow for trying." He finished the last bit of dinner, got up and crossed behind her. He started stroking her hair, something he hadn't done in months, and which she rather liked. He had done it to the others, in years past, as well. "You know how special you are?" he asked.

"Yes," she replied, "but I don't mind a refresher course."

"Okay, where do I begin?" He kept up the stroking. What actors they both were, he thought. She knew he was a fake, and he knew what he was going to do to her. Yet the talk didn't falter, never wavered. What could *possibly* be going on in the woman's mind? How did she manage to conceal her suspicions so well? In an odd way, Marty was impressed, more impressed than he'd ever been with Samantha. He'd never noticed she was a person before.

But he had a question to answer, a scene to play out. He'd do it with style. He'd always done it with style.

"Well," he said, "you're special because you're thoroughly loving."

"Good," Samantha responded. "And?"

"And beautiful."

"Go on."

"I think I'll reserve the rest."

"You mean you can't come up with anything else?"

"Well, all right," Marty said, "there's loyal, trusty, kind, reverent...?"

"Okay, I'm satisfied," Samantha said. Then a question just poured out, as if Samantha couldn't control it. "Marty, what did you do at Fort Polk?"

Marty tightened, although Samantha couldn't detect it. There she goes, he thought.

"I was a hero," he replied.

"Come on."

"No, really. I was given a special commendation for extreme caution under cover."

"Marty..."

"All right. I'll come clean." He stopped stroking her hair. "Clerk-typist. I typed accident reports for jeeps." He laughed. "Does that lower me in your estimation?"

"No. I wasn't expecting a general."

They talked for a few more minutes about nothing in particular, then Marty glanced at his watch. "Hey, if we're not going to the movies, I think I'll get some work done."

"Sure." Now Samantha sensed the tautness inside Marty. It was there in his voice, in the quick rhythm of his speech. He went to his desk in the bedroom, skipping *The CBS Evening News,* which he almost always watched, and pretended to examine a pile of reports. And again the words came back, the words permanently etched in his distorted mind.

"Frankie's a good boy. He's waited a long time."

"Don't gimme that. He's a kid. How long can a kid wait?"

"I want him to be happy."

"Him happy? What about me happy?"

"You know I've tried."

"When have you tried? Yesterday or this morning?"

God, what happened that day! Marty remembered, the picture never losing its clarity, its vividness. Now he'd almost arrived at another special day, when remembrance turned to noble deeds. He felt his hand quiver. The memory wouldn't leave him. It was reinforced as he looked around the room, with its odd arrangement, its bizarre picture frame. Did other men have this thing inside? Did *anyone* else have it?

He found himself staring at the furniture again and again. "Frankie likes it," he whispered to himself. He knew.

Marty lost complete track of time. Finally, Samantha came

in. "What's the crisis?" she asked.

"Huh?" Marty's mind wasn't focused on the possibility of answering questions.

"You've been at this for hours, Marty. Something come up in the office?"

Marty shrugged. "No, it's just a lot of baloney. You know, memos and bills. It was a good chance to catch up. No crisis."

"Sure?"

"Sure."

Samantha felt tempted to look through that pile of papers, if she could get the chance. Maybe, just maybe, there was a clue to Marty's past. Maybe he was doing something in business that would put her on track. She dropped the thought. Too risky. She wasn't a pro.

"Coming to bed?" she asked.

"It's a little early. I think I'll stay up awhile. You don't mind, do you?"

She laughed. "I *always mind.* But I'll forgive you for tonight, as long as I get my share tomorrow."

"I swear," Marty answered. "I'll get the equipment working."

"Well, just don't work it anywhere else." She winked, a charming wink, so thoroughly normal, yet so thoroughly absurd, considering what each of them knew. Here she was, engaged in verbal foreplay with a man who had become the object of her deepest suspicion, whose baby she was carrying, whose life was a mystery. And his responses? Typically Marty, although his mind was on a hammer and chain, and how they would soon be used.

She went to bed.

He gazed at her. She'd live twelve more days.

The next day Samantha made the decision: Go to the police. It came from the gut, yet she had the most rational of reasons—she'd exhausted everything else and her curiosity was turning to fear, fear that whatever was wrong about Marty might someday explode in her face. She could be hurting him by going, but she could also be protecting him. To limit any embarrassment, she decided against telling any of his friends, including Tom. They really had no need to know.

She thought first of going to 20th Precinct headquarters near home. She rejected the idea. Too many friends in the neighborhood. What if someone saw her go in or out? What would people think? No one *really* wanted to be seen in a police station, she thought. It was a sturdy remnant of her middle-class upbringing.

So she took a bumpy, rattling cab to main police headquarters, a modern highrise in lower Manhattan, where Missing Persons had its principal office. Police Plaza was teeming with cops. As Samantha got out of her cab, she saw a veritable sea of blue. At first, the sight frightened her. There was something vaguely military about it; it was as if she were in a fortress, surrounded by a hostile landscape. Of course, the cops were simply going to and from offices, and were generally relaxed. But the scene was unusual in Manhattan, where residents normally saw, at most, small clusters of policemen.

"Yes, ma'am?" asked the officer guarding the front door. Samantha was instantly impressed by his bearing. Main headquarters always got the best.

"I'd like to report a missing person."

"A child, ma'am?"

"No, an adult."

"Okay. Are you absolutely sure he's missing?"

Samantha hesitated. "Yes. No. It's very complicated. It's a man who may be missing, but may not know it. I know that sounds strange."

"That's the business we're in," the officer said. "Take the elevator to the fourth floor, turn left. It's room four eighteen."

"Thanks."

Samantha got into an elevator crammed with husky cops and one handcuffed "perpetrator," there to be questioned. She reached the fourth floor and walked to a solid door marked MISSING PERSONS in gold letters that were beginning to chip. Somehow, the chipped letters seemed right. The modern building surrounding them didn't. A police station, even the *main* police station, should be old and damp, with cracked ceilings and bare bulbs for lighting. There should be "wanted" posters on the walls, not notices of police union meetings. There should be a musty smell, not the purity of filtered air. And there should not, definitely should not, be electronic typewriters and desktop computers. The place didn't fit Samantha's image, and maybe that was good. She felt a little more comfortable once she got to the fourth floor, a little more like a visitor to a midtown office building.

She had to wait more than an hour, all on a cold metal visitor's chair in a plain gray waiting room. There were other cases ahead, and Samantha was struck by the fact that virtually all were women. Why? She couldn't understand it. Was it a fluke this day? Were women more forward about filing reports? Were they there to report missing children? Or were there many Martys, many more than Samantha realized?

Occasionally she heard sobs from the interviewing room, which lay beyond a closed door. And, occasionally, women would come out hiding their faces, leaving quickly, sometimes literally running out. They were either embarrassed, Samantha reasoned, or they had just been given some very bad news. At one point she walked over to the policewoman at the waiting room desk, a young, slim black woman who went out of her way to be courteous.

"It shouldn't be long," the policewoman said, assuming that was what Samantha wanted. "Oh no," Samantha said, "I wasn't concerned about that. I was just wondering..." She stopped, thinking that her question might bring ridicule.

"Yes?"

Samantha forged ahead. "I was wondering how many they...find."

"Not many," the policewoman replied forthrightly.

"Why?"

"The officer will explain it," Samantha was told. "I'm not

authorized to get into those details."

Those details? *What* details? Was there something secret about this? Samantha was annoyed by this little bureaucratic roadblock, but didn't let it show. Don't antagonize them. Not when you need them so much. She returned to her seat.

A few minutes later a tall, middle-aged sergeant stuck his head out the interviewing-room door. He read from a little pink card. "Mrs. Shaw?"

"Yes?" Samantha froze in her seat. Now that her time had come, needles of fright shot through her. He was a *cop*. An officer of the law. A guy with a gun, a nightstick, and a ticket to jail. The reality hit home and Samantha instantly realized how totally out of place, how alien, she felt.

"This way, ma'am," the sergeant said, a slight smile on his face. Samantha looked up at him for a moment, only then realizing that he was Oriental. It was foolish, and juvenile, but as she saw his face she could think only of Charlie Chan. That was the only immediate way she could relate to an Oriental policeman, the only image she had.

Samantha followed him through the door into a large room divided into cubicles, each one paneled with a soundproofing material. It was virtually impossible, from one cubicle, to hear conversations in the next one.

She saw the black identification plate: SERGEANT YANG. Yang gestured for her to sit down, this time on a cushioned visitor's chair.

"Now," he said, "I see you live over in 20th Precinct country. You didn't see Missing Persons over there?"

"No, I was..."

"A little embarrassed."

"Yes."

"I understand." He noticed Samantha staring at him. "My mother was American," he explained, as he'd done to virtually every visitor. My father gave me the eyes. He comes from Taiwan." He smiled broadly. Samantha liked him. "I've never been to the Orient," she said, trying to make small talk.

"Neither have I. I hear there are some nice parts. But if I

go, I have to see my relatives. You know what that's like."

He studied the little pink card, which Samantha had filled out earlier. "A phantom past," he said.

"Yes," Samantha replied.

"And you've sought help elsewhere—professional people?"

"Yes. I tried everything before coming here."

"That's what we like. A lot of people run to us when they could solve the problem at home. Ties up the system, if you get me."

Samantha didn't reply, wondering if she was tying up the system.

Yang finally leaned back, his chair groaning with the agony of age. He flipped the pink card on his desk, ready to give Samantha the standard talk. "Before we get into details," he said, "I want you to be aware of some things. First off, we're not too successful here. We don't find many missing people because most people who are missing *want* to be."

"*Want* to be?"

"Yes. They just decide to change their lives. They drop out, go away. Especially married men. They reach a certain point, the pressure builds up, a lot of bills, and they chuck it all. You've read stories about guys who are last seen at railroad stations?"

"Yes."

"Almost always railroad stations. Most are never seen again."

Samantha realized what a sheltered existence she'd led. No one *she* knew had ever faded away like that. "Marty isn't the type," she told Yang.

He smiled. "No husband ever is," he said. "But look, your husband hasn't disappeared from *you*. Your concern is that he may be missing from somewhere else."

"Yes. Sure."

"All right," Yang went on, "let's list the possibilities. He could be missing voluntarily or involuntarily. If involuntarily, it could be the result of mental illness, or some injury that produced a mental reaction. If voluntarily, he could have been fed up with his old life, or he could be running from something. It doesn't have to be a crime. It could be a personal scandal, even a misunderstanding. Or, he could have had a professional failure that embarrassed him."

"I just don't know," Samantha responded.

"Of course. But let's think hard. Did Marty ever slip out with a name that you didn't recognize?"

"Only business names," Samantha answered. "And he told me who they were."

"He talk in his sleep?"

"No."

"Ever seem confused about his past? You know, saying one thing, then correcting it."

"No, not at all. Marty talks about his past—or what he *says* is his past—all the time. We've even agreed to take a trip to the Midwest, where he says he grew up."

"Oh? That's interesting." Yang jotted down a note about the trip. "Most people who are running wouldn't do that. But I wouldn't put much stock in it."

"Why?"

"Because Marty might genuinely know the areas you're visiting, yet could still be lying to you about having lived there. Where does he say he was born?"

"Elkhart, Indiana."

"You going there?"

"Yes."

"Why?"

"I suggested it. I was really testing him, but he jumped at the chance."

"Well," Yang said, shrugging his shoulder, "I don't know what's in his mind."

"But why *might* he want to go?" Samantha asked.

"Maybe to impress you. He may want to *show* you his made-up past. It may reassure him to see that you believe his story."

Samantha gazed down at the linoleum floor, which hadn't

been polished in months. "This is all theory," she said, not meaning to be rude or ungrateful, but sounding a bit that way.

"Sure," Yang answered. "We're trying to write someone else's story."

"Maybe you...can't help," Samantha suggested.

"You've heard the old proverb—it's from my father's part of the world—that a journey of a thousand miles begins with a single step?"

"I've heard that," Samantha answered.

"Well, we can take that first step here. We might not discover who Marty is, or where he's from, but we can narrow things down. I've already mentioned some possibilities."

"The lawyer I saw, Mr. Grimes, said some of the same things you did," Samantha reported.

"I'm sure he did. There's kind of a standard list. Now, tell me, do you have any voice recordings of your husband?"

"Tapes?"

"Yes. Dictation at the office, that kind."

"I don't know. I can look in his desk. Why?"

"Regional accents. We have an expert here. We might be able to pick up the part of the country he's from."

"I'll try to get something," Samantha said.

"Okay. Now, does he take unusual medicines?"

"No."

"Too bad. Sometimes we can trace old prescriptions." Yang wrote as he spoke, and Samantha could see that his handwriting, done with his left hand, was flawless. He saw from the corner of his eye that she was watching him. "I like penmanship," he said. "I write everything longhand. I don't really believe in typewriters. Too impersonal." Again he smiled. Samantha suddenly felt close to him. Of all those she'd spoken to, Yang was, to her, the most human. The invisible shield that had separated her from Grimes, from Levine, from Marty's friends, even from Tom Edwards, just wasn't there. I can talk to him, she thought. I *want* to talk to him.

"Look, can I say something?" she suddenly blurted.

"Sure."

"I'm pregnant."

"Congratulations. I didn't know."

"Thanks, but that's not the point. I want the baby. It's my baby. It's *ours*." She paused. "But sometimes I don't want the baby. You know what I'm saying."

"Come on," Yang said. "It'll be beautiful."

"Sergeant Yang, it's Marty's baby, believe me. But I don't know who the father is. Do you understand what I'm getting at?"

"Yes, I do."

And then Samantha did what she didn't want to do. She started to cry, just like all those other women she'd seen running from the room, just like the women who cried under stress, the kind she'd never wanted to be. And Yang just sat there and watched her cry, knowing that it was the best purgative. He saw tears every day, the way doctors see blood every day, and they were part of his job. He said nothing, waiting for Samantha to compose herself. Indeed, he used the time to make some additional notes about Marty, yet looked compassionately at Samantha every few seconds to avoid appearing cold.

"I'm sorry," she finally said, taking a tissue that Yang offered and dabbing her eyes. "This is hell. It never came out like that."

"I'm glad it came out here," Yang said.

She couldn't cry in front of Lynne, or Tom. Even a psychiatrist's office was too forbidding. Here she cried.

"I waited for Marty," she continued, trying to hold back the sobs. "All my life I waited for him. Okay, I try to convince myself that it'll all work out, but I know it won't. I tell myself that he's this great knight I knew he was, but I really know he isn't. And I've got his baby, and I wonder what I'm going to say to it when the time comes. Marty won't be there. I just feel he won't."

Yang did not interrupt. This was the way victims resolved things in their minds, he knew. Best not to intervene until the right moment.

"I had other chances to get married," Samantha continued. Now she just wanted to talk, even if she wavered off the subject. "One of the guys was a foreign correspondent. Now, wouldn't that have been nice? But I had to wait for Martin Everett Shaw. No one else was good enough for cute little Samantha."

"Don't say that about yourself," Yang cautioned. "We all wait for the best. I think you were right."

Samantha stared at Yang, stared deeply into his eyes. "You see a lot like me, don't you?" she asked.

"All the time," he replied. "And I want you to avoid the usual pattern. Many women start feeling that *they're* at fault if their husband disappears, or has Marty's kind of problem. I see this beginning in you. The problem is *his*, not yours. If he's done something wrong, you share no blame."

"Thank you," Samantha said quietly. For the second time she'd met a man who was totally understanding and sympathetic. The first time had been Marty.

"Why don't we go on," Yang suggested.

"Sure. I'm sorry I'm taking so much time."

"Not at all." Yang paused. He knew there was a piece of unfinished business from before Samantha's breakdown. "About your baby," he said, "is everything healthy?"

"Yes," Samantha replied.

"Please keep it."

There was a long silence. The Oriental eyes were so sincere, so caring, so impossible to defy. "I will," Samantha promised, and she knew she could *never* break that promise.

"I want to ask some financial questions," Yang went on, "if that's all right."

"Yes."

"Have you examined your tax returns?"

"Well, Marty takes care of that, but I look at them every year. I check the arithmetic."

"Is there any sizable amount that Marty doesn't declare? You can tell me."

"No, he's honest."

"Can you account for his earnings?"

"What do you mean?"

"Well, does any important money disappear?"

Samantha thought. "I don't think so, but I really haven't calculated. Why?"

"If your husband has a problem, and has to pay someone, even to stay alive, it might show up."

"My God," Samantha groaned.

"Please don't jump to conclusions. I'd like to have any financial records you can supply without tipping your husband."

"I'll get them."

The conversation lasted a full hour more, with Yang, impeccably polite, asking the standard questions and coming up with nothing of great importance. He was pessimistic about solving this case. Samantha's verbal portrait of Marty told him that this was a shrewd, calculating man, the kind who'd cover his tracks well and who probably had sought a new life, with a new identity, to escape some unpleasantness in his past.

"We have access to a nationwide computer bank," he told Samantha. "It has pictures of thousands of missing persons. It's only a shot, but I'd like you to look at some of the pictures."

"Some?"

"They're catalogued. I'll only show you men around Marty's age. There's no point in looking at kids, or eighty-year-olds. Are you willing?"

"I'll try anything."

Yang escorted Samantha out of Missing Persons to a photographic library down the hall. As they walked, he put his arm about her shoulder, once again showing the concern that she appreciated so much, that had been the missing ingredient in her life before Marty.

She noticed how the other cops glanced at Yang—the tall

Oriental with his arm on a "complainant," the policeman who could easily have been a psychologist, a clergyman, or a social worker.

The photographic library consisted of long metal file drawers filled with pictures of missing persons, with a few tables and chairs for people like Samantha to study the collection. Yang selected the right batch and Samantha started her search, not expecting any results whatever.

"Remember," Yang told her, "your husband could have changed his appearance. Try to study facial contours and skin markings. Anything that looks familiar. Watch the hairlines also, and the size of the ears."

"Okay," Samantha said. Despite her pessimism, she felt good about looking through the pictures. At least she was taking *action*, not just talking philosophy with friends or abstractions with paid, *well*-paid professionals. She was amazed at the sheer number of photos—thousands of them, all eight-by-ten glossies. They were not, however, "mug shots." There are no mug shots of missing persons. They were mostly family pictures reproduced by police departments around the country. Some were pathetic, others heartrending. They showed men with their wives and children, in happier times. Almost all the men seemed ordinary, not the kind to melt away or get into trouble. Yet, by Yang's account, most abandoned those around them and simply started again.

"Many of these men probably have new wives and kids," Yang explained. "Sometimes they do it again and again. We had one case of a man who'd left three separate families."

"But aren't there *legitimate* missing persons?" Samantha asked.

"Oh, of course. A lot of children. That's a national scandal. Grown-ups disappear too, sometimes after they're robbed. They're just disposed of so they can't testify later. And there's the head injury thing we talked about."

As he had promised, Yang showed Samantha pictures of men about Marty's age. But he also showed her pictures of younger men taken years before, men who would *now* be Marty's age.

Yang stayed with Samantha, going over each picture. Soon they were joined by another policeman and another woman, this one a bride in her early twenties whose new husband had suddenly disappeared. Samantha overheard their conversation, peppered with words like "bankruptcy," "creditors," "loan sharks." That sounded logical. Man in financial trouble just chucks it all.

After a time, the pictures began to look like blurs. Besides, Samantha saw nothing familiar. None of those men even remotely resembled Marty. She didn't know whether to be happy or depressed. Some clue, however grim, would be better than this perpetual mystery, this wondering, this not knowing. Or would it? She doggedly went through pile after pile, one minute hoping to recognize Marty, another minute hoping not to.

The pictures of the younger men fascinated her, for here was a chance to encounter Marty's past. Some of the pictures had been taken 10 or 15 years earlier. Marty would have been in his late twenties, the time when many men marry and have their first children. She'd watched Marty at friends' houses holding *their* children. He'd always seemed awkward, unaware of what to do. No, it didn't seem possible that he'd been one of those with a family before.

And then ...

A picture came up.

A man in jeans, with a sport shirt, two little boys beside him, in front of a large ranch house.

Samantha held the picture, studied it. She blinked her searching eyes a few times to clear them, to fight the fatigue and double vision.

Marty liked ranch houses. He'd said so. A ranch house in the country. That's what he wanted for summers.

Maybe he'd *always* liked them.

Maybe he'd lived in one.

The facial features in the picture were so familiar. Yang caught Samantha's reaction. Once again he remained silent. Let the witness study. Let the witness ponder. Don't suggest or lead.

There was a companion picture. The same man, this time with a young woman, brutally attractive. Once more Samantha felt the tears well up. Could it be? The pictures weren't that clear. They'd been taken in 1970. But that face, and the build, and the shape of the shoulders, and the ranch house.

With a slow, gentle motion, meant not to disturb or jar, Yang reached over to a shelf and took down a loupe, a small magnifier. He slid it over to Samantha. She placed it over the face in the second picture and bent her head down, centering her eye in the glass. She clenched her fists, then bit her lip. Her body seemed to stiffen, as if receiving a sudden, stabbing wound.

"Marty," she whispered, "I found you."

10

"Wait one moment," Yang advised Samantha. He showed no jubilation at her discovery. He knew the meaning of the moment. She was going through agony. It was the low point of her life, a discovery that would change her forever, probably destroy her marriage, possibly lead her to try something drastic. It wasn't the time for celebration or cries of "Eureka." It rarely is in missing-person-cases, for the familiar picture usually confirms the darkest fears.

Yang went to another file and took out a brief written report whose serial number linked it to the pictures Samantha had just identified. As he pulled it out, he glanced back at her. Now she sat motionless, staring at the pictures, her face blank except for the moist eyes, her hands not even trembling. It was the shock effect, Yang knew. She was probably looking more at the kids and the woman, especially the woman, than at the man. She was meeting people who, inevitably, were very important to her.

Samantha felt more numb than angry, but one question gnawed at her: Was that woman, were those children, still alive? Maybe they weren't. Maybe there'd been a tragedy—a fire, a car crash, something. Maybe that's why Marty...

What should she hope for?

What was right?

Was it right to pray that they were dead, that Marty had escaped a horrible past and found his Samantha? Was it cruel, immoral, obscene, to think that way? It was, but it was also natural. And so, with no embarrassment, Samantha secretly hoped that this was a family of the past, no longer on earth, residing in the recesses of Marty's mind and the cause of constant anguish—but gone forever.

Yang brought her the report, contained in a yellow folder marked BRANNEN, KENNETH.

"Your husband know anything about banking?" Yang asked.

Samantha shrugged. "He knows about money. We've never talked about banks, except to open accounts."

"The man in the pictures was a banker. He had this wife and two kids. They were living in Green Bay, Wisconsin—they have a football team, you know."

"I've heard of it. Marty sometimes watches..."

"He does?"

"But he watches other teams too."

"I see. The report says that this man disappeared in 1969 on his way home from an Army Reserve meeting. He was in a finance unit."

Samantha's heart suddenly sank. "You mean...the family was alive when he disappeared?"

"Yes, I suppose so. There's nothing here to contradict that."

"I see," Samantha said quietly. Yang knew she had crossed the river into that world of ugly reality where men do indeed leave their families and start new lives. He knew it was best to keep her mind focused on the problem at hand, not to let her eat her insides out.

"Does Marty talk about the Army?" he asked.

"Yes, but nothing about finance. He says he was other

places. It wasn't true."

"Please look at the pictures again. Are you sure it's Marty?"

Samantha glanced at the photos, and studied them through the loupe. "It sure looks like him," she said, ice in her voice. "I mean, he hasn't changed that much. Yes, that's Marty." Now the reality was building, grasping her, overpowering her. "*That's* Marty. And *that's* his wife. And *those're* his kids. He's certainly good at keeping secrets, isn't he? Never even a slip of the tongue. Real good, this Marty. This *husband.* What he did to her. What he did to them. To *me*!"

"Try to control yourself," Yang suggested softly. "Remember, there's no positive identification."

"*I'm* the positive identification," Samantha snapped. She felt rationality slip away. It was all emotion now, but she didn't want to sob again. She controlled it, held it in.

"There's very little in this man's folder," Yang told her. "It's incomplete, which happens when we're depending on a small police department. Of course, he's committed a felony."

"He has?"

"Abandonment. He abandoned his family. If this is your Marty, there might be charges in Wisconsin."

Now Samantha thought back to lawyer Grimes. He had cautioned about this—that she might get Marty into trouble by going to the police. But she cared no longer. If he could do what he'd done, he deserved the worst.

"I've got to get more data on this man," Yang said. "I need an ironclad identification, even with your testimony."

Yang took Samantha, with the photos, back to his office. Using his desktop Hewlett-Packard computer terminal, he tried to search out more information on Brannen, Kenneth, in national crime files. He drew a blank. While he worked, Samantha could hear a man in another cubicle pleading, half in English, half in Spanish, for information on his missing son. The boy had left his upper Manhattan apartment for a job at Macy's, and had never reached the store. Samantha suffered with the man, who kept moaning over and over that this was his only child, that his wife was dead, that he was alone and afraid. Some have it worse than I do, Samantha thought. Losing a son is worse than acquiring a criminal for a husband.

The computer search kept turning up nothing. Yang gave up and decided to call the police department in Green Bay, Wisconsin, directly.

He was connected in less than a minute. The sergeant-in-charge located the old missing-persons file on Kenneth Brannen, but it was also incomplete. Data was missing—borrowed over the years, not returned, then lost. However, there *were* some things that Yang could use. "The subject has a short scar on his right knee from surgery," the sergeant in Green Bay said, in a raspy, cigarette-ruined voice. Yang jotted it down, then turned to Samantha.

"Does your husband have a scar on his right knee?"

"No," Samantha answered.

"This man does. But plastic surgery could've changed that."

The sergeant in Green Bay went on. "This man had an interest in railroads."

"Your husband like railroads?" Yang asked Samantha.

She almost jumped. The trains. Those silly trains. "Yes. Definitely yes!" She knew this was the right man.

The rest of the data from Green Bay was nondescript—it could have applied to most men. Kenneth Brannen liked to talk about sports. He'd served a two-year hitch in the Army, mostly in Europe. He'd always gone to church and had insisted his family go too. The medical and dental records were missing, but might be located if an official search were conducted. There was one piece of information, though, that Yang had to pass on to Samantha, no matter how much pain it might cause, no matter how much bitterness. A 1982 memo inserted to update the file read:

Mrs. Kenneth Brannen (Kathleen) has not remarried although she had her husband declared legally dead after the usual seven-year period. She works as a bookkeeper and resides at 27 Mulberry Drive West. Both her sons are in college, on scholarships. Mrs. Brannen still seeks information about the whereabouts of her husband, and his fraternal order continues to offer a $5,000 reward.

Yang repeated the memo to Samantha. "She would be the main supplier of any information," he said. "Unless you object, I'm going to check with her. By putting everything together, I hope to get positive identification...if this is Marty."

Samantha was exasperated. "It's him. Believe me. But... do you think she'll cooperate?"

"She still seeks information," Yang repeated from the memo.

"Does she seek it from the new Mrs. Brannen, or Mrs. Shaw, or whatever my name is?"

Yang hadn't thought about that one. He'd never had a case where the old wife and the new were converging on the same target. "I can't answer that," he said. "But my hunch is that any woman in her position would cooperate. The only complication is her having had her husband declared legally dead. If there was an insurance payment, and Marty is the man, the insurance company might decide to sue her."

"Could they win?"

"I'm not a lawyer. But let's play dumb and go at it. Okay?"

Samantha sighed. The turmoil inside made any careful decision-making impossible. "I guess so," she said.

Yang was about to get back on the line with Green Bay when Samantha suddenly reached forward and touched his arm, restraining him. "Wait," she said.

"What's wrong?"

She took a deep breath. She knew that what she was about to say might sound silly, or worse. "I want to talk to her."

"You *what*?"

"I want to talk with Mrs. Kenneth Brannen, the first wife of my husband...his only legal wife."

"You sure?"

"Yes," Samantha said firmly. She was amazed at her own control. If life was shattered, she told herself, pick up the pieces with style. Her mother would have said that. But how long would her nerves hold? How long before the pain became too much?

"It could be difficult," Yang cautioned.

"I'm ready. We have a lot in common."

Yang nodded, sensing Samantha's resolve. He got back on the line to Green Bay. "My subject wants to talk with Mrs. Brannen," he said. "Can it be arranged?"

The sergeant at the other end laughed, a hoarse laugh that dissolved into a throaty cough. "I never heard of that," he said.

"This is her wish," Yang insisted, now Samantha's advocate. "Can it be arranged?"

"I can try," Green Bay replied. "I'll get back to you."

"Thank you, Green Bay."

Yang hung up. "Now we wait," he said.

One floor below, Spencer Cross-Wade checked off another day on his calendar. Eleven days to December fifth, and he had absolutely nothing new. He was reduced to going over evidence from past murders and trying to find some new twist. Arthur P. Loggins sat heavily in a visitor's chair, equally stumped. Cross-Wade began to pace, his shoulders rounded, his head down, a man who, seemingly, had lost.

"I am humiliated," he announced. "Even my flowers look sad. They'll say upstairs that I'm not modern enough, that I haven't used the computers properly, that I'm depending on old-fashioned police work. Well, they're right. That's what I know. That's what I believe in."

"Yes, sir," Loggins answered, with his usual dullness.

"You have reinterviewed all the witnesses, and only the whistle shows up?"

"Not exactly a whistle, sir."

"You know what I'm talking about, Arthur."

"Yes, sir. The lady who was near last year's murder site

said she heard a person sounding like a train horn."

"It could have been anyone," Cross-Wade said.

"Yes sir. But this was right off Route I-95 in Greenwich, Connecticut. The lady said very few people walk there. We've confirmed that. And it was around the time of the murder."

"So? Do we put out an all-points for anyone who impersonates trains?"

Loggins didn't answer. Like Cross-Wade, he was humiliated.

"I'm considering a very quiet request, passed by local patrolmen, to all beauty shop owners," Cross-Wade announced. "They'd be on the lookout for auburn-haired-women. We might have the local precincts visit them. But...I'm afraid word would get out and we'd have the same problem as with a general alert. A freak show."

"Yes, sir."

"It's a bad idea. I'm glad I thought of how bad it is. Look, Arthur, there must be a picture of this man as a boy. We *know* where he lived. I can't believe all pictures have disappeared."

"They have, sir, except for that grainy newspaper picture, and even that negative is gone. The picture is very blurry. We talked about that."

"Yes. Well, I have nothing else. This is a man who makes no mistakes, who leaves no real clues. He could even strike in Alaska this year, for all we know. He may even be dead."

"Sir," Loggins said, "this may be one of those cases where the killings just go on until the guy messes up, like 'Son of Sam.' Remember? He got caught 'cause he got a parking ticket."

Cross-Wade stopped pacing and slumped down in his desk chair, fatigued by the ordeal. "You're right, of course," he said. "A life might be saved, or lost, because of luck."

The room fell silent, each man lost in his own thoughts—thoughts of failure, of another victim. Finally, quietly, Cross-Wade spoke up, in terms he had never used before. He hated himself for what he was saying, but he knew he had clear responsibilities.

"Let us, Arthur, draw up a plan of action to follow the next murder. We must know exactly how to react, what questions to ask, what steps to take. Witnesses's memories fade quickly."

"I'll draw something up," Loggins said.

"Do that."

Samantha waited.

Yang did paperwork while the sergeant in Green Bay tried to reach Kathleen Brannen. But Yang's mind was on Samantha, and her emotional condition. He saw the delayed reaction setting in, as it does when someone loses a relative, handles all the arrangements calmly, then dissolves when the reality hits home. Yang could see Samantha's hands trembling slightly, and her skin losing its color. Then he saw her reach down to her stomach.

"What's wrong?"

"A little pain," she replied, her voice quivering. She thought back to Fromer's warnings. The stress could cost her the baby. "I'll be all right."

"We have paramedics," Yang said, with a touch of alarm. "You want me to call?"

"No. Please." Samantha feared they'd take her to a hospital, and she'd miss Kathleen Brannen. "It'll go away. I'm just nervous."

"I can understand," Yang said.

His phone rang.

They both stared at it. Yang was now emotionally intertwined with his "subject." He let the phone ring again, then picked up.

"Yang."

There was a pause. Yang was expressionless. "I see," he replied to the caller. "I appreciate this." And then he hung up. "She's calling here," he told Samantha. "Any time."

"Did he say how she sounded?" Samantha asked.

"Dazed, confused."

Then the phone rang again.

Yang reached out, but Samantha reached first. Yang made no effort to stop her.

She picked up the receiver. "Hello?"

There was static at the other end, but the voice came through clearly. It was a lazy voice, common, not what Samantha had expected of Marty's first wife. "Can I talk to Sergeant Yan?" Kathleen Brannen asked, dropping the last letter of Yang's name.

"Is this... Mrs. Brannen?" Samantha replied.

"Yeah."

"This is..." Samantha hesitated. What should she say? How should she introduce herself? My God, she thought, *I'm* the other woman. The *other woman*—right out of a romance novel or a soap opera. She knew what Kathleen would think of her. She'd think the same thing if *she* were in Green Bay, abandoned, with two children.

"This is Mrs. Martin Shaw," she finally blurted out. "I'm the one."

"Oh," Kathleen answered, subdued but not angry. "I guess maybe we... know the same fella."

"I think we do," Samantha replied. She felt a sudden kinship with Kathleen, something she hadn't expected. They'd both been cheated by the same man. What stories they could tell. "Was he interested in trains then, too?" she asked cynically.

"Yeah. A lot of the guys here are. Y'know?"

"I know. Did he have his little model trains?"

"Nah. He liked the regular ones."

"Well, he's graduated to toy trains, you'll be happy to know."

It was a bizarre conversation, neither knowing what to say, how to say it, precisely how to get down to the business of positive identification.

"Look," Kathleen said, "I'm not angry or nothin'. I'm not interested in him anymore. What he did. I had him declared a corpse."

"I know."

"Why'd you go to the cops?"

"A long story," Samantha answered.

"With Kenny everything's a long story. The booze is a long story. The other women. The gambling. Even the eye."

"The eye?"

"Yeah. He loved to tell how he got it."

"It?"

"Miss, you readin' me?" Kathleen asked. "The glass eye."

"What! What are you talking about?" Samantha's heart pounded like a repeating cannon. She suddenly gasped for breath.

"His left eye," Kathleen replied. There was a silence. She finally caught on. "Hey, lady, are we talking about the same guy?"

Samantha didn't immediately reply. This was impossible. It couldn't happen. Again she looked at the pictures. That was Marty. It *was* Marty. Was it Marty? Maybe this Kathleen was making something up. "There was *nothing* in your husband's file about a glass eye," she said, her voice cutting.

"I know," Kathleen said. "I didn't tell the cops."

"You didn't? *Why*?"

"I thought if Kenny came back he'd be steamed. *He* talked about the eye, but he got crazy if I did. Look, I'll give you his doctor's name. He'll tell you, Miss."

She was telling the truth. In her gut, Samantha knew that. The pictures *weren't* Marty. It was a mistake, a terrible, wrenching mistake. The camera had lied. Or her eyes had lied. Or maybe something inside her had been wishing too hard.

"The doctor won't be necessary," Samantha said. "I'm not married to your husband. It was my mistake. I'm sorry if I upset you."

"Upset me? I'm beyond upset," Kathleen said. "I get calls like this every couple years. It's life."

"Thank you. I wish you luck."

"Yeah," Kathleen replied. "You back."

They both hung up. "I'm sorry," Samantha said to Yang. "I thought it was him." The tears came again.

"Don't apologize," Yang told her. "It happens all the time. *I'm* sorry we put you through this."

"I'd better be going," Samantha said. She was humbled.

Yang felt for her, but understood her need to be alone with her own feelings. "All right," he replied. "You need some rest now anyway. But I want to stay in touch. Okay?"

"Okay." Finally Samantha smiled. It was a weak smile, not deeply felt, filtered through the torture she had just endured. But she knew she had a friend. "I wonder what'll become of her?" she asked, gesturing toward the phone.

Yang couldn't possibly answer. He saw so many tragedies, and the problems of a single woman in Green Bay seemed remote by comparison. He helped Samantha up and held on to her as they walked slowly back to the hallway. "I'm okay," she said to him. "I really am."

As a gesture of confidence, Yang let go of her. She walked alone, more quickly and evenly, as if her old defense mechanism had taken over. But Yang was still concerned. "I can have a squad car take you home," he told her.

"Oh no," Samantha insisted. "I'd be mortified if someone saw. I mean, nothing against the police."

Yang laughed. "I understand. I guess I wouldn't want to be seen in a squad car myself. Can I at least get you a cab?"

"Sure. Thanks."

They walked down the hall and rounded a corner. Samantha accidentally brushed against a man walking in the other direction. "Sorry," she said.

"Perfectly all right," Spencer Cross-Wade replied, and continued on.

Samantha returned home exhausted. She told Lynne she'd simply been shopping—looking at baby things—and had overdone it. She lay down and slept, knowing she had, in a sense, come to the end of her rope. Going to the police was the ultimate act. Yes, she could hire a private investigator, but she'd decided that the risk of Marty's finding out was too great. Besides, he was probably expert enough to cover his tracks thoroughly, leaving nothing for an investigator to investigate. No, the trip to Yang had been the final action. If he could come up with nothing, she might live the rest of her days married to a mystery, living in dread fear, wondering what horrid surprise could be next. She recalled an Alfred Hitchcock film, *The Wrong Man*, in which Henry Fonda was imprisoned for a crime he didn't commit. It was almost the same thing, Samantha mused—she too was suffering a kind of imprisonment, although she'd done nothing wrong. She too had lost control of her own fate. She too lived in fear that things could stay the same, or even get worse.

She cried herself to sleep that afternoon. And, as she did, she occasionally broke out in a nervous, spontaneous laugh. It was sick, nightmarish, weird. That night she would have to make love to this man. And tomorrow she would resume planning his party. It was as if Henry Fonda were getting ready to celebrate his prosecutor's birthday.

"It has to be a Model thirty," Marty snapped into the phone in the sweaty booth under Rockefeller Center. It was the kind of call he'd *never* make from his office—not when a secretary could be listening in. "I'm not interested in a substitute."

He surprised himself. He was rarely this short-tempered. He knew the tension was getting to him. Control it, he told himself. It's less than two weeks away. Just last until then. Don't fail Dad now. He never failed *you*.

"And it has to work?" asked the voice on the other end.

"Yes. I only buy sets that work," Marty replied. It was a fairly obvious comment, but not so obvious in these circumstances, for Marty was trying to buy a thirty-four-year-old, ten-inch RCA Model 30 television set, one of the first classics of the television age. It was the set he'd been watching the night of December 5, 1952. You didn't buy this kind of thing from a TV shop, or even an antiques store. You went to a collector. They were dotted around the United States, placing their little three-line ads in hobby magazines, offering to trade an RCA this for an Admiral that, or bidding large dollars for the old Philco console radios that symbolized the era of sound-only.

Marty waited impatiently, tapping the glass of the booth, throwing in another dime to be sure he wasn't cut off. The guy on the other end sounded like a nut. A lot of them were nuts—the kind who could tell you every tube used in the Model 30, and its function.

"All right," the guy said, "I can locate one. I know somebody. But it'll cost you."

"How much?"

"I gotta see three thou."

"Jesus. Three thousand dollars."

"Two grand if it's unrepairable. Look, fella, you're talkin' Model thirty, not crap. You're talkin' classic."

"I know, I know," Marty shot back, resenting a lecture from a New Jersey crackpot. "How soon can you get it?"

"How soon you got three thou?"

"Tonight, in cash."

"Then you got it. My friend is right here in town. You want delivery?"

"No, I'll pick it up."

"How do I know you'll show?"

"I'll send you a deposit by messenger within an hour." Marty didn't realize it, but he was breathing heavily—a combination of the stuffy booth and the excitement of the buy. My God, it was coming together.

"Sold," the guy said. They exchanged names...except Marty gave an alias. Then they hung up.

Marty already had the videotape machine.

And he already had the tape—made up by a company doing a history of television for home tape libraries: Douglas Edwards with the news, sponsored by Oldsmobile. That's what they'd been watching the night of December 5, 1952.

Dad had always liked Doug Edwards. *"Frankie, this is about winter in Korea," he'd said that night as Edwards came on. "You ought to watch it."*

Frankie watched, and now would watch again.

11

"Frankie Nelson," Cross-Wade said, speaking on his office phone. "That was his name, although we assume he's changed it. We've checked every Frank Nelson in the United States, without result. The incident occurred just outside Omaha, Nebraska, on December fifth, 1952."

He waited for the party on the other end to ask a question.

"There are *no* available, legible pictures," Cross-Wade replied, "even as a child. Don't ask me why. What I'm simply going on is a hunch—that my target may live outside the United States part of the time. You see, in the Yard this is a common problem because there are so many countries in the Commonwealth. I thought that if the Passport Office could keep watch, we might come up with something." He paused again. "Thanks."

The conversation ended. Of all the shots in the dark, this was the darkest. The Passport Office of the U.S. State Department was hardly a criminal investigation agency, but everything had to be tried.

Cross-Wade knew that thousands of interviews over a period of months, or years, would probably lead to some useful clues. But he didn't have months, or years, or even weeks. He had days.

And then another day passed. Another day without progress.

He checked off the date on his calendar. Murder minus nine.

A batch of memos appeared on his desk. Routinely, Cross-Wade went through missing-persons reports, not in search of the calendar schizophrenic, but in search of his victim—some woman with auburn hair who might be missing, lured by her potential murderer. He'd checked out a small number of missing auburn-haired women without result. Most had shown up, had sent goodbye notes, or had been found dead far from home, usually the victims of alcohol or drugs.

He went through the reports quickly, yet thoroughly, a dogged believer in detail. It was just after 3 P.M. on a sunny, unusually warm autumn day, with the heat at headquarters naturally turned up much too high. Cross-Wade felt a bead of perspiration on his brow, and the increasing dampness of his wilting collar.

And then...

He almost went past it. It was a memo, impeccably written by Sergeant Yang, whom he knew and respected. The subject: one Samantha Shaw. It wasn't the physical description of Samantha that grabbed Cross-Wade. In fact, her hair color wasn't even mentioned. It was something else, something far more intriguing. He reached for his phone and was connected to Yang.

"Yang, this is Cross-Wade."

"Yes, sir," Yang responded in a clipped, military style. He was in awe of the living legend.

"Yang, my dear boy," the legend asked, "do you recall a Samantha Shaw?"

"Do I?" Yang replied. "One of my toughest, sir."

"Ah, so she's in your memory. A question: This December

fifth reference, did she elaborate?"

"No, sir. Just what's in the report."

"Ah. Tell me, Yang, do you recall her hair color?"

Yang thought for a moment. "Uh, no Mr. Cross-Wade. She wore one of those babushka-type objects. We're kind of more interested in the missing person's description."

"Of course," Cross-Wade commented. "Did the lady feel she was in any danger?"

"No, not directly. She was just concerned about her husband's past."

"Yes. A fine report. Look, I'm working on a case where this date is significant. I may ask the lady a few questions."

"Sure," Yang said. "But could I request that you go easy, sir? There's a lot of pain there."

"Gentleness is my middle name," Cross-Wade answered. He hung up and flipped on his intercom. "Fetch Loggins, please!"

Minutes later Arthur Loggins waddled in. "You called, sir?"

"Yes. A chair, Arthur. Be quick."

Loggins could see the glint in Cross-Wade's eye. Something had happened. Loggins assessed the glint—it was medium, somewhere between "big event" and "possibly significant." Assessing glints was a Loggins specialty. You learn in homicide to figure the story behind the expression.

"Something new, sir?" Loggins asked, knowing the answer.

"Possibly, Arthur, and possibly important." Right again, Loggins thought, with pride. "A missing-persons dispatch," Cross-Wade continued.

"Oh?"

"A woman came in several days ago with a curious complaint. She was scheduling a party for her husband—fortieth birthday, the usual. She wanted to find friends and teachers from his past."

"A lovely gesture, sir."

"But she couldn't. The gentleman's past simply didn't

exist. None of the things he'd told her checked out."

"Interesting, sir. But..."

"How does it apply to us?"

"Yes, sir."

"The husband's birthday is December fifth."

"Wow, sir."

"Yes...wow. We know our killer's birthday is December fifth."

"Could be a coincidence, sir."

"I'm aware of that, Arthur. It probably *is*. But it's the only strand I have—a man with the right birthday, with no detectable past, about the right age."

"Any physical description, sir?"

"Yes. He's a large man. In general, he meets the descriptions we have. But so would many men."

"Anything about auburn hair with the gent?"

"I don't know yet. Look, Arthur, be a sport for me. Go visit this lady, this Mrs. Shaw, and ask her the usual questions."

"I will, sir."

"Today, Arthur."

Loggins left and Cross-Wade was once again alone with his thoughts. The new thread was so tenuous, the lead so vague, and yet he felt a certain excitement. He knew the danger of deluding himself, convincing himself he had something, just to create the satisfaction of movement. Instinctively, he braced for disappointment. He had once calculated that only one out of twenty-two leads actually turned out to be significant in most investigations. No matter how much he wished, he didn't expect much from Samantha Shaw.

Loggins took the subway to 72nd Street and Central Park West, stopping at one of the transfer points to pick up a copy of the *New York Post* and a package of Bazooka bubble gum, to which he was mildly addicted. The *Post* headline, KILLS TWO, RAPES ONE, was pretty standard for the paper.

Loggins skipped to the sports pages. He knew Samantha's

neighborhood. He'd worked in the 20th Precinct as a homicide detective ten years before, when the area wasn't as pricey and the population was somewhat younger. He hadn't been there in three years, and was amazed at the changes. Lots of gold chains, babies with nurses, boutiques all over the place, people rushing around with the vacant look of those afraid of losing their first million. The middle West Side had once been artists, the retired, young folks, and just plain "guys," with a rich strip along the park. Now the money was spreading out, and Loggins didn't feel much at home on his old beat.

He'd called ahead to make sure Samantha was in the apartment and Marty wasn't, and was directed by a doorman to Samantha's floor. He rang her buzzer. Just then Lynne Gould came out of her apartment down the hall, heading for the elevator. Loggins smiled at her with his round, bland face, and Lynne shot back an awkward, curious nod. Must be a tradesman or a repairman, or maybe someone selling something for the party, Lynne thought as she stepped past him and took the elevator down.

"Who is it?" Samantha asked automatically, although she already knew.

"Detective Loggins, ma'am." He pulled out his identification, ready to flash it. He saw the eyehole open and an eyeball look through, sizing him up carefully. Then, a sliding chain, a clicking lock. The door opened slightly. Loggins thrust the ID through. The door opened wider. And then Arthur Loggins saw.

"Jesus Christ."

"What?" Samantha asked.

Loggins quickly regained his official poise. "Uh, sorry, ma'am. I was just thinkin' of something. May I come in, ma'am?"

"Yes, of course."

Loggins stepped in, but couldn't take his eyes off Samantha's long auburn hair. He walked awkwardly, realizing that any questions he might ask were probably unnecessary. The auburn hair—that was the whole thing, the complete pizza as he liked to say. It changed everything, made everything possible, created a link where none had existed before.

"Please sit down," Samantha said.

"Thank you, Mrs. Shaw."

"Some coffee?"

"Oh, no thank you, ma'am. I just had my break." Loggins glanced around. To him this was great wealth—his attached house was on Staten Island and not in a glittering neighborhood. He looked into the dining room. There were little scraps of paper on the table, arranged in short rows. Samantha saw that they attracted his attention.

"I'm planning a party," she said. "That's a possible seating plan. Maybe Sergeant Yang told you."

"I read the report, ma'am," Loggins said. "I'm awfully sorry to be subjecting you to questions."

"You're not doing it," Samantha assured him. "He is." She gestured toward a picture of Marty on a glass table. Samantha was remarkably composed, emotionally recovered from her ordeal with Yang, plunging back into planning the party, ever toying—in her own stressed mind—with that recurring fantasy that all would be resolved happily.

"Ma'am, I came over to clear up a few things," Loggins said. "But...well, I wonder if I could make a phone call. Privately, ma'am."

Samantha was baffled. Loggins still stared at her hair. "About me?" she asked.

"Official business, Mrs. Shaw."

"Yes, of course," Samantha told him. "There's a phone in the kitchen. I'll go in the bedroom."

"Sorry to inconvenience you."

"It's all right."

What could Samantha do? The man wanted to make a call, and you don't say no to a cop. She feared him. Even after feeling the warmth of Sergeant Yang, she couldn't get over that fear of police. She walked quickly to the bedroom and closed the door behind her.

Loggins went into the kitchen. For a moment, he forgot Cross-Wade's direct number and had to look it up in his crammed, dog-eared little address book. Then, quickly, he dialed. The man himself answered.

"Mr. Cross-Wade here."

"Sir, Loggins."

"Yes, Arthur?"

"Sir, you won't believe."

"What won't I believe?"

"This lady I went to—she's got long, auburn hair."

There was a silence on the line. Cross-Wade sat up, as if he had received divine revelation: an auburn haired woman married to a man with no past whose birthday was December fifth.

"Arthur, we might be onto something. I want you to wait there. I want to handle this personally—I'll be there as soon as possible."

"That's what I'd hoped, sir."

They both hung up. Cross-Wade restrained his emotions as he sped toward Central Park West in a commandeered squad car. Was her hair auburn or red? Loggins might have made a mistake. The two are similar and men weren't that perceptive about subtle differences in hair color. And did it really matter? The color might simply be a coincidence—a remarkable one, but a coincidence just the same. Some women had auburn hair, and a certain percentage, maybe one out of a few thousand, would have husbands born on December fifth. And maybe all the business about the man's having no past just reflected his wife's ineptitude in checking things. Maybe she was reckless and sloppy, someone whose probes into her husband's past went awry because of her own mistakes. Anything could be possible, Cross-Wade knew, and it would be foolish to get his hopes up.

He arrived at the building and rode up by elevator. Instinctively, he made a visual sweep of the hallway outside Samantha's apartment. There was an umbrella rack, with a black umbrella in it. Were there any reports of umbrellas used by the calendar schizophrenic? He didn't think so, but made a note to check. There was nothing else of interest. He rang the doorbell.

Samantha, alerted by the doorman and with the protection of Loggins in the apartment, simply opened. She stared at Cross-Wade, eye level. In a way, she was disappointed. She'd expected the senior man to be tall, tough-looking, something out of a movie. But only his trenchcoat fit the image.

"Cross-Wade," he said. Like Loggins, he looked at Samantha's hair. It was auburn.

"Come in," Samantha said.

They went to the living room and joined Loggins. "I know it may seem unusual for me to rush over here, Mrs. Shaw," Cross-Wade explained, while removing his coat and placing it neatly on a chair, "and I apologize for the inconvenience. But Mr. Loggins called with a most important point and I wanted to speak to you myself."

Loggins had said little, not wanting to pre-empt the boss, so Samantha had no idea what Cross-Wade was talking about. "I appreciate your coming," she said, feeling it was the only thing she could say.

Cross-Wade sat down. So did Samantha. Both instantly felt the tension rise. There was something unspoken between them, with both afraid to hope, yet afraid not to.

"Mrs. Shaw," Cross-Wade began, "has Mr. Loggins told you anything of our interest?"

"Just that he got my name from Sergeant Yang. After he called you he went over the sergeant's report with me, checking facts. He said he wanted to wait for you."

"And you got the feeling that something important had happened."

"He said there was something new. I...I really don't understand this."

"Mrs. Shaw," Cross-Wade said, looking at Samantha grimly, "we have a problem. It *may* be related to your situation."

Samantha sighed. She didn't want to bring up a point prematurely, but had to. "Mr. Loggins told me you're from homicide," she said.

"That's correct."

"What does this have to do with that?"

"I'll be glad to explain, madam. But I must caution you—it's a very disturbing story. You must brace yourself."

"I'm ready," Samantha replied, almost in a whisper. "After the last few weeks, I'm ready for anything."

Cross-Wade framed his words carefully. He wanted to be as gentle as possible, yet precise. "Madam," he asked, "have you ever heard of a man named Bleuler?"

"No."

"He was an early experimenter in psychiatry. Brilliant chap. I mention him because he devised a number of categories of the mental illness known as schizophrenia. Are you familiar with that?"

"I've heard of it, of course," Samantha answered. "I took a psychology course once, but I really don't know much about it."

"Neither do I. But there's a subcategory known as anniversary-excitement schizophrenia. You probably haven't heard of that one."

"Afraid not."

"It's a rare thing. It's when people have a disturbance only on a particular calendar day. It's usually related to something that's happened on that day in their past."

"I see," Samantha said. "Like feeling sad on the anniversary of someone's death."

"Precisely. But it sometimes goes beyond feeling sad. These people can do strange things."

"Like?"

"Some of them can kill."

Samantha didn't react. The whole idea of murder was outside her frame of reference. Illness she understood. Maybe even treachery or cheating. But murder? That happened in other families, other worlds.

"What *else* can they do?" she asked.

"Why don't we stick to killing," Cross-Wade replied, and saw the shock in Samantha's eyes. It wasn't the answer she'd wanted. "I know that may be frightening," he told her.

"To put it mildly."

"Well, one cannot hide from the truth. That's what we're talking about. Our police psychologists believe that someone with this condition is loose. Let's call him a calendar schizophrenic for short. His crimes occur on one calendar day of the year. That day, Mrs. Shaw, is December fifth."

"Marty!" Samantha blurted out. She felt the blood rush from her head. For a moment, consciousness seemed to melt away. Hold on, she told herself. Bear up!

She recovered. She'd be bigger than they expected her to be. "My husband's birthday," she said, trying to control the quiver in her voice. "I think you knew that. It was in Sergeant Yang's report."

"That's what attracted us," Cross-Wade answered in a soft, healing voice. "That and his...unusual past. And now something else."

"What's that?"

"Mrs. Shaw, this individual we seek is a murderer. His victims are all women. They all have the same color hair. That color is auburn."

"Oh, no, no, no," Samantha cried. "I can believe almost anything, but not that my Marty...Marty...is out to *kill* me. I may not know him as well as I'd thought, but I know him well enough. No, not that. Not..."

She stopped. She looked at Cross-Wade, then Loggins, then back at Cross-Wade. They'd seen all this before. She knew it. She felt it. They'd seen the wives who deny, who can't face, who reject. They'd seen the mothers who told them "But my Johnny's a good boy." They'd seen all those who shout no, only to admit later that it was yes all along.

"I know how you feel," Cross-Wade said. "I'd feel the same way." He saw the denial fade from Samantha's face, replaced by a valiant attempt to stay calm.

"Tell me the whole story," she asked.

"All right. It's best that you know, that you understand." Cross-Wade slowly got up and walked over to the part of the sectional couch where Samantha was sitting. He sat down next to her, trying to show his concern, his feeling. "There have been six of these murders," he revealed to her, "one in each of the last six years. All have been carried out with a blunt instrument and a chain."

Samantha winced.

"May I ask if your husband has any weapons?"

"Not that I know of."

"Does he have a bicycle chain?"

"No. He doesn't even have a bike."

"Let me go on. These murders have occurred in North America, the last three in or near New York. We expect another woman to die the night of December fifth."

"That's the night of Marty's party," Samantha said. "He *insisted* on that night."

"Insisted?"

"Yes. Even though it was during the week."

Cross-Wade thought that odd. *All* the murders had occurred at night. Why would Marty, if he was the murderer, fill his night with a party? Of course, Cross-Wade reasoned, he might be changing his tactics and planning the murder in the daytime. But if Samantha was the target, he certainly wouldn't kill her during the day, then have a party at home that night, without her. Contradictions were starting to appear, but Cross-Wade pushed ahead.

"I deduced that the December fifth date had some special significance," he said, "so I had my people check back in criminal history. We found what we were looking for."

"Marty?"

Samantha was almost frantic. Cross-Wade held up his hand to calm her. "Let me continue," he gently insisted, and she settled back. "It seems," he went on, "that there was a murder just outside Omaha on December fifth, 1952. The victim was an unemployed laborer. He'd bought his older son a set of electric trains..."

Samantha gasped.

"What's wrong?"

"Trains."

"What do you mean, madam?"

"Marty bought trains."

"What trains?"

"Just recently he brought home electric trains. He set them up on the rug. He stained it. There, you can see the stain." She pointed to a grease spot on the carpet.

"Did he say *why* he wanted the trains?" Cross-Wade asked.

"Just that he'd always wanted trains. It was a big hobby. That sort of thing. He ran them, let me run them, then put them away."

"I'll want to see them," Cross-Wade said, "but let me continue with the background."

"Please." Samantha was breathing heavily now, and the news about the trains even made Cross-Wade feel a sense of lunging anticipation. Yet once again he tempered it. Coincidence, he reminded himself, was the curse of criminal cases. Don't get trapped. Don't get overconfident.

"This unemployed gentleman came home with the trains and gave them to the boy," Cross-Wade continued. "His wife resented the gift. With all their money worries, she couldn't understand spending on electric trains. They argued. It got violent. The wife picked up a hammer and struck her husband in the head. He fell, but apparently was still alive. So she choked him with her younger son's bicycle chain."

"My God," Samantha whispered.

"The older boy witnessed the whole thing," Cross-Wade said.

"What happened to those kids?" Samantha asked.

"They were taken by relatives and separated. The mother was sent to prison, and died there a few years later. We haven't been able to track down even one member of the family. They simply melted into the landscape. The whereabouts of the boys is unknown."

"What was their name?"

"Nelson. The older boy was Frankie Nelson. Of course, it could be different now."

"And how does this...?"

"I'm getting to that. The mother had auburn hair...like yours." Samantha squirmed at those words. "We believe," Cross-Wade continued, "that the older son is the calendar schizophrenic, that the date December fifth triggers an uncontrollable frenzy in his mind. He seeks out auburn-haired women because they represent his mother. In his mind, they *become* his mother. The rest of the year he's probably perfectly normal. We don't know why he began killing only six years ago, but our psychologists tell us almost anything is possible in these cases."

"And you believe," Samantha said somberly, "that Marty is this man."

"I didn't say that," Cross-Wade replied. "It's just something worth looking into. He would be about the right age... although we can't be sure of your husband's real age since he's altered so many personal facts. The December fifth date is obviously significant to him. Witness his insistence that the party be held on that date. And *you* have auburn hair."

"Why can't you check it?" Samantha asked.

"I'm not sure what you mean, madam."

"Well, there are medical records and pictures. A picture of this Frankie Nelson should tell you if Marty resembles him."

"Of course, but there are no pictures. The family albums disappeared. Taken by relatives, no doubt. The medical people are gone, and with them their records. This was a small community. Very informal. Some evidence from the murder trial was kept, but it tells us nothing. We assume that Frank Nelson grew up, left whomever he was living with, and went into the world. The only thing we have is a newspaper photo from the day of the father's funeral. It shows Frankie and his younger brother in the distance. Much too blurry to be of use. So you see, we have no practical way of checking your husband by going into the past."

"Yes, I see."

"We'd pieced together the information we do have through routine police work. What was missing was a real suspect. We now have that because you were wise enough to come to the police."

Strangely, Samantha felt suddenly revolted. Cross-Wade had meant his remark as a compliment, but it triggered painful thoughts. She *had* gotten Marty into trouble. Well, he deserved it...maybe. *Maybe.* She still was a wife who'd betrayed her husband. She couldn't shake the thought, the shame. Yes, it was irrational. She knew she shouldn't feel that way. But if it was irrational, it was also understandable. It was that middle-class upbringing again. The family comes first. We don't wash our dirty linen outside.

She suddenly resented Cross-Wade, loathed the little man, blamed the messenger for the message. This cop had come to tell her she might be murdered by her own husband, by the man she'd waited for, loved, revered, whose baby she carried. Who was he? Who was he to come in, with his clunking assistant, and say these filthy things? She didn't realize it, but her face was melting into hostility and contempt. Loggins spotted it. So did Cross-Wade.

"I understand your reaction," Cross-Wade said quietly, sounding like the grandfather he would never have a chance to be. "I'm sure you resent what I've said, but I can only tell you what we know. This is only an inquiry. No one is being charged. It was important that you know the background. My main concern now is *you* and your safety."

He'd said the right things. He was on his way back to winning her trust.

"What should I do?" she asked, realizing how erratic her feelings were becoming.

"Very little. It's what *we* should do. We're going to follow your husband and study his movements. Something he does might tell us what he's planning, if anything. I *do* hope he's innocent."

Cross-Wade really didn't. In fact, he fervently hoped he'd found his man. His feelings were a spinning mix of genuine concern for Samantha and sparkling visions of glory, of last-minute capture. But he had to say those right things. Only experience taught him what words to use, what pauses to insert, what expressions to register. It was all critical, all part of the art.

"And," he continued to Samantha, "I'd like permission to search the apartment."

"Why?"

"First, to get a feel for the way your husband lives. That might tell us something. Second, to see if anything reminds us of young Frankie Nelson's life in Omaha. Third, because we might find something even *you* don't know is here."

"Like what?"

"Like a hammer and chain."

"Go ahead," Samantha said.

Cross-Wade had Samantha sign a statement agreeing to the search, for it might come up in court later. After all, Samantha could turn out to be a hostile witness, even *involved* in the crimes rather than a victim. Cross-Wade had seen that twist too often. "Please accompany me," he requested. "I may have questions."

Samantha started leading Cross-Wade and Loggins around the apartment. Her resentment receded. She knew her own life might be at stake.

"The trains," Cross-Wade suggested. Samantha led the detectives to a closet where Marty had stored the electric trains. Cross-Wade examined them, handling almost every piece, studying small details. "Remarkable," he finally said, turning to Loggins. "Arthur, what do you make of these?"

Loggins examined the trains. "Old Lionel," he replied. "When they were still the original company. This stuff comes from the fifties."

"Did Marty tell you why he bought an *old* set?" Cross-Wade asked Samantha.

"He said he preferred the older models. He said the old

Lionel stuff was terrific."

"He's right," Loggins agreed.

"Arthur," Cross-Wade asked, "is there any record of the trains that caused the fatal dispute in the Nelson household?"

"No, sir. I remember reading about that. They kept the trains as evidence at the trial, then gave them to Frankie to keep. But there was no description."

"What about sales receipts?"

"None turned up. There was a notation that the store where they were bought went out of business a few years later."

"Damn," Cross-Wade said quietly. History had even blotted *this* out. He could have compared Marty's trains to the ones owned by Frankie Nelson, but the lack of records made that impossible. Then a thought struck him. "Mrs. Shaw, are you *sure* your husband bought these recently?"

"Of course. They weren't here."

"No, you misunderstand. I know they weren't *here*. But are you sure he didn't own them?"

"Well..."

"He could've kept them in his office, or somewhere else."

"What are you suggesting?"

"That these may be the very trains Frank Nelson owned as a child, the very trains that led to his father's death."

Samantha stepped back, as if the trains were contaminated. "Why would he bring these *things* home?" she asked.

"I don't know," Cross-Wade admitted. Once again he turned to Loggins. "Arthur, there couldn't be that many used-train stores in New York. Make a list of these trains. Check to see if anyone has bought them recently."

"Yes, sir," Loggins replied.

Cross-Wade entered the bedroom. He was startled by the bizarre arrangement, especially the headboard's being against the radiator and the bureau's blocking a window. His eyes focused on the gaudy picture frame. "Interesting," he commented.

"I know what you're thinking," Samantha said. "It's God-awful."

"That's a matter of taste, madam."

"This is Marty's taste."

"Beg pardon?"

"He insisted on re-doing the room this way. Recently."

"How recently?"

"Oh, a couple of weeks, I think."

"Why?"

"He said he wanted to try it, that he saw this in an architectural magazine."

"He must've been joking."

"It didn't sound like a joke, any more than the trains did."

"With all the room layouts, why this one, madam?"

"I don't know," Samantha sighed.

"Has he done anything else... unusual?"

"Nothing that I can think of. I mean, nothing obvious like that."

"Is that his desk?" Cross-Wade asked, pointing.

"Yes."

"May I look through it?"

Samantha gestured her approval. Cross-Wade searched the desk and found only a batch of normal business papers. "Nothing here," he said, "but I wouldn't expect anything unusual. No one leaves clues in a desk at home."

He went through the rest of the apartment. "Only the trains give cause for suspicion," he finally pronounced. "But there's certainly nothing decisive."

"I really didn't think so," Samantha said.

"What we have here is a pattern of circumstance," Cross-Wade continued. "It needs more investigation."

Again, Samantha had no firm answers. The agony of doubt, of suspicion, continued.

Cross-Wade prepared to leave. But, before he did, he had some firm advice for Samantha. "Madam," he said, "I must ask your cooperation."

"Of course."

"Please listen carefully. Change nothing in your schedule. That might just tip Mr. Shaw that he's being watched. Try to show happiness. Talk about the trip you've planned. Oh, by the way, have you told anyone that you've seen us?"

"No."

"Good. Of course, the doormen downstairs know. Before I leave I'll instruct them. I have ways to influence people to cooperate. Your husband must not find out we were here. Now, on December fifth..."

"God, it's so close," Samantha moaned.

"Yes, a bit more than a week. We'll have men in the building that day and night to insure your safety. There'll be listening devices here. Are there empty apartments on this floor?"

"No, but someone down the hall is away for a month."

"That's all we need. We'll contact the building manager. We'll be able to hear everything going on between you and your husband. If anything unusual occurs, we'd be on the scene in seconds."

Then Cross-Wade did something no other detective on the New York force did, or would do. He took Samantha's hand and kissed it. "You are a lady," he said. "It pains me to see this happening to you."

"Thank you," Samantha replied. "Thank you so much." She was genuinely touched.

"Help us so we can help you," Cross-Wade concluded. It was his standard exit line, spoken in perfect cadence, perfected over the years.

And he was gone. With one visit to Sergeant Yang, Samantha Shaw had stepped to the center of an intense, massive, criminal investigation. A mistake could destroy her life. A victory would destroy her marriage.

12

"I don't believe it," Samantha said.

"Isn't it beautiful?"

"Well...it's nice. But what goes, Martin Everett Shaw? You becoming an antiques dealer?"

"Say again?"

"First the old electric trains, then this old TV. You didn't ask me first. Well, okay. You've got your hobbies. But I don't understand."

They stood in the living room, the old Model 30 on the carpet, its brown wood cabinet gleaming with a new coat of polish, its ten-inch screen yellowed with age, the ancient tubes still visible through the air holes in its dust-encrusted back.

"It's a collector's item," Marty explained. "This was one of the very first commercial sets in regular use. It practically built the TV industry."

"Bully for it."

"This was the set Uncle Milty was on."

"I'm moved," Samantha replied. In ordinary times she

would have burst out laughing at Marty's sales pitch, his boyish enthusiasm for an old black-and-white set that probably didn't even work. But these weren't ordinary times, and her first thought was reporting the purchase to Cross-Wade. Like the trains, this was something from the fifties.

"It works," Marty assured her. "I tested it myself."

"Wonderful."

She delivered her lines, but she was far away. Jesus, she thought, I love him, but he may be planning to kill me. *Kill* me! "What are you going to do with it?" she asked.

"Set it up. Look, it cost fifty bucks. It's a conversation piece. People *will* be interested. You'll see at the party."

The word "party" sent an electric jolt through Samantha, and suddenly she felt the heat of fear. Afraid of him? Of Marty? Yes, she was afraid of him, and she hadn't fully realized it until this moment. That flaming reality was punching through the emotional barrier that was still strung up inside her. She could never have dreamed that this moment would come. Afraid of Marty. Afraid of a date on the calendar. Afraid, yet not really accepting that this hunk of enthusiasm with an old TV set could really do what Cross-Wade thought he could do.

"I like it," she finally told him, hoping to close the subject. "It's...quaint. Put it anywhere you want."

He smiled. Phony, as always.

They made love that night, and in its physical aspects nothing had changed. For Samantha, though, all the emotion and heat had been drained. Suddenly Marty felt like some crawling, panting creature, some intruder preying on her like a lusting animal. Cross-Wade's revelations would not leave her, even for an intimate instant. "I can't believe I'm doing this," she thought, as she played along, which is precisely what Cross-Wade would have wanted her to do.

The next morning Samantha called Cross-Wade to report the television set. Cross-Wade called back a short time later.

His report: an RCA Model 30 had been found in the Nelson home after the murder.

Another link.

Another blow for Samantha.

But another word of caution from Cross-Wade: The Model 30 had been common. It had been in millions of homes. A coincidence maybe. Some cases had many coincidences.

Cross-Wade also reported to Samantha that Loggins had checked the used-train stores around New York. Marty had indeed bought his set recently. "The salesman remembered him," Cross-Wade said. "He described him exactly. But again, we must be cautious about drawing conclusions."

Cross-Wade told Samantha that he was showing pictures of Marty to friends and relatives of the calendar murderer's other victims. It turned Samantha's stomach. *Her* husband's picture, like some common mug shot, would be circulated among those who lived in grief. How low things had sunk. How disgusting all this was. She had to remember it was only an inquiry. She had to try to stay calm. But how much restraint was any human being supposed to handle?

Samantha took Cross-Wade's advice and plunged once more into the party planning. But from now on, she knew, it was simply going through the motions. A job. An assignment. A show. Cross-Wade had thrown the thunderbolt. So she was making a party for a man she loved and feared at the same time, and the ambivalence was tearing at her like a ragged blade. It seemed so strange to prepare a gala that could turn into a night of terror. She felt unique. Surely no wife had ever been put in this position before, at least none whom she'd ever read about or heard of. It was unfair, so horribly unfair, and yet she felt suddenly juvenile for letting a minor word like "unfair" cross her mind. "Catastrophic" would have been better.

Tom Edwards volunteered to help. He had some vacation

days, with nothing special to do, so he came over. He'd been upset since their lunch, he told Samantha, but could think of no real way to help her uncover Marty's past. At least he could help with the party.

Samantha appreciated that. Tom knew Marty's business friends better than she did, and was a godsend in working out table arrangements and avoiding awkward combinations. While he concentrated on strategy, Samantha made final choices of menus and trimmings. Inevitably, though, the talk got around to "the problem," as Samantha preferred to call it.

"Anything, uh, turn up?" Tom delicately asked in that naive manner that Samantha found so affecting.

"Nothing," Samantha replied. "I'm sweeping it under the rug."

"Wise move."

"Knew you'd say that."

"Well, Sam, it's like I told you. Either forget it or confront the man. You didn't confront him, did you?"

"No."

"I didn't think so. I'm glad you didn't. You've got a great marriage. Don't ruin it. The man's past is his own. Make up a fantasy. Say he was a spy on a critical mission that saved his country. You might just be right."

"I've thought of that, believe me. You think chocolate chip ice cream is good enough for dessert?"

Tom thought for a moment, raising his eyes from the stack of place cards he was arranging. "Yes, that's great, but only if the chips are big. You know, monsters. But have an alternative. If it's a cold, wet night, no one goes for ice cream."

"Chocolate mousse?"

"Overdone, my dear Samantha."

"Yeah, overdone. You're right. Too fancy." Samantha crossed the choice off. "Hey, I need a request list for that little band I'm having—you know, the three players."

"Show tunes. Always safe," Tom said. "And that's what

Marty likes. Just stay away from rock, and, God, no country. Show tunes. You can throw in the Beatles. I went to a great party a few weeks ago and they really did the music right. I'll get the song list."

"Would you?"

"Sure."

"You're a doll. And such taste."

Samantha was right. Tom, gentler and more sensitive than Marty, did have exquisite taste in virtually everything. And he never had to hire anyone to help him—not with his apartment or with his little country house in Connecticut. Some described him as "artistic," but "sensitive" was probably the best word. The fact that he wasn't married gave "sensitive" a delicate meaning, and even as close a friend as Samantha wasn't sure precisely what his proclivities were. He seemed "okay," but never talked about women, and when she'd hinted that he might consider marrying, he'd always changed the subject. In a way, she was attracted to him, the more so since her marriage to Marty had turned so bizarre. But she was of no mind to do anything about it, so his orientation was hardly a pressing matter.

"When are you and Marty going on your Midwestern trip?" he asked.

"I'm not sure of the dates," she replied. "You think it's a good idea?"

"Oh sure. A great idea. It could straighten things out. He might tip you on a couple of secrets."

"You think so?"

"I'm guessing."

Samantha felt the urge to reveal the baby. After all, she'd told the New York Police Department. Why not Tom? But she still planned, despite all that had happened, to make the announcement at the bash, and couldn't bring herself to tell Tom before Marty. What she couldn't resist, though, was a little gentle probing, another subtle attempt to make something of Marty's past.

"Tom," she asked, after a long period of silence, "were you surprised when Marty married me?"

Tom seemed flustered by the question. "Why do you ask?"

"I just want to know."

He shrugged. "I don't remember. I wasn't collapsing on the floor in shock, old Sam. I mean, he had discussed you in rather *favorable* terms."

"Yes, I can imagine."

"And Marty wanted to settle down. Likes kids, you know."

"I know." Don't let on about the baby, Samantha kept telling herself. Don't let on.

"So, no, I guess I wasn't surprised. Were you surprised when he asked you?"

"I felt it coming."

"Yeah. Women always do."

"Is he happy, Tom?"

Tom turned fully to Samantha, a curious look on his face. "Hey," he said, "I thought we're putting all the agony to sleep."

"Tom, this isn't agony. It's just a question. All wives want to know."

"Doesn't he tell you?"

"Sure. But maybe he has a concern, a worry, that he talks to you about. I mean, I don't want to probe..."

"Sam, this Marty Shaw is a happy man. And you're making him even happier with the party. It's the only thing he talks about. I'm bored stiff with it. Get the damned thing over with, will you?" He laughed.

So did she.

There was no more agony talk.

"Do you know this man?" Cross-Wade asked, sitting on a kitchen chair, with beef stew cooking in a pot no more than six feet away.

Alice Carrione broke down in tears, looked away, and simply groaned "Maryanne."

Cross-Wade waited. Never rush them. Not when they're like this. Put yourself in *her* position. A mother. Happy. A family type. And then, one night, a policeman arrives to say that your auburn-haired daughter, your only child, has been found dead in an empty lot in Queens. The grief never dies. It may even get worse as months pass. Any suggestion of the crime brings the tears. Give her a chance. Give her all the time she needs.

"I sympathize," Cross-Wade said. "She was such a beautiful young woman. I share your rage. That's why I want to capture the animal that did this." He looked at Maryanne Carrione's mother. She was only fifty-four, but looked ten years older—the effect of grief, of a life destroyed emotionally just as her child's had been destroyed physically. He sensed the emptiness in the little attached house in Brooklyn, on a block where everyone took care of everyone else, and crime was rare.

Mrs. Carrione regained her composure and looked at the picture of Martin Everett Shaw that Cross-Wade had brought. "Let me ask you again," he said, "do you remember this man? Was he ever in your daughter's presence?"

She took the picture and held it in her damp, trembling hands. "She had a lot of gentleman friends," she said, "if you know what I mean."

"I do."

"Very fine men. Always very fine."

"Of course. She would."

"This one I can't be sure of. You know, she didn't bring them all home. Sometimes she met them at work, especially during the week."

"Do you remember discussing their backgrounds with Maryanne?"

"Oh sure. Mother-daughter talk. What a man did for a living. What he had in his future."

"Were any of them interested in public relations?"

"I think a few. So many boys are."

"Yes. What about trains?"

"Trains?"

"Some men like trains as a hobby."

"This I don't remember."

"Did Maryanne ever say that one of her friends went to journalism school? Or grew up in Indiana?"

Mrs. Carrione thought for a few moments, then shrugged. "Most of these young men came from New York. You know, we're an Italian family. We don't like goin' too far from home."

"Ah, Italia," Cross-Wade reacted. "How well I understand."

"But some may have come from other places. I just don't remember."

"Were any in the Army?"

"Sure. Most."

"Do you remember where, madam?"

"No." Then Mrs. Carrione stared once again at the picture. "Do you think this man killed my girl?"

"We don't know," Cross-Wade replied.

"Let me look again."

Cross-Wade knew it was fruitless. It was common for a witness to want a second look after learning that the subject of a picture was a suspect. People wanted to help. They wanted the psychological honor of putting a killer behind bars. But it was the first reaction to a photo that really told the story.

"It's hard for me to say," Mrs. Carrione finally admitted.

And Cross-Wade left.

He had a list of appointments—more friends and relatives of victims. He'd also sent Marty's photo to police departments who'd been investigating victims of the calendar killer outside New York, but without result. He wondered whether the pictures had actually been shown around. He knew that many departments were lax in investigating crimes that were no longer on the front page. It was frustrating, but there was nothing Cross-Wade could do. Cooperation among departments depended entirely on how cooperative the cooperators were.

He stopped at a Riverdale apartment, where the unemployed brother of one victim lived. She was the girl whose body had been discovered just off the Interstate in Greenwich, Connecticut. The brother, Steve Lewis, was twenty-two, thin, and cocky, and greeted Cross-Wade with a can of Miller's and not a stitch of clothing above the waist. He was not the kind of son Cross-Wade would have been proud of, but the seasoned detective didn't wince, didn't even frown, as he entered the messy apartment. Never show contempt for a witness, he knew. Never make him afraid, hostile, or suspicious. You didn't have to be an altar boy to testify at a trial.

Cross-Wade and Lewis sat down. "Ever see this man?" Cross-Wade asked, handing the picture of Marty to Lewis, who continued drinking his beer.

"Yeah," Lewis replied.

"Where?"

"Where?" Lewis repeated. "I dunno. I seen him."

"I have to know where," Cross-Wade insisted.

Lewis looked at the photo again. "Beer?" he asked.

"No, thank you," Cross-Wade replied.

"I can't place the guy," Lewis finally admitted.

"Was he with your sister?"

"Who the Christ knows? I didn't see much of my sister. Know what I mean?"

"I think so."

"She didn't like...approve of me. Know what I mean?"

"I still think so."

"She hung out with guys who went to school 'n stuff. When I was at my mom's I sometimes saw her."

"Did she bring dates there?"

"Oh yeah. My mom, she wanted to look 'em over. Old-timer, like you."

"Yes," Cross-Wade said.

"Yeah," Lewis said. He closed one eye to look again at the picture, his face taking on a contorted, weird expression. "Yeah," he said again, "I know him. My sister dated him."

"You sure?" Cross-Wade remained calm and professional.

"You asked me, didn't you?"

"What was his name?"

"Name?"

"Yes. What we call people."

"Uh, lemme see. Name. Arnie or somethin'. Yeah, Arnie."

"Marty?"

"That's it."

"Last name?"

"That I couldn't spot."

"Shaw?"

"Sounds right."

So now Cross-Wade had a man who said he remembered Marty Shaw as having dated his sister. He asked a few more questions, then left the Riverdale apartment. While still in the hallway he crossed Steve Lewis off his list. He hadn't believed Lewis for a second. Lewis was one of "those." Show them any picture, and they know the guy. Tell them any name, and they remember it. A waste. A fraud. An irresponsible kid who'd say anything. Cross-Wade knew him from instinct, from a career devoted to separating the liars from the other ten percent. A lot of people came close to going to prison, and some did, Cross-Wade knew, because of the Steve Lewises of the world.

It took another full day for Cross-Wade to interview the friends and relatives he wanted to cover, and he insisted on doing it himself. He needed to get the "feel" of their answers, their emotional reactions to Marty's picture—things he couldn't get from written reports. But he came up with nothing. Sure, some said Marty "looked familiar," but a lot of people look familiar. And some said the name "Marty Shaw" sounded familiar, but what did that mean? The calendar killer probably used false names. Indeed, Cross-Wade knew, the murderer might not have even known his victims. He might simply have followed them and trapped them on December fifth because of the color of their flowing hair.

It was November twenty-eighth.

Thanksgiving.

Cross-Wade was so completely focused on the case that he hardly noticed. He still had nothing on Martin Shaw but suspicion and coincidence.

It was Marty and Samantha's first Thanksgiving together, but, with Marty having no family at all and Samantha having no one close, it wasn't the same as in other households. They declined an invitation from Lynne and spent the holiday quietly, watching a bit of the Macy's parade as it passed along Central Park West, and having a modest turkey dinner. The peace inside their apartment was in stark contrast to the storms going on inside their minds.

November twenty-ninth.

A setback for Cross-Wade. Grasping at anything, he had sent the one grainy newspaper photo of the two young Nelson boys at their father's funeral to a high-tech lab in New Jersey that specialized in a technique developed by Minolta of Japan. By using old photographs the lab could "project" images years into the future and show how people would look as they matured. But it could do nothing for Cross-Wade. The old picture he'd sent was too blurry, too washed out, the faces too vague.

November thirtieth.

Loggins came into Cross-Wade's office at midday. "Surveillance report," he told the boss. Loggins himself had tailed Marty during the morning shift, relieved by another sergeant for the afternoon and evening.

"Anything?" Cross-Wade asked.

"No, sir. He's a regular person."

"A regular person," Cross-Wade echoed. He reveled in the Loggins eloquence.

"Yes, Mr. Cross-Wade. This subject..."

"Man, Arthur. *Man.* Let's try to be civilized around headquarters."

"I apologize, sir. Anyway, this particular man gets up at a normal hour and proceeds to his office in midtown, the address known to you. He sometimes proceeds by taxi, but sometimes walks. Depends on the weather."

"Does he ever go *with* anyone?"

"No, sir. We haven't observed that. He arrives in his office and usually works until twelve-thirty, when he proceeds to lunch."

"Usually?"

"Sometimes he proceeds to business appointments. We check out where he's going. They're corporations where his company has work. When he has lunch, it's alone or with other business personnel. A very normal pattern, sir. Of course, he sometimes goes into stores, but no place that would concern us."

"And our night reports show the same, I believe."

"He returns home. That's usually it."

"So far, we haven't advanced beyond the interview with Mrs. Shaw," Cross-Wade said.

"I regret that, sir."

"And there's something else, Arthur. People like this, with mental compulsions, usually have definite rituals. Isn't it so?"

"I suppose so, sir."

"This killer has murdered women he hardly knew, or didn't know at all, and just left them. Now we theorize that his new target is his wife. This is entirely out of character. It doesn't fit. For the first time he'd be focusing attention on himself. He'd have to flee, but we would have his name. Why would he do that?"

Loggins just shrugged. The question couldn't be answered.

"You know, Arthur," Cross-Wade continued, "I think we might have here a major set of coincidences. Shaw may not be our target. Lord God knows, it's happened before—which is why we sometimes lock up the wrong man. But I've never seen anything quite like this. The trains. The December fifth date. The auburn-haired wife. Might all be coincidence, Arthur.

"You know, this is a shrewd killer. Look at the way he manages to remove his fingerprints from every murder scene. An intelligent man. Thoughtful. He might be schizoid, but only on that one calendar day. He may just be too good for us."

"Too good for *you*, sir?" Loggins asked.

Cross-Wade needed that compliment. "We'll see," he replied. "We have five days to go. Five days to save a life."

13

Cross-Wade was depressed on December first.

"It's the date," he told Loggins. "We're into December. I feel," he said, with his devilish little laugh, "like a calendar schizophrenic. The *date* is affecting me." The laugh faded. His face became grim. "Depression, you know, is the most common symptom of the malady."

His staff continued the investigation, and Cross-Wade himself spoke again, by phone, to several relatives of the victims, trying any possible angle. Surveillance reports on Marty came in every two hours, but always showed the activity of a typical businessman.

It was that afternoon, though—December first—that the investigation took a new turn, one that Cross-Wade had feared, one he loathed, yet one that finally answered the fundamental question that had haunted him since he spoke with Samantha: What was the truth about Martin Shaw?

As he'd told Samantha, he'd assumed that little Frankie Nelson's medical records had been lost forever. But he'd also asked the Omaha police to keep checking, on an urgent basis, and not to give up. On December first a large brown envelope arrived at police headquarters by express mail. An accompanying letter explained that Frankie Nelson's medical records had been found. They'd been misfiled, kept in the storage room of the criminal court.

They were enclosed.

Rapidly, police experts compared them with records obtained from Marty's doctor. They compared eye color, skin markings and surgical scars.

The records didn't match.

That was it.

Proof positive.

For Cross-Wade, the question had been answered. His investigation collapsed. He fought being overcome by despair. With the discipline of a good soldier, he reached for the phone and dialed Samantha Shaw.

Samantha was asleep when the call came, feeling the fatigue of pregnancy, of a party, of a marriage in crisis. She reached over to the night table to grab the Trimline phone, accidentally pushing it off the receiver and hearing it bounce on the table. She lifted her head, tried again, and grasped it firmly, bringing it to her ear.

"Hello?"

Cross-Wade sensed her grogginess. "Mrs. Shaw?"

His voice did not immediately register. "Yes?"

"Mr. Cross-Wade here."

Samantha sat up sharply. "*Yes*."

"Mrs. Shaw, I have some news for you."

Samantha's face froze with tension. It was about Marty, it was bad, it was the final word that would seal the fate of her trembling marriage. "Please tell me," she said, putting up the brave front.

"Mr. Martin Shaw is *not* the man."

It was a thunderbolt, totally unexpected.

Samantha winced, then stared straight ahead, then looked into the phone, as if for confirmation of the strange words she had just heard. "He's not...please say that again."

"I say, Mrs. Shaw, your husband is not the man. We have absolute proof. There's been some coincidence here, but there's nothing to worry about."

A sea of relief washed over Samantha for the moment. She literally felt a burden lifted. Marty wasn't a killer. He wasn't a mass murderer. He wasn't the object of a police manhunt. God, that was good news, news that permitted some hope that she could see the marriage through, restore it to its unsullied glory. But another truth prevented the moment from erupting into joy. All right, he wasn't that horrible thing Cross-Wade was searching for. But then, who *was* he? That question hadn't been touched. *Who was he*?

"I'm a little relieved," Samantha said to Cross-Wade. "But, now could you tell me a little about my husband? I mean, you must've learned about him to come to your answer."

"I'm afraid not," Cross-Wade replied. "We learned who he *wasn't* by medical records that finally turned up. We actually have nothing new on him. From your point of view, you're back to square one."

"Yes, I guess I am," Samantha agreed.

"But Mrs. Shaw, think of it this way. At least you are safe. I feel for your other problem. But your safety is of paramount importance."

"Yes."

"I am at your disposal, madam. If there is anything I can do to help, please call me. Even though I'm in homicide, I might have suggestions."

"I appreciate that," Samantha told him. "I really do. You know, in a strange way I'd almost hoped you'd tell me Marty *was* the man, and that you'd learned all about his past."

"That's a natural feeling," Cross-Wade replied. "We all want news. Uncertainty is awful."

"Yes, it is."

"Good luck, Mrs. Shaw. I hope you find your answers soon."

"Thank you for your help," Samantha responded.

They hung up. Samantha had actually wanted to talk more, to go over her problem once again with Cross-Wade, but sensed it was the wrong time. The man still had a killer to catch. She stayed up, and did a few things for the party. Cross-Wade was right. She may have been back to square one, but at least she didn't have to worry about her husband's killing her.

Cross-Wade sealed the investigation of Martin Everett Shaw. He canceled the surveillance and started looking for another suspect. He all but wrote off the chance for success.

Marty still worried about those calls Samantha had made. Was she still making them? Was she still probing? He'd know with the next phone bill, but that wouldn't come until after December fifth. He could call the phone company and check the records, but that might arouse suspicion. So he simply was left wondering.

But, since it was already December first, the questions were rapidly becoming academic. Hold out, he kept telling himself. This is for *Dad*. You can hold out for Dad, can't you, Frankie? You'd do anything for Dad.

He walked into a jewelry store near Rockefeller Center. A tiny lady, a Russian immigrant with a thick yet charming accent, stood behind a counter dressed in a simple gray dress. Her cold, watchful eyes followed Marty as he walked to a display case where the gold necklaces were laid out, each one snaking itself over the blue velvet under it. He looked at each necklace intently. The lady knew this was a gift, and an important one. She knew the moves men made at display cases the way Arthur Loggins knew the moves they made in murder cases. Yes, this was a *major* gift. Anniversary. Birthday. Birth of baby day. The man would spend for the right piece. She slid toward Marty slowly, but deliberately. Don't rush him, but help out.

"Are you looking for something in particular?" she asked.

For a moment, Marty didn't answer, so intently was he

staring into the case. "Uh, yes," he finally said. "I need a thin gold chain with a pendant. A red stone with gold around it. You know."

"Of course," the lady said, rolling her "r" in the Slavic manner. "We have a very fine selection. This, naturally, is for a special person."

"Naturally."

"You will want something of quality. Let me, I will show you." She reached into a drawer under the case and slid out a tray with pendants attached to gold chains. Two or three fit Marty's general requirements. "Here are some fine pieces," she said. "Of course, everything we handle is guaranteed absolutely."

"Oh, I know," Marty said. "I've shopped here before."

He studied the selections carefully. His mind drifted back. Dad had saved so long to buy that pendant for Mother. She'd hardly said thank-you. Wasn't as big as her sister's, she'd muttered. But she'd worn it. She'd worn it that night, that December fifth. How it swung as she'd raised the hammer over her head. How it swung back and forth, wildly, on its thin chain.

Marty's eyes focused on one piece. "There's a nice one," he said. Ask the price, he reminded himself. Make it look like an ordinary purchase. "Uh, what is the price?"

The lady picked up the piece, slinking it over her chubby little hand. "This would be one hundred twenty-five dollars, plus tax." She smiled at Marty, as if signaling that she agreed with his selection. She always agreed with selections above a hundred dollars.

"That's fine," Marty said. He whipped out his American Express gold card and flipped it onto the counter. Be a sport. Charge it. The bill would never be paid anyway.

The necklace was carefully gift-wrapped in a white box and tied with a blue ribbon, at Marty's request. He'd give it to Samantha, and she'd wear it at the party. Everything was falling into place.

Marty returned to his office, and, as he had often done

during this season of rituals, locked the door and ordered that all calls be held. Then he took out pen and paper and wrote still another letter to the only person who'd ever meant anything to him in his four decades of life, the person whose presence he still felt wherever he walked:

Dear Dad,

The day approaches. Isn't that wonderful? There's been some trouble with Sam, though. She may know that I've made up a lot of what I've told her, but she loves me. She's no real threat. I'm doing the best I can for you. Someday we'll be together.

Your loving son,

Frankie

P.S. I got the trains.

He placed the letter in his safe. Then he unlocked his door and buzzed the intercom four times. Moments later, Lois entered.

"Lo," Marty said, "I know you've got a big family, a lot of Christmas shopping. Look, you take two or three days off before the holidays. Whatever days you like."

Lois was genuinely touched by the thought. "Thank you," she said warmly. "Thank you so much."

Marty smiled, almost blushing. He really liked to do things like this. "It's okay," he answered. "And, something else. You've really helped me, and I know I can be demanding at times."

"Oh no, you're not at all."

"Sure I am." Marty reached into his pocket and pulled out a bill. "I don't know what to buy. Do something for yourself. Something you'd really like."

He handed Lois the bill.

It was a hundred dollars, and Marty felt great.

December first passed. So did December second.

As Spencer Cross-Wade agonized over his failing investigation, Martin Shaw prepared to carry out the last great ritual before the fateful day. First step: the phone call to Samantha from his office on the morning of December third. The urgent voice. The tinge of regret.

"Sam," Marty said, "guess what?"

Samantha was sitting amidst catering tables that had already arrived, their metal tops not yet covered with linens. She'd heard that tone in Marty's voice before. It portended bad news, disruption.

"What's wrong, Marty?" she asked.

"A little problem in St. Louis," Marty replied. He sat tensely at his desk, watching every word. "One of our clients out there got involved in a lawsuit, and it's a public-relations mess. I've got to go. Today."

"Marty!"

"Hey, don't worry about the party. I'll be back in twenty-four hours. *No* client could keep me from that."

"Well, that's a relief. For a minute..."

"Sam, *you* before business." For an instant it was the old Marty, smooth and sentimental, affectionate and caring, the one Samantha wished would somehow re-emerge from the layers of mystery that had enveloped him.

"Where are you staying?" she asked, grabbing a pencil.

"Don't know yet. I may be out of touch most of today anyway. My client isn't taking calls at his office and has checked into a hotel to avoid the press. I'll have to be with him. I'll contact you as soon as I can."

"Sure. Okay."

"And, Sam...the staff here doesn't know the real reason I'm going out. We want to keep this under control. You know, people talk. I've told them just that I'm going for a fast confab. If you call the office, remember."

"I'll remember," Samantha said. "Sweet, I'm sorry you have to go like this, right before the party."

"Yeah, so am I. You know, I wanted to be home tonight to help out. I really looked forward to that. Godammit, those jerks out there...you'd think with all their lawyers they'd stay out of trouble."

He sounded so genuine, so filled with emotion, his voice trembling, his anger spilling out. "It's okay," Sam told him. "You'll be back tomorrow, love. I'll take care of everything. You know I will."

"That I know," Marty said. "Look, no strain. Hear me? It doesn't have to be the Inaugural Ball."

"No strain," Samantha agreed. "Not with the..."

She stopped. She'd almost tipped the baby.

"Not with what?" Marty asked.

"Not with a caterer doing all the real work." Great save, Samantha thought. Top save.

Marty blew a kiss into the phone. It's something he rarely did. It was affecting, moving, so right for the moment. Again Samantha's lingering optimism surfaced. Maybe his secrets were *good* secrets, for a good cause, something to be proud of. Maybe. It was always maybe. But Samantha blew a kiss back.

The United flight glided in over St. Louis in early afternoon, giving Marty a glistening view of the great arch that symbolized the city. He was on the ground a few minutes later. He entered the terminal, and waited. He did not go into town.

His secretary had booked the flight to St. Louis under, of course, the name Martin Shaw. But when Marty had arrived at LaGuardia Airport he'd bought an additional ticket, paying in cash, under the name Frank Nelson. It was his tribute, his homage to his family name, his deference to Dad. The ticket he'd bought was for a flight from St. Louis to Omaha. Now, in St. Louis, he glanced at his watch, already set to Omaha time. It was 1:55 P.M. The flight to Omaha would leave at 2:30. He was Frank Nelson now. Frank Nelson again. It felt wonderful. Emotionally he was home, and soon he would be home physically as well. He checked to make sure his sunglasses were in his jacket pocket. He needed them for security. Someone on an Omaha flight might recognize his face, even though a generation had passed since he'd lived there.

He walked to the American Airlines terminal section and boarded the Boeing 727 for "home."

Marty felt his heart pound as the jet engines lifted the plane into the air, heading west to Omaha. He looked around him, peering over the seats at the other passengers. Could anyone guess? Could anyone know what was going through his mind? How would they react if they knew a mass murderer was on the plane? What would they say if they were told a ritual was being performed—a ritual that would end with the bludgeoning of an innocent woman in a New York apartment?

"Something to drink, sir?" the stewardess asked, as she rolled the serving cart down the aisle.

"No, thanks," Marty answered. He couldn't think about food.

He glanced out the window as the city gray turned into country green, miles of green, hundreds of miles of green, the green of the Midwest where he grew up, where he had been scarred for life.

"Live in Omaha?" the man next to him inquired. He was an old man, with a thick, gray mustache that needed combing. "Uh, no," Marty answered. "Visiting."

"Oh."

The Boeing took a sudden dip—an air pocket—and the old man gulped, ending, Marty thought, the brief conversation.

"Bad one," the man said, proving Marty wrong.

"Yeah."

"How long you live in Omaha?" the man asked.

Marty turned sharply towards him. "How did you know...?"

"Don't get all steamed. It's in your voice. I can tell even with a few words. You can't erase it completely. You probably live East."

"Yes."

"That's right. When they go East they try to erase it.

Really too bad, young fella. Omaha's a great town. You should be proud you came from there." He winked at Marty, a reprimanding wink.

"I *am* proud," Marty replied. He felt he had to say it. "I left when I was young. The accent melted."

"Yeah," the old man said. "I've lived there all my life. Don't need anyplace else."

Wonderful, Marty thought. A local booster. He didn't want to change seats and make his discomfort obvious, but he didn't want this pep talk either.

"What part you come from?" the man asked. Now he turned completely toward Marty and Marty could look into his bloodshot, alcoholic eyes and get the full scent of Scotch head-on.

"Upper north," Marty replied, then quickly pulled the airline magazine out of the seat pocket in front of him.

"So do I," the local booster said.

Christ, Marty thought, I needed this. Then he felt a sharp chill race through him. Hey, maybe this guy recognizes me. Maybe he *knew* me as a child. Maybe I look familiar and he's just probing to place the face. Even with the sunglasses, he may know.

"That's nice," Marty replied, flipping through the magazine.

"What's your name?"

Marty stopped reading for a moment. This was becoming serious. "Harvey," he answered. "Len Harvey."

"Durant is mine."

"Hello, Mr. Durant."

"You goin' to that part of town?"

Think fast, Marty thought. You've got to shake him. "Not immediately," he said.

"Oh, that's too bad. I could've given you a lift."

"Thanks," Marty replied. "That's real nice. Real Omaha nice."

"That's the spirit," Durant said. "I like you."

"You're very kind to say that."

"I'd like to drive you wherever you're goin'. Doesn't matter. It's Omaha nice."

"Oh, I couldn't accept that."

"Sure you could."

"No, really. I'm meeting people. It's business."

"Okay," Durant answered. "Tryin' to be helpful. I'll be lookin' for you in our part of town."

Marty didn't answer. Stay rational, he thought. The old guy's a certifiable drunk. He's no threat. Even if you run into him again, what can he do? He can *bother.* That's what he can do. He can cramp a killer's style. Marty swore to do anything to avoid him.

It was a bumpy landing in Omaha. Marty stepped out of the plane ahead of Durant, walking briskly, losing him in the crowd. Durant headed for the baggage area, Marty did not. He'd always kept a small overnight case in the office, with two days' supply of basic needs. He'd taken it right on the plane. Goodbye, Mr. Durant, he mused. Hope you drink a lot in the next few days and forget everything.

Marty walked to the Hertz counter to rent a car, and once again he used his American Express card. He planned to be far away when the bill came in the little windowed envelope.

"Preference?" the blue-uniformed lady at the counter asked.

"Buick Century," Marty replied.

The lady checked the computer. "We're out of that type," she said. "I can give you a Chrysler LeBaron."

"That'll be fine," he answered. He presented his license and credit card, and a Hertz bus took him to the car pick-up station.

The car was a late-model, two-door LeBaron, blue, with the dashboard ashtray missing. Hertz could put Marty in the driver's seat, as long as he didn't smoke.

He knew the route. He'd driven it before on a few visits back, just as he knew the routes into places like Elkhart,

Indiana, and Evanston, Illinois—towns he'd used to construct his falsified past. He drove slowly and carefully. This was not the time to have an accident or attract the attention of an Omaha traffic cop. A few drops of rain began to splatter the windshield, instantly heightening his sense of caution. He checked the gas gauge. Full. He wouldn't need more gas during his stay.

He flipped on the radio.

"And now for the daily farm report..."

He changed stations.

Frank Sinatra. "Love and Marriage." A fifties song, played by one of those nostalgia stations. *That* was the correct mood. Marty rode with that music all the way to his old neighborhood.

The old neighborhood.

Clapboard houses. Some close together. Some on isolated lots. A rural feel, though it was only eleven miles from Omaha's center. Not a neighborhood in the block-after-block sense, with parallel streets and a group of stores. This was more of an area, a state of mind—one main street and a few side roads, none with streetlights. There was a row of stores, including a supermarket and a hardware store, and the inevitable bar, where the boys from a local aircraft-parts plant liked to hang out after work. It was one of those desolate sections that any respectable, ambitious person wanted to leave, yet always come home to, for it was a part of the countryside that seemed never to change, never to go with the tide, never to join the modern world. Nowhere, USA.

Marty saw the house—that strange green clapboard with pink trim that Mother had demanded, set apart from the others, on a small hill with no trees.

Abandoned.

Partially boarded up.

Home.

14

"I'm here. I'm here, Frankie."

Marty remembered the voice. He stood on the same spot, at the side of the house. Dad had taken the bus home—the car had been broken and there'd been no money to fix it.

"Frankie, where are you?"

The voice had been cheerful. It had always been cheerful, no matter how hard times were. Now Marty ran to the front of the house, as he had that December fifth.

"Hi, Dad." He remembered saying it.

Dad had the big carton cradled in both arms. *"Happy birthday, Frankie."* Frankie'd known instantly what was in the box. All he'd been talking about was trains, trains, trains. And Dad had promised: *"for your next birthday, if we can afford it."* He'd gone ahead and gotten the trains anyway, even though he'd known he *couldn't* afford it. A broken-down car in the garage, brand-new electric trains in his arms. All right, Dad had been a dreamer. Impractical.

"Come on inside, Frankie," he'd said.

Marty walked up the front steps. The house was locked,

as it had been for years, known as a murder site, unsalable. He couldn't go in, but he could *look* in. God, everything was always the same. The vandals never touched this house. There were rumors of ghosts, spirits that hung around protecting it. Strange how people believed those things.

He remembered.

The door had opened. Mom was there. No smile. Never a smile. She saw the carton with the trains, and exploded. "*Bum!*" she'd screamed. She'd screamed it about Dad, to his face.

Marty didn't want to think about the rest just then. He only wanted to look through the windows and remember the good times—Dad pillow-fighting with him and Jamie, his younger brother; Dad playing his old banjo and singing war songs from Europe; Dad making those phone calls, those endless phone calls, trying to get work. The phone wire was still connected to the wall in the living room, Marty saw, although the phone had been ripped out long ago. And there was still an old dusty pillow in the floor, just where it had lain the night of December fifth. Yes, everything *was* the same, really—even the old RCA Model 30 television set. The ghosts were such good protectors, such reverent watchers in the night. Fine. Nothing should disturb what Dad had touched.

Then, Marty heard a staccato voice behind him. "Hey, you lookin' for something, Mister?"

He spun around. Incredible, but he hadn't heard the car engine as it pulled up. An Omaha police cruiser was idling, its patrolman-driver looking right at him from behind mirrored sunglasses.

"Just curious," Marty replied, trying to smile, his own sunglasses his only disguise. But instantly he sensed that his answer was ridiculous, more likely to arouse suspicion than quench it. "I like this neighborhood," he went on. "This old house for sale?"

The cop shrugged. "You'll have to see the county assessor, son." He was younger than Marty, but insisted on the "son." "That old house has quite a story behind it."

"Oh?"

"Lady wasted her old man in there."

"Jesus."

"Big story—back in the fifties, I think."

"Pretty spooky."

"Yo. Nobody really wants that house. There's a real-estate broker about a mile down that there road—Calman Brothers —if you want to ask about anything else."

"Thanks," Marty said. "I appreciate that."

"Okay," the cop concluded, and drove off.

Imagine, Marty thought: Here was a cop within thirty feet of him, as he went through the most profound ritual of his season of death, and the guy never suspected a thing. That's planning.

Marty decided to take a stroll through the neighborhood, past his elementary school, its grassy playground filled with kids learning the rudiments of football, past the Avery house, where he'd spent some of his happiest hours playing, and past Doc Marsh's house. He stopped at that one—wood and brick, belonging to a dentist now—and he stared at the front door. Marsh had tried so hard to save Dad. He'd been one of the good guys.

There were plenty of people out walking, some on their way to Christmas shopping. Marty recognized a few of the old-timers, but none recognized him behind his glasses. None of them meant anything to him anyway. He felt no visceral urge to speak with them, even about the old days, before December 5, 1952. These people hadn't helped after Mom killed Dad. They'd stayed away. They'd avoided Frankie and his brother on the street. They hadn't been nice, the way church-going people should've been.

Marty suddenly felt a lump form in his throat. He knew why. The cemetery was just around the corner. He began feeling closer to Dad. The hearse had traveled up this bumpy, broken street, and people had stared out their windows. It wasn't normal to have a funeral procession with police cars, but this had been a special funeral, the funeral of a murder victim. The police had been there in case the crackpots came to disturb the family. A few had come anyway, with their leering eyes and pointing fingers. Frankie had heard one of them shout that Dad must've been an evil man. It wasn't true.

The old cemetery was poorly kept. A lot of people had moved from Omaha, leaving graves behind them, not keeping up with maintenance payments, depending on the largesse of churches and the goodwill of the cemetery management to show proper respect for the remains of mothers, fathers, spouses, and children. Some respect was shown, but there were financial limits, so the grass was uncut, some stones were overturned, the obscenities scribbled on one monument went unscrubbed. Marty was angry. Dad shouldn't have to lie in a place like this. He deserved better. He deserved one of those hillside graves with olive trees around, with green grass good enough for a golf course, with flowerbeds and soft breezes. That's what Dad deserved. Marty gritted his teeth. He had the money to move Dad, but couldn't. To move a body required a court order. He'd have to reveal himself, ruin everything. Even an anonymous contribution for upkeep of Dad's plot might arouse suspicion. So things would have to stay as they were, at least for a time.

There wasn't even a groundskeeper. Marty walked through the rusted, broken gate and stood for a moment, looking over the depressing place. He started walking again, taking the same route he'd taken that bitter December day in 1952. He heard the grass rustling under him. None of it was trampled, for rarely did anyone come to the cemetery, especially in the cold. A black dog jumped from behind a gravestone and started yelping. Marty froze. It had no collar, no license. A stray, and mean looking. Marty tried smiling at it. It kept yelping, then finally turned and ran.

Marty walked on again. He felt the wind, and it triggered an almost photographic image in his mind of that day at the cemetery in 1952. There, to his left, was Al Ryder's grave. He remembered that American flag mounted on it in 1952, just after Al's body had been returned from Korea. It was one of the few graves still kept up. His parents must still be alive, Marty thought.

And then...

Dad. Squeezed amidst a bunch of others was a small, thin headstone, the cheapest available at the time. Now it was tilted toward the body at a 15-degree angle, and its base looked like it was coming out of the ground. The inscription was partly filled in with dirt, but was still clear: JOHN ALBERT NELSON, 1916—1952. He didn't live nearly long enough, Marty said to himself.

He looked around. If anyone saw him now, there might be suspicion. But no one did. It was pure emptiness. So Marty knelt down reverently beside the grave, ignoring the tilt of the headstone.

How did Dad lie? He still wondered, as he had at Dad's funeral, although he knew by now, as an adult, that bodies are placed face up. But always? Was there some law that required it? Dad's coffin had been closed during the service, so who was to know? Maybe the undertaker had put him face down. And once again Marty wondered if there was an expression on Dad's face, and whether it was that curious look he'd had just before it happened.

"Like the lumber loader, Frankie?"

Marty heard Dad's voice. It was so clear, so alive, as if carried on the wind as it swept over the gravestones.

"It's the new lumber loader. Automatic. I saw it work at the store. Don't lose any of the logs, though. Okay?"

Marty remembered that he'd never lost any of the logs. Even when he'd had to leave the set behind, when he went into the world, he'd kept the logs—because Dad had said never to lose them.

"Dad, I may be away a long while," he now whispered, staring at the gravestone. "But I'll be back. You know I will. We're showing that Mom hasn't gotten away with this, aren't we? We're sure showing it."

He edged over and tried to straighten the stone, but his

strength wasn't enough. All he could do was clean the dirt off the front. "I want you to rest easy, Dad. I've got things under control. I'm playing with the trains. I'll even answer the Christmas cards for you. And I got that RCA Model 30 this time. We have things called video cassette recorders now. They play tapes of television programs. I got this old tape of Doug Edwards. Remember how you watched him? I'll play it the night of December fifth... for you, Dad."

Suddenly, a vision of Samantha flashed through Marty's mind, but all he could see beneath her auburn hair was the face of his mother, and all he could hear was his mother's screaming voice. Samantha's transformation in the twisted depths of his psyche was beginning.

"I failed you once, Dad," he said. "I failed you on December fifth, 1952. I should have saved you, but I failed. I'll never fail you again."

He got up and stepped back.

"Goodbye, Dad. Next time I see you it'll all be over." He left the cemetery.

15

The clatter of metal against metal rang through the Shaw apartment as the caterer's men brought in the last of the chairs and tables for the December fifth gala. Samantha and Lynne watched, assuming that the well-recommended caterer knew what he was doing. But Samantha held a floor plan in her hand, occasionally directing the placement of a particular piece.

She didn't know what to feel. What *do* you feel in a situation like this? A great party coming up, a husband cleared of a ghastly crime, that husband shrouded in mystery, and yet, on the other hand, that same husband about to be a father. As linens started appearing on tabletops, Samantha slowly felt restraint slipping away and anticipation overtaking her. It was natural. Parties bring with them their own psychology. And Lynne was a great cheerleader. She still knew nothing of the trauma over Marty's past. Samantha had simply told her that the probing for Marty's old friends had never worked out—that they'd been too hard to find and too expensive to bring in. Lynne had bought it.

"Over here," Samantha commanded, and a hauler switched direction and brought a round table to the front of the living room. He didn't acknowledge the order. People who haul for caterers never say much of anything.

"I think you got a broken one," Lynne whispered as she saw a worker trying to steady a table that wouldn't get steadied. Samantha looked at him, he looked back, and again without a word, refolded the table and replaced it with another.

Some of the furniture had been pushed to the sides of the living room, with some pieces stored in Lynne's apartment. "It looks so...commercial," Samantha commented as the workmen were just about finished.

"You just watch," Lynne said. "I run four parties a month for my gallery. They start getting it together and you'll have the Waldorf right in your living room."

"Think Marty'll like it?" Samantha asked.

"He'll love it. *Everyone* loves a party in their honor. It's the American way, baby."

Samantha knew that Marty was flying back to New York that very moment, only a day before the party. She'd spoken with him the previous night, when he'd called from a St. Louis hotel. He'd checked into the hotel to maintain absolute credibility to the last possible minute. Marty Shaw overlooked nothing.

Of course he'd love the party, Samantha mused, just as Lynne said he would. And maybe—just maybe—he'd choose the special night, December fifth, to reveal his great secrets. It would be wonderful to end the mystery the night of the party. Of course, that was precisely what Marty had planned, but his interpretation was rather different.

"Mrs. Shaw?"

Samantha heard the voice and turned. A young, smallish man, about twenty, was at the door, which had been wedged open by the caterers. "Yes?"

"Nick Auerbach, Dimension Video. The doorman thought I was with the caterer and sent me up."

"Oh, yes," Samantha said with her ever-gracious smile. The name took a few seconds to register, but she knew Auerbach would be making the videotape of the party, and had come to scout the apartment for shots. "Please come in," she said. "The place is yours."

Auerbach had no video equipment with him—only a clipboard and a pencil. Samantha showed him the apartment, and he made little sketches, noting measurements, table locations, and the colors of walls. After finishing, he sat down with Samantha at one of the tables. "I'll need some information from you," he told her.

"Like what?"

"Like whether there'll be any ceremonies or presentations."

"Oh no, nothing like that," Samantha replied.

"I beg your little pardon," Lynne interrupted. "Aren't we forgetting something?"

Samantha didn't realize what Lynne was talking about, so Lynne pointed to her own stomach. Samantha felt like a fool for forgetting. "Of course," she told Auerbach. "I'm going to make an announcement from the head table. A special thing. Shall I signal you when?"

"I'd appreciate that," Auerbach said. Samantha was amazed at his wiry youth. She'd expected someone much older. She hadn't realized Auerbach was a college student who did this in his spare time.

He asked many more questions. Did Samantha have a list of people who *had* to have close-ups? Did she want "interviews" with guests? Were any subjects to be avoided? Were there things or people who *shouldn't* be included?

The tone bespoke more experience than Samantha would have imagined. Auerbach knew that parties were very political events, that the videotapes had to reflect the right point of view, show people in the light that the host intended. The tape was the modern version of the wedding album, whose pictures were often selected to make this family member or that look good... or bad.

"Would you like a history?" Auerbach finally asked.

"A history?" Samantha replied, as the clatter of the last table being set up punctuated her question.

"Yes. Sometimes people like us to include stills from a person's past—in this case your husband's. You know, if you have old yearbooks or albums or even home movies..."

My God, Samantha thought, the little guy hit it right on the head, didn't he? A history. Now that would be a lark. Sure, he could do a history...if he could *find* it. She felt like telling him that, but didn't.

"No, my husband is pretty shy about those things," she replied. "I'd better pass on it."

"Okay. Of course, we could do it in titles alone."

"I don't follow."

"Just a stream of words showing his past, floating across the screen. Home town. College. Companies. Stuff like that."

Samantha didn't know whether to laugh or cry, or do both at the same time. "I still think we'd better do without it," she said.

"Fine," Auerbach said. "You may have an awfully cold tape, though. Like, just a lot of people buzzin' around."

"I'll have to take that risk," Samantha told him. "It'll be a lively party. I think we'll have all the warmth we'll need."

"I hear you," Auerbach said. He left a few minutes later.

The workmen finished putting the white tablecloths on the tables and Samantha saw the elegance that Lynne had talked about. The apartment took on a formal quality, a brightness combined with high style. Samantha could imagine what the rest would look like—the place settings, the centerpieces, the silver service, the small band off to the side. It would have to be a party to remember.

It *would* all work out.

It had to.

The police cruiser sped through Manhattan streets, its lights flashing and siren blaring. Traffic ahead lurched to the right to let it pass. Inside the cruiser, a young patrolman sat at the wheel.

Spencer Cross-Wade sat in the back of the cruiser with Arthur Loggins. Cross-Wade gripped a large brown envelope in his right hand, gripped it tightly, as if it contained some state secret. Neither man spoke or gestured. They sat motionless, expressionless, contemplating what had just happened, how they would explain it, what it might lead to. Cross-Wade felt an embarrassment, a humiliation, that he had never experienced before, even during the darkest days of the calendar killer probe.

The car lurched onto Central Park West and sped uptown. Now Cross-Wade dreaded what was about to happen. He phrased his words in his mind and silently rehearsed every point. He knew there was a ray of hope amidst the embarrassment, but he felt for Samantha, for she would bear the brunt of the latest bulletin.

He had the doorman announce him by intercom. At first, Samantha was startled to hear that he'd returned. For a moment, in fact, she wondered if it was actually him. So he got on the intercom, assuring her, in his distinct style, that he had to see her on "police business."

He and Loggins rushed to the apartment.

Samantha opened.

She had never seen Cross-Wade so grim, so ashen, so obviously agitated. It was about Marty. That had to be it.

"Come in," she said nervously.

The detectives entered. The workmen and Lynne had already left.

"I'm sorry we had to disturb you," Cross-Wade said.

"I understand," Samantha replied. "Please sit down."

They all sat, and they all sensed it was no time for small talk. Cross-Wade turned immediately and urgently to Samantha, still clutching the brown envelope in his hand. "Mrs. Shaw," he said, "I know you're surprised to see us."

"Yes," Samantha agreed.

"I'm sure you wished we'd gone away and never returned."

"Well, in a way." Samantha studied Cross-Wade's face

closely and felt his distress. "I think you found out something about Marty," she said, "something that clears up a lot about his past. And I think it isn't good."

"You're very perceptive," Cross-Wade answered.

Samantha sighed. "I'd hoped his secrets were good secrets. What'd he do, steal some money?"

Cross-Wade realized that Samantha didn't fully understand. She thought he'd simply discovered some minor transgression, some forgivable lapse.

"You can tell me," she went on, when he didn't immediately answer. She felt a sudden depression. The high she'd been on as the party tables were set up fell apart. "I guess I'd have preferred finding out *after* the party, but I want to know."

"Mrs. Shaw," Cross-Wade said, "before discussing this, I do want to be sure of something. May I see your bedroom again?"

Samantha was startled. "Why?"

"It's important."

Without saying a word, Samantha led Cross-Wade to the bedroom. He had only to stand in the doorway. "Yes," he said after looking around, "we're right."

"About what?" Samantha asked.

Before answering, Cross-Wade led Samantha back to the couch. He sat close to her. "Madam," he said, "as you know, I canceled the investigation of your husband after we received those medical records. It was the proper move."

"Of course."

"But, the way things are in the bureaucracy, some actions just went forward automatically. I had asked the Omaha authorities for pictures of Frankie Nelson's house, inside and out. They supplied the outside pictures, but neglected the interiors. So, last week I asked again for pictures of the inside. They finally arrived today. I have them here." He raised the brown envelope.

"So?" Samantha asked.

Slowly, grimly, Cross-Wade opened the envelope. Inside was a set of eight-by-ten glossies. He gently handed them to Samantha.

She gazed down.

Her eyes widened.

"Oh my God," she whispered. She looked up at Cross-Wade in sudden panic. "Oh my good God!"

Cross-Wade just nodded, agreeing with her reaction.

She studied the pictures once more, holding one up. It showed a bedroom in the old Nelson house—arranged precisely as Marty had arranged the bedroom in the apartment. On one wall was the gaudy picture frame, identical to the one Marty had put up.

There was even the same obstructing of the windows and radiators by furniture, the same bizarre layout.

And there was, in another picture, the RCA Model 30, ancient, dusty, but recognizable.

Samantha shook her head, dismayed, shocked, baffled by it all. "I don't understand," she said.

"It's self-evident," Cross-Wade replied.

"But... you have his medical records."

"We thought so."

"Thought?"

Cross-Wade had a forlorn look as he tried to explain to Samantha. "Mrs. Shaw," he said, "I've been in police work long enough to know that not everyone in our profession is completely reliable. Yes, we received a set of records with the name of Frankie Nelson on them. We compared them with Marty's and they didn't match. But when we look at your bedroom, and then at these pictures of the Nelson house, the truth becomes clear. Why didn't the medical records match? I suspect we were sent the wrong records, mislabeled with the Nelson name. Someone simply made a mistake. Mrs. Shaw, your husband *is* Frankie Nelson."

Samantha got up slowly and walked back to the bedroom. Cross-Wade and Loggins followed her, not saying a word. Samantha gazed around the room, then down at the photos, which she still held. "Why would Marty do this?" she asked, accepting the basic facts. "Why would he decorate the room the same way?"

"I would surmise it's part of some ritual," Cross-Wade answered. "Perhaps it reflects an attachment to his youth, the youth that existed before..."

"Before he saw his mother murder his father," Samantha said.

"I'm afraid that is the situation we must face."

Samantha lowered her head. "A murderer," she whispered bitterly. "I thought we'd jumped that hurdle. My husband is a murderer." She felt slightly faint and rushed to sit down on the bed. "I can't believe it."

"That's human," Cross-Wade told her, his voice filled with a genuine sympathy. He knew he'd taken Samantha on a roller-coaster ride, first suspecting Marty, then exonerating him, now accusing him again. It had been savage, if unintended. "I know this has been very difficult for you," he went on. "You've been brave. You'll have to be brave a little longer."

Samantha knew what Cross-Wade was saying. It was December fourth. "I guess I'm a target," she said. "*His* target."

"We must assume that. It's all in his mind. You're simply not his wife any longer. Now..." Cross-Wade hesitated. He was entering the vague recesses of Marty Shaw's abnormal psyche. "Now," he continued, "you've become his mother."

Samantha simply stared. "His mother," she repeated. "Isn't that just fine? I've got two babies...and one carries a hammer and chain."

Cross-Wade and Loggins glanced at each other briefly, each almost wishing he could take Samantha's hurt on himself.

"Well," Samantha asked, "what do you want me to do?"

"I want you to help us stop your husband," Cross-Wade answered.

"Me? Stop *him*? Why don't you just arrest him for his other murders?"

"Because," Cross-Wade sighed, "we still don't have a single shred of hard evidence linking your husband to those murders. The evidence is all circumstantial. We need something solid."

"And I'm to help you get it."

"Yes," Cross-Wade said. "Mrs. Shaw, I know what's going through your mind. This is the end of your marriage."

Again, as on earlier occasions, the tears started filling Samantha's eyes. Cross-Wade had stated the reality so well. "Yes," she said softly.

"I would want only to leave you alone, not to bother you in these sad circumstances," Cross-Wade went on. "But we can't confront your husband before the party and charge him. He'd never admit anything and we might lose the whole case."

"How do you do it then?"

"By asking you to go through with the party as if nothing has happened, and letting him reveal himself tomorrow, his crucial day, December fifth."

"Jesus."

"I know it's hard, but we must make an airtight case. It's for your own safety. Marty's a threat to you...and to the baby."

That one hit home. It jolted Samantha into facing what Cross-Wade wanted her to face. The baby. Something *could* happen to the baby if Marty weren't stopped, if he somehow escaped prosecution. She now wanted that baby so much. Even if she couldn't share it with Marty, the Marty she thought had been, she still wanted it. It was a part of her now. She had to protect it.

"We'll have the apartment entirely covered," Cross-Wade continued. "It'll be wired with our advanced sound equipment. We'll be down the hall in the apartment where the residents are away. When something begins to happen here, we'll be in within seconds. Everything will be on tape. Marty will be caught."

"Trying to *kill* me?" Samantha asked, shocked as she visualized the scene.

"We'd never let it go that far. We're very good at what we do."

"I can't believe he'd do it during the party," Samantha said.

"Neither can I," Cross-Wade agreed. "He'll undoubtedly make his move after the guests leave, but before midnight of the fifth. However, we'll have him under surveillance the entire day. Indeed, we'll have one additional form of protection. In the morning, before Marty leaves for work, a telephone repairman will be in your apartment, supposedly to make a repair on a circuit. Of course, he'll actually be one of our men."

Samantha glanced at her watch, her hand shaking, her arm coated with the first glisten of a cold sweat. "It'll all be over in a little more than thirty-two hours," she said. She buried her head in her hands. "Marty will be out of my life."

"It gives me no pleasure," Cross-Wade told her. "But I hope I can have your help."

"Yes," Samantha muttered. Now the anger she'd previously felt when Marty was under suspicion began to surface again. He'd betrayed her. He'd betrayed her by being something other than what she'd thought. "I'll help," she said, her voice trembling.

"You're a great lady," Cross-Wade said.

They spoke for a few more minutes and Cross-Wade called his headquarters to order the sound equipment installed in Samantha's apartment. He also ordered visual surveillance of Marty resumed upon Marty's return, and alerted a squad of men to spend all of December fifth in an apartment on Samantha's floor, prepared to protect her in an instant. Then he returned to Samantha, who now had drifted back to the living room with Loggins. She was sitting on the couch, staring at all the preparations for the party, all the useless, meaningless gaiety.

"Madam," Cross-Wade told her, "I think it's wise that I take the photographs back. We wouldn't want your husband to discover them."

Samantha hardly realized she was still holding the pictures. She handed them over, and Cross-Wade instantly saw that the side of the envelope was crumpled and almost punched through from Samantha's tight, horrified grip.

"Do you have to leave now?" she asked, not really wanting to be alone.

"We must," Cross-Wade told her. "We have procedures to prepare."

"Yes, procedures," Samantha lamented. "Always procedures."

"You know, Mrs. Shaw," Cross-Wade said gently, "it has been my lot to visit many women who've suddenly found themselves without partners. Normally it's a murder situation. I've seen their despair and their emptiness. But there is a tomorrow. Believe me. The wound will never heal completely, but there will be an easing. Even now, you must think about tomorrow. For the baby."

Samantha barely comprehended Cross-Wade's words, so completely was she absorbed by the shock she'd just received. He was so decent a man, so caring, so unlike the stereotype of the tough, indifferent cop. But for now the only "tomorrow" that mattered was December fifth. "I appreciate your thoughts," she answered him. "It's hard for me to think right now." Cross-Wade nodded his sympathy. "We'll be in close contact," he said. "We must have our equipment in here before your husband comes home. Once the clock strikes December fifth, everything has to be heard by our men...even when you're sleeping."

"I understand."

"We wish you the best, Mrs. Shaw."

And then Cross-Wade and Loggins left.

Samantha heard only silence.

Everything had changed once more. In the course of a

few minutes her hope that Marty's secrets were good secrets had been dashed. His secrets weren't good secrets. They were the worst kind of secrets. She contemplated the horror of what she faced—watching the police take him away, answering the probing questions from Lynne and other friends and neighbors, the whispers, the speculation about *her* and her part in the ugly mess. She'd have to move. No doubt about that. She'd have to give up the life she'd dreamed of for years. And she'd have to face the loneliness again.

She looked down at her stomach and wondered whether the baby had some way of knowing that something was wrong. She'd once heard that babies in the womb could feel the tension of the mother. Would the baby be hurt by this? Would there be some psychological damage that would come out years later?

Would the baby ultimately blame *her* for what was happening to its father?

My God, Samantha thought, it could be a replay. Maybe the baby *would* blame her, the way Marty blamed his own mother.

Samantha suddenly had the terrifying thought that she might be afraid of her own child.

This couldn't be happening, she said to herself over and over, as she had before.

There had to be a way out.

Somewhere there was a glimmer of light.

Maybe...just *maybe* Cross-Wade had made another mistake.

Her rational side didn't believe that for a moment, but part of her had to believe it to survive.

Exhausted, she fell asleep.

16

December Fifth

The Day came.

It would appear, if Marty Shaw had his way, on Samantha's tombstone.

It would appear, if Spencer Cross-Wade had his way, on a commendation marking the date he solved a major mass murder.

It would appear, if Samantha had her way, on nothing out of the ordinary—for she wished the whole nightmare would go away.

The day was cold, with occasional driving rain that cut through to the bone and turned a brief walk outside into shivering misery. Tom Edwards had been right. It wasn't a day to serve ice cream for dessert.

The rain pelted against the windows of the Shaw apartment as Marty and Samantha awakened. Marty staggered to the window and looked out, gazing at a sea of gray that blocked every building on the New York skyline. "Great day!" he exclaimed, and smiled back at Samantha. She looked skeptically at him, determined to play the part Cross-Wade asked her to play. "No, I mean it!" Marty said. "The hell with the weather. *This* is a great day for both of us!"

Samantha smiled, forcing it. "You're right. Happy birthday, love!" She rushed out of bed to kiss him, and gave him an embrace that any man would remember. God, she thought, this is sick. The man is a monster, and I'm kissing him.

And yet, she still had something for Marty inside. She couldn't erase it. This was a form of torture.

The doorbell rang.

Marty frowned. "At this hour?" he asked, seemingly annoyed that this great day was being disrupted right at the start. "Don't the doormen announce people anymore?" He started for the door.

"Oh, wait," Samantha interrupted. "I think I know who that is."

"For the party?"

"No. The phone company called yesterday and said they'd traced a problem to our phone line. The woman told me they might be here early."

Marty shrugged and continued walking toward the door. "Who is it?" he asked.

"Phone company," the voice answered, confirming Samantha's story.

Marty opened. A tall, muscular "repairman" stood before him, holding a telephone company ID card. "Repair," he said. "We called."

"Sure," Marty replied.

The man entered and went to work in the dining room. Samantha felt temporarily safe.

Marty walked back to the bedroom, determined to resume the spirit of the morning, just as it was before the doorbell rang.

"You know," he said to Samantha, "I don't feel forty. I feel fifteen, tops." A devilish grin came over his face. "I even have my electric trains."

"Marty," Samantha kidded, "please, not at the party."

Marty looked hurt. It, too, was a fake, of course. "Why not? I thought I'd give everyone a chance."

"Marty... no."

"Okay, no. Birthday boy doesn't get what he wants. Birthday boy might cry."

"Before you cry," Samantha said, "what do you want for breakfast?"

"Steak," Marty replied.

"You want *steak* for breakfast?"

"Why not? Hey, I'll take you out. I know where you can get steak at this hour."

"Forget it. I've got it here."

"No kidding!"

"You once told me you thought a birthday would be perfect with steak for breakfast. I remembered, love."

Now it was Marty's turn to go through the motions of rushing over to kiss Samantha. "I don't know what I'd do if I hadn't found you," he said.

"You'd starve."

They were both such magnificent fakes, Samantha for a good cause, Marty for an evil one. And both had worries. Something *could* go wrong, Samantha knew, and her life could end in a violent second. Samantha *could* know more than he thought, Marty realized, and his plan to kill her might backfire.

Unconsciously, Samantha kept glancing at an air vent high on one wall, where Cross-Wade's men had planted one of their microphones. Strange, but she worried about saying something embarrassing, something that might make the cops in the empty apartment down the hall laugh. Even those in mortal danger worry about their pride.

"I'll start cooking," she told Marty as he began to unbutton his pajamas.

"Wait a second," he said.

"Something wrong?"

Marty stopped unbuttoning and walked briskly to his

desk. He opened a drawer and took out the gift box that he'd gotten at the jeweler's.

"What's that?" Samantha asked.

"Well, my dear," Marty replied, "I was thinking recently... and you know how dangerous *that* is."

"I sure do."

"So... here." Marty handed the box to Samantha.

"Marty... thank you," she said, genuinely surprised. "You didn't have to do this."

"I wanted to. You deserve it."

"I'm just so, so shocked."

"Hey, forget the shock. Go ahead and open it."

For a flash, Samantha almost forgot the horror she faced. This was so old-fashioned, so romantic, so typical of the Marty she'd known. A present on his birthday... for *her*. But why? Why was he going to all this trouble if he planned to murder her? What motivated his bizarre mind?

She opened the box, as she'd opened so many other presents from Marty during the time she'd known him, carefully removing the ribbon and setting it aside, as if there were some real reason to save it. Then she took off the top and folded the wrapping tissue aside. She gazed down at the pendant at the end of its slim gold chain.

"Marty, this is beautiful."

"I thought you'd like it."

"Like it! I *love* it!"

"You sure? If it isn't just right, I can always get you something else."

What were the cops thinking as they listened to this soap opera, Samantha wondered. The man was actually talking about exchanging a gift for a wife about to be a corpse.

"Don't you dare take this back!" she said.

"Put it on," Marty requested.

"Sure." Samantha walked to a mirror and slipped the pendant around her neck, letting it hang gently over her nightgown. Neither she nor Marty said anything for a few moments, the slapping of the rain the only sound.

"It's perfect," Samantha finally said.

Marty still said nothing. He just stood behind Samantha and smiled. It was a vague smile, very distant. Samantha caught it in the mirror. She never recalled Marty's smiling like that. Usually his smile was forceful, direct, up front, almost bursting out. This one seemed more inside than out, a smile that reflected a private thought. Samantha kept staring at that smile as if it were some clue she couldn't comprehend.

Marty, through the smile, stared at the image of Samantha in the mirror. Yeah, that was Mom. Sure it was. The long auburn hair. That pendant hanging from her neck. Too bad about Mom. Too bad about the kind of person she was. Too bad Mom had to be punished, and punished for good.

"I'll wear it tonight," Samantha promised.

"I'd like that," Marty replied. "It looks great on you."

Samantha turned around to Marty. "How about that steak?"

"Sure," Marty replied. But he still wore that strange grin.

Samantha gently removed the pendant and returned it to its box, where it would remain until evening. Then she went into the kitchen to prepare Marty's special breakfast, something she'd planned since she conceived of the party.

In the empty apartment down the hall, four of Cross-Wade's men listened on surveillance equipment. All wore shoulder holsters. All had keys to Samantha's apartment, made during the night at a Police Department machine shop. They could be at Samantha's side within twenty-five seconds if they heard anything suspicious, although, with the "repairman" in the apartment, it was improbable that they would be needed during the morning. Two of them carried plumber's wrenches and the other two carpenter's tools. They were, as far as the people in the building knew, doing some repair work.

Marty began to dress and inevitably went over the day's

details in his mind. Hammer, chain, Doug Edwards tape, ticket to Rome for the next morning. Everything was in order. The demon had taken over. The "5" in his calendar watch was enough to trigger the passionate lust for revenge that he felt every year on this date. *This* was the only anniversary that counted, the only important date in his wretched, tortured life. He felt close to Dad, closer than he'd ever felt since Dad went away in 1952. Yes, there was always a side of Marty/Frankie that wanted him to stop, to resume the normal life of a successful New York businessman. But that side couldn't overpower the demon, the superheated part of his psyche that made him take revenge on December fifth.

Inevitably, he thought back to his first victim, that smiling, auburn-haired librarian in a Philadelphia suburb who'd left the library one evening and was later found dead in a wooded area two blocks away. How exhilarated he'd felt at this first tribute to Dad, how powerful he'd imagined himself when he realized he could get away with it, not just once, but many times.

He'd recently reasoned that, with precise planning, he might get away with Samantha's murder as well. But he would inevitably come under police scrutiny, and the instinct for survival that had kept him free for six years told him to make the trip to Rome, change his physical appearance and begin again under a new name. Within hours he would no longer be Martin Everett Shaw.

"Now *that's* the way to begin a day," he said, walking into the kitchen and smelling the steak being grilled. "I should be forty more often."

It was all so normal, so typical, not different, really, from any domestic scene in a television show or a nineteen-fifties movie.

Marty and Samantha had breakfast, marred only by one incident—Samantha suddenly knocked over a full cup of coffee, sending it splattering to the floor. "Nerves," she explained. "The party."

It was a half lie. It was nerves, but it wasn't the party that made Samantha knock over the cup. It was the vision of Marty wielding a hammer and chain.

After breakfast, Marty put on a brown wool coat and left for the office. Outside, in unmarked parked cars, and across the street on the rim of Central Park, were plainclothesmen from Cross-Wade's office. A few of them, in an old blue Chevrolet Impala, trailed Marty's cab downtown, where other plainclothesmen, posted outside his office building, watched him enter. It was Marty's normal routine, reported in detail to Spencer Cross-Wade, who coordinated the operation from his office.

Marty took the elevator upstairs to his firm's headquarters and made his usual walk down the hall, opening the main door with a flourish. Then the normalcy of the morning evaporated.

"Surprise!"

It was a cliché, but it was heartfelt.

The office staff had wanted to throw Marty a party before-the-party, just for the people in the firm. The offices were alive with streamers, crepe paper, balloons, food tables, and a large ice sculpture of the head of Martin Everett Shaw. Before Marty could even get inside he was smothered by the kisses of secretaries and the backslaps of more restrained employees.

"My God!" he exclaimed, caught off-guard, "what have you people done?"

"A warm-up for tonight," someone said, and that set the tone for the rest of the day. Not much work would get done, but everyone was sure Marty wouldn't mind.

And Marty didn't mind. Once December fifth was over, he'd never see these people again.

A police surveillance team in a building across the street, armed with carefully concealed telescopic lenses, was able to see into the windows of Marty's firm and report the surprise party to Cross-Wade.

Leonard Ross, Marty's vice-president for media relations, a whiz kid of thirty with a well-trimmed beard and an abnormally deep voice, called for silence as Marty stepped in and beamed at the assembly. "Folks, can I have your attention?" Ross called out, raising his right arm and stretching his new Pierre Cardin blue blazer. "I'm just as anxious to get the party going as you are, but I need about a minute of your time." He gestured for Marty to stay close to him.

The staff of ten women and eight men stopped talking and turned their attention to Ross, whose bright eyes, well-rehearsed charm, and style of command made him ideal for these moments.

But then someone started singing "Happy Birthday," and almost instantly everyone joined in. It wasn't what Ross had wanted, but it would have been poor taste to stop it. He started leading the song.

"Okay," he said when it ended, "that was great. Just great. Now, is everybody here?"

Faces turned toward each other and a few staffers counted heads.

"Looks like it," Marty said.

"Nobody in the little boys' room or little girls' room?" Ross asked.

"If they are, they've got more important things to do," Marty quipped. There was much laughter.

The staff gathered round in a semi-circle, waiting for Ross to resume speaking.

"Marty," Ross finally began, "I know this is a great surprise to you. And maybe the morning isn't the best time for a party, but our guys and gals were eager."

"I appreciate that," Marty replied.

"Besides," Ross continued, "we have to get this food down before the big feast tonight."

"Right on!" someone shouted. More laughter.

"Marty," Ross continued, "our people wanted to show you their respect, their loyalty and their love. You may be the boss, but to us you've always been a good friend."

Marty smiled modestly as the room burst out in strong applause.

"So we're having this little party to help you celebrate your fortieth birthday, with the wish that you have at least eighty more..."

Further applause.

"...and that we get raises during that whole time."

Everyone laughed, Marty more than any of them. Ross slapped him on the back and someone took a picture with a Polaroid camera. Then Marty stepped forward to speak. "I'm shocked," he said. "I didn't think anyone liked me." He knew how to get that obligatory laugh. "But I really want to thank you. Having your loyalty means so much to me. It's been a long struggle from journalism school, through the Army and a lot of jobs I'd like to forget. But I'm proud of this firm, proud of what we do, and proud to be associated with all of you. Let's not just celebrate my fortieth birthday. Let's celebrate our success now and into the future."

It was a good little speech and the applause was sustained. There were even some loud cheers, a certain sign that the right things had been said. People began breaking up to start the serious eating, but once again Ross raised his right hand.

"Wait a minute. Please. All. Just one minute. We have a little something for Marty."

The buzzing stopped. Everyone turned back to Ross. Marty looked surprised again.

"Marty," Ross said, "we weren't going to let you get away without showing you a permanent token of our affection and esteem. Carol..."

Carol, a tall, blond secretary who worked for Ross, walked quickly into Ross's office and emerged a few moments later with a large, flat package, gift-wrapped with a blue ribbon, and the number "40" drawn on the side in bright red.

"Now *this* you didn't have to do," Marty said.

"Marty," Ross replied, "we thought that if you could have anything hanging in your office to remind you of this occasion, it would be this. We hope you like it." He handed Marty the gift.

"Well, thank you," Marty said, knowing he'd never hang anything in that office again.

"Open it!" someone shouted.

"I will!" With a broad smile, Marty began unwrapping the gift. Ross helped. The wrappings came off slowly, accompanied by the crackling sound of the paper. Finally, the edge of a picture frame showed. Then more of the frame. Then the back of a picture. The last wrappings fell away. Marty was looking at the rear of the picture, so he turned it around.

"Magnificent!" he exclaimed, shaking his head from side to side as if filled with emotion. "This is wonderful. *This* is something to treasure. It will be with me for the rest of my life."

He gazed down at the portrait of Samantha, her auburn hair flowing gently over her graceful, innocent neck. Her face glowed with the soft smile of one looking forward to a lifetime of happiness and love.

"We had a painter do it," Ross explained. "When you were on a trip we took that little picture of Sam from your office and gave it to him. He made a copy."

"Beautiful," Marty said.

"It's oil color," Ross told him.

"Beautiful," Marty said again. "I want to hang it today. Then I want to bring Sam in to see it. Tomorrow. After the party. It'll be a perfect climax to a wonderful time. She'll love it."

"We hope so," Ross said.

It was almost hilarious, Marty thought. What a great news story it would make after Samantha's body was discovered—HUSBAND KILLER GOT PORTRAIT OF WIFE BEFORE BLUDGEONING HER. He was sure the portrait would be reproduced in the papers.

"I'm taking it to my office right now," he announced. "And thank you all again, from the bottom of my heart. Now, enjoy!"

Marty raised the picture so all could see, then marched into his office as the staff raced to the food tables to fill up. Once inside, he closed the door behind him. To carry out his promise to hang the picture immediately he removed a small mosaic from his northern wall and replaced it with the portrait. Then he stepped back and surveyed it. "Dad," he whispered, "this is a great omen. It's as if some force made those fools out there realize Samantha wouldn't be long for this world. What a scene, Dad. What a great scene."

Marty rejoined the party, but couldn't keep the irony of the portrait out of his mind. And that recurring thought made him change his plans. "You know," he told Ross at one point, as they both sipped Bloody Marys, "I think I'll take the portrait home tonight. It's so gorgeous I want everyone at the party to see it."

"That's a very nice gesture," Ross said. "Everyone on the team will get a charge out of that."

"Right," Marty said. "A charge."

As festivities were winding down, Marty returned to his office, alone again. Now he began preparing the items he would need to carry out the ultimate ritual planned for that evening. He opened his safe and took out the hammer and chain, placing them in his attaché case, under some business papers. He also took out the videotape of the old Doug Edwards news show, placing it on the hammer and chain. Finally he took out the ticket to Rome for December sixth, and placed it in a side pocket of the case, which had a lock. He snapped the lock shut.

He'd take the picture down, he decided, just before leaving for home. Bringing it home would be the last thing he'd ever do to make Samantha happy.

The clock was counting down. Nothing could stop him now. It was 10:45 AM when he placed his attaché case in a corner of his office and walked to the reception area, where a few staff members lingered. "Great day," he told them.

"Right," one of them said, "and a great night ahead."

"Oh yes," Marty replied. "It'll be all I've ever dreamed of."

"That sounds like it comes from the heart," a young secretary said.

"Oh, it does," Marty answered. "Tonight comes straight from the heart."

Samantha's time had almost run out.

The apartment was humming. The caterer was there, the delivery men, the florist, the advance man for the musicians ...and then Auerbach came over, setting up his videotape shots with all the pomp of a self-proclaimed cinema artist. Samantha was moved out of her own kitchen by cooks who began preparing for the feast. The building superintendent came up several times to ask what he could do, knowing there was nothing he could do, but that making an appearance guaranteed a tip.

Spencer Cross-Wade appeared just after 1:00 PM. He surveyed the apartment—tables covered with elegant cloths and centerpieces, a small bandstand in what had been the dining room, colored lights replacing standard bulbs—and for a moment it reminded him of an elegant British dinner party. It seemed incredible that this affair would be a prelude to murder. Dressed in plainclothes, Cross-Wade was indistinguishable from a number of others who came in and out, and only Samantha knew he was a detective. They went into the bedroom to talk privately.

"Beautiful arrangements," Cross-Wade said, knowing that anything he said to begin the conversation would be awkward and strained.

"Thanks," Samantha replied. "Too bad it's all going to waste." Cross-Wade thought she looked remarkably calm considering the circumstances. She was dressed in a pink silk housecoat and her hair was perfectly combed back. She was determined to do the whole thing in style, no matter what the horror that absorbed her mind.

"Let's hope something good comes of it," Cross-Wade

said, "if only bringing one man to justice."

Samantha lowered her eyes. Why did "one man" have to be Marty?

"I wanted to talk with you a few minutes," Cross-Wade explained. "There are some last-minute instructions."

"Go ahead."

"You've been told where all the microphones are?"

"Yes."

"We'll also have video people in a Fifth Avenue apartment across the park. It's a long distance and their image might be clouded. Make sure your curtains stay open."

"They'll be open," Samantha assured him. "Everyone likes the view."

"Good. The video people are in instant communication with our men here. We're covered both ways. If we hear or see something, we can act."

"That's very reassuring," Samantha said. She was trying her best to accommodate Cross-Wade, but she felt numb. All this was just washing past her, part of the bad dream she wished would go away, the bad dream she still thought *might*, by some miracle, be untrue.

"Who locks up at night?" Cross-Wade asked.

"Usually me."

"Good. After the party, leave the lock open, but pretend to close it. Do you follow my logic?"

"I think so," Samantha replied. "You don't want Marty to suspect that I'm doing anything unusual."

"Precisely."

"Now," Cross-Wade continued, "please listen. As I said, we can hear what's going on, and, if you're near a window, we can see. But if you're in this bedroom after the party, the curtains would logically be closed."

"Yes."

"And your husband might be very silent about his actions."

"In what way?"

"He'll have a hammer and chain. They may not make noise when he takes them out."

A shiver raced up Samantha's spine. "Then what can you do?" she asked nervously.

"We'll depend on you. As soon as you see the first sign of a weapon, even a suspicious gesture on Marty's part, I want you to say the words, 'I think I'm getting a headache.' Of course, if he actually has the weapon in his hand, grab something in the room. It'll take us a few seconds to get in. We'll shout, 'Police! Freeze!' That'll stop him. He'll turn his attention on us."

"I sure hope so," Samantha said.

"Madam, I assure you," Cross-Wade told her, "if I thought were were any real risk, I wouldn't let you do this. But to increase your safety even further, I've brought something." Cross-Wade reached into his pocket and took out a slim, palm-sized cylinder with a small red valve on top. "This is Mace. I'm sure you've heard of it."

"I remember the name," Samantha replied.

"It has the combined effect of a tear gas and nerve gas," Cross-Wade explained. "I will ask you to clip it inside your clothing. If a desperate moment should occur, simply spray it in your husband's face. It will stop him, believe me."

"I believe you," Samantha replied, horrified that she might have to use such a weapon.

"Also," Cross-Wade continued, "you must observe your husband at all times. Am I clear?"

"Yes. Very clear."

"And I will tell you this: If we must rush in, please dive to the floor. I know that's unladylike, but it's for your own safety."

If she weren't so appalled at the situation, Samantha would have been amused at Cross-Wade's elegance.

"If an arrest is made," Cross-Wade continued, "there will be procedures that have to be followed. Please watch as best you can. You would be a witness."

Samantha shook her head, utterly dismayed. "I still can't believe this is happening," she said. "I feel like a robot, with other people controlling me."

"I'm sorry," Cross-Wade replied, "If I seem manipulative..."

"Oh no. I didn't mean that. I appreciate everything you're doing—you and Detective Loggins and Sergeant Yang. If it weren't for you..."

She stopped. Contemplating her own murder was not easy.

"Tomorrow at this time," Cross-Wade said, "I trust you'll be free. And madam, I wish you a happy life after that."

"Thank you," Samantha replied.

And then Cross-Wade kissed her hand.

They started to leave the bedroom, Cross-Wade still amazed at Samantha's stamina. But then, as if it were inevitable, he saw her hands turning white and her body starting to tremble. The numbness she'd felt gave way to the starkness of her predicament. Cross-Wade took her arm gently. "I know," he said softly, no other words being necessary.

Then she drew close to him and he could hear the soft sobbing. "Sit down," he told her. "Don't go out there like this."

She sat down on the bed, trying to stop the sobs, trying to restrain the anger. "Why?" she asked, almost in a whisper. "Why *me*?"

Cross-Wade sighed. "Why anyone?" he replied. "Why anyone?"

17

Marty came home at 6:30.

Samantha had pulled herself together and regained her strength in time to greet him at the door. She was a vision—long blue velvet gown, a magnificent contrast to her equally magnificent auburn hair, the pendant Marty had given her glistening around her neck. She had never looked better. Yes, this was a performance—a superb, spirited performance that she would give once in her life, and would give for keeps.

"You're gorgeous," Marty said, standing in the door.

Samantha just smiled. She stepped aside so Marty could see how his apartment had been transformed into a magical arena for the great affair that had been weeks in the planning. She glanced down at a section of bunched fabric on her gown. The Mace was behind it.

"Hey," Marty said, not yet stepping in. "I'm in some wonderland. Oh..." He rushed forward to embrace Samantha as he had never done before. Anyone watching would have thought this was a true love couple, unencumbered by doubts, by fears, by any serious problems. But for Marty this, too, was a performance, and he was every bit the actor Samantha was.

"I'm glad you're happy," Samantha said.

"There's not a word in the language to describe it," Marty answered. Samantha suspected nothing, he assured himself. "I've got something for you," he said.

Samantha looked surprised. "For me? On *your* birthday?" She gazed down at the pendant. "Again?"

"It's not exactly from me," Marty explained. He stepped back outside the apartment, where he had leaned the portrait, now rewrapped, against a wall. He brought it inside. "The crew at the office threw me a surprise party this morning. They gave me this." He retrieved his attaché case from outside, closed the door, and started unwrapping the portrait, as he had done that morning. The wrappings fell away quickly.

Samantha gazed excitedly at the portrait. "Marty, they gave you *that*?"

"Sure did."

"Does it look like me?"

"Exactly. It's a wonderful job. Do you like it?"

"Of course I do! Isn't that nice of them. Where do we put it?"

"In my office. I just wanted it home tonight so you and all the others could see it. But tomorrow morning it goes up behind my desk."

Was she hearing it right? Were Cross-Wade, Loggins, and the others down the hall hearing it right? Did Marty really say that he was bringing the portrait back to his office the next morning? Samantha felt nauseated. The man was totally gone. What was this, a form of sadism? Of self-gratification?

"Will it look all right behind your desk?" Samantha asked.

"I tried it out," Marty replied. "It was splendid." What a piece of cake, he thought. A little joke before death.

"Let's put it over there, in the corner, so people can see it,"

Samantha suggested. "I want everyone to know it came from the staff."

"Great." Marty put it exactly where Samantha wanted it. Then he went back for his attaché case and picked it up, ready to take it to the bedroom. Samantha watched him, just as Cross-Wade had asked her to. She saw how tightly he grasped the case. Of *course,* she thought. That's why Cross-Wade hadn't been able to find the murder weapons anywhere in the apartment. They were with Marty, in the case. They had to be. She stared at the case, then snapped her eyes away, fearful that Marty would notice.

"Want me to take your case for you?" she asked, hoping Cross-Wade, listening, would catch on.

"Hey, what are you, my valet?" Marty asked. "Of course not."

"Just trying to help the birthday boy. That case looks heavy."

"Just business papers, Sam." Before going into the bedroom Marty stopped to look around once more. He turned to Samantha. "I can't wait. Can you?"

"No," she giggled.

"Let me wash up and change." Marty took the case into the bedroom and closed the door.

Samantha studied the portrait. It *was* a good likeness. If the marriage hadn't been destroyed it would have looked good behind Marty's desk. It would have been so romantic, so perfect. Marty would've talked about it to visitors. It would've become a conversation piece and a family heirloom. Now it would probably wind up in the police property office, part of the evidence of Marty's last day.

The catering staff, the musicians, Auerbach the video man, and the bartender had been out on their own dinner break, but, as Marty was getting ready, they started filtering in. Guests were due at 7:45. Samantha rushed around seeing to last-minute preparations and replacing a few wilting flowers with an extra supply she'd kept in the kitchen. The food was already cooked and had only to be heated. Samantha had ordered Marty's mundane favorites—meat and potatoes, with green salad. Always safe.

The first real sign of action was the musicians' tuning up. Samantha felt a sudden thrill, as if this really *was* a celebration. She felt almost like dreaming, like pretending, like trying to make the reality as painless as possible. In the bedroom, she knew, was a mass murderer, and she was his victim, while out here was a feast.

But for a few remarkable seconds she visualized a very different party filled with *very* special guests—relatives of the women Marty had killed in his streak of psychotic revenge. Wouldn't *that* be grand? Wouldn't that be *right*? Wouldn't it be perfect if they could see Marty *taken* away?

A ringing doorbell brought Samantha back to reality. It was only 7:03. Was someone rude enough to come this early?

She walked to the door. The bell was the signal for the orchestra, which started up with "Gary, Indiana," from *The Music Man*. The bandleader thought it would be appropriate to have something from Marty's home state.

Samantha opened the door. There was Tom Edwards, with a beaming smile. "I thought I could help," he said.

The guy was terrific. If there was one person who was easing Samantha through this period, it was Tom and his almost naive, old-fashioned earnestness, his just being there.

"You're great," Samantha told him as she ushered him inside. "But I don't want you helping. You just relax."

"Me? Impossible." He was awed, as Marty had been, by the party set-up. "Hey, now we're talking class," he said. "When the Queen comes, nudge me, will you?"

"I'll do that," Samantha replied. "You'll know her by the little crown."

The band finished its first tune, then stopped. It had been a false alarm. One guest didn't require full music.

Despite Samantha's admonition, Tom walked around, straightening place settings and cards, arranging flowers and generally getting things tight. Samantha glanced at him from the kitchen, watching him work. She'd developed such a strong fondness for him.

Marty washed and shaved, filled with anticipation. He'd slipped the attaché case under the bed, assuming that Samantha would never notice. After combing his hair, he changed to a blue suit. It was his only real compromise of the evening. He'd wanted to wear khakis and a lumberjack shirt, as he had the other murder nights. It was the outfit Dad had worn on that night in 1952. But tonight, at the party, he'd never get away with it. It was out of the question.

He left the bedroom and saw Tom. "Hey," he shouted, "what are you doing here?"

"Just acting as advance man," Tom replied.

"Well stop it. Have a drink." Marty rushed over and slapped Tom on the back. "You think I'd let my best pal do the dusting?"

"Oh, just helping out."

Samantha came out of the kitchen. "He's been a gem," she said. "Without Thomas, I would've fallen apart."

"I'm getting jealous," Marty said. "I don't like all that good feeling."

Tom gestured to Samantha, with a wink. "I think he knows about us."

They all had a good laugh as the last of the catering staff began filing back in. Auerbach, without announcing a thing, started his JVC videotape system and did some closeups of Samantha and Marty preparing for the party.

7:28.

The phone rang. Samantha answered. "Oh, I'm sorry," she replied to the caller. "I know Marty will be *very* disappointed. But I hope he feels better." She hung up. It was the first and only cancellation, a newspaper editor from New Jersey, not one of Marty's greater friends.

"Probably a fake," Marty reacted. "He never goes to parties. I didn't really expect him."

A few guests arrived early, each with a reason. "I came direct from work," one said. "We couldn't wait," said another.

"Why hang around downstairs?" was the most honest answer. The band swung into a medley from *A Chorus Line,* and the buzz level of the small crowd increased. Auerbach stuck his camera into everyone's face, prompting Samantha to think that she might have made a mistake in hiring him.

7:45. The hour. Now the most insistent rhythm was the ringing of the doorbell. The party began to jump as Marty's friends started streaming in. He was beaming. Samantha was radiant. No one could have guessed what was going on in their minds. No one could have realized that every word was being recorded down the hall. No one could have known that each movement, each gesture, was being watched through long lenses across Central Park.

Three large tables were spread with food and wine, with waiters to dispense the delicacies. The small band hit a rapid beat, mixing show tunes with the Beatles, taking requests and giving the evening a thoroughly festive feeling. The presents started piling up in one corner of the living room, with Marty realizing he'd have to open more than thirty before the party was over. He made sure to take each guest to see the portrait of Samantha. One woman, the wife of one of Marty's biggest clients, was especially taken by the richness of Samantha's hair in the picture. "Lovely!" she exclaimed. "I didn't realize Samantha's hair was so, so reddish."

"Auburn," Marty replied. On this night, in particular, that had to be right.

"Yes, auburn," the lady said. "A very pretty shade."

8:36.

By now there were more than seventy people in the apartment, straining the air system. Marty went to open a window, letting out some smoke and stuffiness.

"Dinner is served," the captain announced, and people began sitting down, bringing their drinks, assessing the apartment with each other, mugging for Auerbach's ever-present video camera. It may have been a great party in Marty's honor, but to many in the living room it was a business event—a chance to rub shoulders with media people, public relations types, and others who might advance careers. Ordinarily Marty would have noticed, even studied, the political maneuverings, the attempts to get someone's ear, the backslapping and false compliments. But now he could only rehearse in his mind how he would attack Samantha. He would do it while she was in bed, he knew. That would be easiest, quickest, and least likely to make noise.

Marty suddenly felt a thud on his back. He spun around and looked into the smiling face of Leonard Ross. "Spectacular party," Ross said. "Utterly spectacular. And thanks for bringing the portrait home. Did Sam like it?"

"Loved it," Marty answered. "So did everyone else. It really made the day, Len."

Ross slapped Marty on the back again. He felt he had made the correct career move with the boss. Then he sat down at his table and Marty sat at the small dais at the front of the living room.

Samantha was seated beside Marty, and Tom Edwards beside Samantha. Lynne and her husband completed the dais. Samantha had insisted that Lynne share the honors, considering the work she'd put in.

After everyone was seated, Tom Edwards started clinking a spoon against his wine glass. "May I have your attention please?" he asked. For Marty, it was almost a replay of the surprise party that morning.

The room quieted. This was tradition. Even Auerbach tried to be discreet, standing off to the side while taping the dais.

Tom rose, then lifted his wine glass. "I'd like to propose a toast," he said. Everyone else stood up. "To Marty, on his fortieth birthday." He drank. Everyone drank. "And now," he went on, "to Samantha, without whom Marty would be just a guy."

Laughter. More drinking, then applause.

"May I respond?" Marty asked.

"No," someone shouted.

The banter had begun. Everyone sensed it would be a fun evening.

"I'm claiming squatter's rights," Marty announced. "I demand to be heard."

"Speech!" someone else shouted.

"That's more like it," Marty responded. "I, too, would like to propose a toast. To all of you, my good friends, who have made this night so wonderful."

He drank, then everyone followed, somewhat awkward about toasting themselves.

"And there's one more toast that I must make," Marty said.

The room fell silent as the smile melted from Marty's face. Everyone assumed he would say something serious, maybe about his parents, maybe about his hard beginnings, about some secret mentor. But, instead, he turned slowly toward Samantha and raised his glass. "Little more than a year ago there was an emptiness in my life," he said. "And then this lady came in and filled it. Without her, this fortieth birthday would be very lonely, completely meaningless. *With* her, I couldn't be happier. To you, Sam."

He raised his glass. There were misty eyes in the room, including Samantha's.

Down the hall, Spencer Cross-Wade, Arthur Loggins, Sergeant Yang, and two other officers listened, surrounded by the lavish and showy furnishings of the apartment they were using.

"Disgraceful," Cross-Wade said. "The man is treating her like rubbish."

"I wonder what *she's* thinking," Loggins said.

"What could she be thinking? Her husband is toasting her, yet he'll try to kill her within hours. This is a little exercise to him, a little diversion. I suppose, Arthur, that even murderers like to have fun."

"Yes, sir."

But Samantha wasn't really concerned with the twisted

irony of Marty's toast. By now she'd written off that side of him, the same side that had brought home the portrait. She thought only of the time. It was 8:59. In a bit more than three hours it would all be over.

Someone started singing "For He's a Jolly Good Fellow," and everyone joined. The apartment shook with happy sound. The little band followed the tune. Spirits rose even more as the guests waited for the elaborate roast beef dinner, whose aroma was floating through the apartment.

But there'd be something else before dinner.

"May *I* have your attention please?"

The voice was weaker than the others, and, though Samantha tried to control it, it had a nervous shake. Her friends just assumed it was from the excitement of the evening. People shushed each other, and the room quieted once again.

"I have something to say," Samantha announced. Unlike Tom or Marty, she did not rise. "This is Marty's night," she continued. "He's a terrific guy and, as you just heard, a very special husband—more special than you can ever know."

Applause.

"He's so special, in fact, that it's really unfair that there's only one Marty."

"Yeah!" someone shouted.

"I knew you'd agree. And I kind of thought it was time to do something about that. And I did, with Marty's help." She quickly lifted her glass, broke out in a broad smile, and turned to Marty. "Here's to you... Daddy."

For a moment, utter silence.

Samantha bit her lip as if overcome with feeling, forcing herself to act it to the hilt. Marty was expressionless, stunned. The whole room gazed at him as Auerbach caught the frozen look on his face.

And then the reaction. "Ah!" and "Wonderful!" and "Congratulations!" Voices filled the room. And then, sustained applause.

Marty's face finally dissolved to a winning, delighted grin. Then he reached over to kiss Samantha.

"Kiss her again!" Leonard Ross yelled.

And he did.

And the band played "Rockabye Baby."

It was a glittering moment, warm and touching. But Samantha felt hollow. The moment meant nothing, nothing but a baby who wouldn't have a father.

Marty's insides exploded in chaos. He hid it. He could hide anything. But this was a thunderbolt, a curse, the worst possible news. This was something *Mom* would do.

A baby?

His baby?

Inside *this* woman?

No, he couldn't have heard it right. Yes, he'd heard it right. Of course he'd heard it right, and even smiled, and even kissed Mom.

Everything had changed. *Everything*. It wasn't only Samantha who would die. It was the baby as well. But was that important? Was a little fetus something he should even worry about?

Yes.

For it was the first direct descendant of Dad.

It would have Dad's blood, probably his features. Maybe its eyes would be Dad's warm eyes, maybe its voice would be Dad's voice. Maybe it would move like Dad or even laugh like Dad. Maybe it would be generous, the way Dad had been generous. Maybe, when he looked into its face, Marty would see Dad.

For the first time since the calendar schizophrenia madness gripped him, Marty was torn. He *had* to kill Samantha. Samantha was Mom. He'd married her *because* she triggered the image of Mom in his mind, *because* she was so ideal for the role he'd envisioned for her—the role of his final victim. It would be obscene, a violation of all he'd promised Dad in his letters, in his visits to the cemetery, to let Samantha get away on this December fifth.

But the baby.

Would he be violating Dad by killing his direct descendant? Would Dad be angry rather than proud? How perfect it would be if Dad could find some way to signal his wishes. But that was impossible, Marty knew. He would have to make this decision by himself.

He felt the slaps on his back. Those people were always slapping him on the back, and now they had a very special reason. He remained at the dais wearing that put-on smile, shaking the outstretched hands, getting kisses from well-wishing women, accepting a few cigars. "Thank you," he kept saying to the chorus of congratulations. "Thank you, it's really great." His insides continued to boil. "Thank you. Yes, it was a complete surprise. No, I haven't got any favorite names. Not yet."

Auerbach stuck his camera into his face and Marty broadened his smile. "This is the happiest night of my life," he said to Auerbach's microphone, his insincerity recorded for all time.

He hated Samantha.

He hated her more than ever.

He wanted so much to kill her, to watch life rush from her body.

But now she carried Dad's bloodline.

Everything *had* changed.

Or had it?

18

Only time mattered to Marty now. Get the party over with, get these people out of here, get to the end of December fifth. But he was still in shock over Samantha's announcement, and wasn't sure what he would do. He smiled, he greeted, he did the small talk, he heard the run of baby jokes that seemed to go on endlessly, but his eyes were forever switching between two points—Samantha's stomach and his gold watch. Leonard Ross, increasingly obnoxious, saw him glancing at his watch every few minutes.

"Hey, you got somewhere to go, Marty?" Ross asked.

Marty shook his head in a kind of mock sadness. "Just watching how quickly time goes by," he replied. "I wish this would last forever."

"You'll have the memories," Ross said. "You'll be able to tell your child."

"That's very touching, Len."

It was 10:00 P.M.

"Sweetheart, isn't it wonderful?" Samantha asked, still

playing her role, and playing it to the microphones hidden in flowers, in a radiator, in lighting fixtures, even under her chair on the dais.

"More than wonderful," Marty answered. "This is a story we'll tell our child." It wasn't often that Marty borrowed lines from others, but he saw no great need for originality. "I want to start making financial plans in the morning," he went on to Samantha, squeezed into a corner of the living room. "This kid isn't going to have to worry."

He meant it. If he decided against killing Samantha, making financial plans was precisely what he'd do. No kid of his would drift the way he had drifted. No kid of his would have to struggle. Any kid of his would have some security, a business to enter...and a father who'd take care of him. Most important, this kid wouldn't go through life with a psychosis that forced him to kill women who bore a physical resemblance to his mother. If Samantha were permitted to live, if the baby lived, Marty would be a father in the grand style.

10:30.

He began to sweat. It wasn't much at first, just a glisten on the forehead, but then his face seemed to ooze perspiration from every pore, as if he had just finished jogging or pedaling an exercise bike. Samantha, by now talking to friends, glanced over and noticed. She broke off and came to Marty, who sat down in a vacant chair to rest.

"Marty, what's wrong?" she asked.

"The excitement," Marty answered. "You know, these things can get to you."

"Do you feel all right?"

"Oh sure. Just fine. I just overdid it, that's all."

By now some friends were gathering round, each looking concerned. "Some water?" one of them asked.

"Oh no, I'm all right," Marty answered. He didn't like attracting this kind of attention. He wanted to seem normal, relaxed, happy. He turned to Samantha and smiled. "I should be asking *you* how you feel?"

"Just great," Samantha answered.

"Good, but why don't *you* sit down. You're breathing for two, you know."

She smiled, and did sit down beside Marty. He edged his chair over and put his arm around her. "You still going to pay attention to me when the baby is born?" he asked, making sure some of the others overheard the question.

"Not really," Samantha teased.

"Yeah, that's what I thought. The father always gets the raw end."

"But Marty," someone said, "think of the bills you'll have the privilege of paying."

"I'm thinking," Marty answered with a wink. "If it's a girl, I'll need a second job."

And so the laughs continued, but so did Marty's sweating. It was the sweat of indecision, of disruption of a ritual that had become holy to him.

10:53.

"Maybe we ought to wrap it up," he told Samantha. The next day was a business day, some of the guests who lived in the suburbs had already left, and others appeared tired. Those were good reasons for wrapping it up, but the time was the greatest reason. December fifth would end in 67 minutes.

Samantha really didn't want to wrap it up. She wished that time would stand still, for she knew what was coming when the guests left, when she would be alone with Marty. She barely responded to Marty's comment and pretended to be distracted by a somewhat pushy guest. So it was Marty who walked over to Tom Edwards, deep in conversation with one of the bartenders on the subject of French wines. "Tom," he said, "we'd better wind it down. Could you possibly drop some loud hints?"

"Sure," Tom answered, always the obliging Tom. But then he glanced across the room and saw a look on Samantha's face that he'd never seen before. It was more than tiredness, certainly not the fatigue of a pregnant woman. He couldn't quite figure out how to read her, but her eyes seemed wider than normal, glazed, only partially focused. He finally guessed that she'd just been overtaken by the excitement. It was all right.

But Samantha was terrified.

Now she became *obsessed* with time.

It was 11:01.

"Wonderful party," Tom said loudly to a friend as he dropped his coat over his arm. "But it's getting awfully late. Work in the morning."

He actually lingered, but the necessary hint had been dropped. Everyone knew the party was nearing its end.

Now the exodus began, and Marty glanced over to the corner where the gifts were piled. God, he said to himself, we didn't open the gifts! He'd planned to. He'd thought it would burn some time, but the party went by too quickly. No one objected. Not yet. But he worried, and sweated. What if someone demanded that he open the gifts, and sat himself down to watch. Could Marty really refuse?

He decided to stand right near the door with Samantha, literally forcing attention away from the pile of presents, most of them with high-status Fifth Avenue store wrappings. But, certain as clockwork, one ad man did notice the oversight. "Hey, we didn't open the presents!" he announced. But the other guests were tired, and no one took up his war cry.

"Thank you," Marty kept saying as guests filed out. "I'll always remember this." His act continued.

"And I'll remember it too," Samantha told everyone. So did hers.

11:08.

The band members were gone, and so was most of the catering staff. Samantha had arranged that the tables and equipment would be removed the next morning.

11:13. Only a few stragglers remained, Leonard Ross among them. He would, Marty thought to himself. Ross was trying to impress, to show that *he* enjoyed the party so much he was reluctant to leave. The man was becoming insufferable in his machinations. It had probably been his idea to have the portrait painted, and he probably planned to drop that point into his next private conversation in Marty's office.

Marty walked over to him. "Len," he said, "if I had *my* way, a couple of us—y'know, the inside group—would hang around all night. But I'm sending you home. I don't want you exhausted in this weather and getting sick."

Ross couldn't refuse. With the effusiveness of an international diplomat, he spread around a last volley of praise and thanks, and finally left.

By 11:19, only Tom Edwards remained. He was sprawled out on a Barcelona chair that had been shoved to the side of the living room, still holding a Manhattan in his right hand, looking thoroughly spent. Samantha understood why he wanted to be the last guest to leave: He felt a proprietary interest in Marty, and in the party. He'd been present at the creation, and felt more like family than friend. Since Samantha felt the same way, there was no awkwardness about Tom's lingering. In fact, Samantha walked over and sprawled out on a chair next to him.

"When does the fun start?" Tom asked.

"Ha, ha," Samantha replied. "If you haven't had your share, Thomas, you'll have to find another stand."

"Those're fightin' words."

Marty came over and joined them. "Do I hear an argument?" he asked.

"Tom wants more circuses," Samantha answered.

Marty smiled playfully at Samantha. "Well, if I weren't married..."

He's keeping it up, Samantha thought. A thespian to the last. He'll keep it up right until Tom leaves. Mustn't raise any suspicions in Tom.

"It *was* a great party," Tom said. "Martin, I've never seen people have such a terrific time."

"Makes me feel good," Marty answered. "Of course, the prime architect here deserves the credit." He gestured toward Samantha, as if presenting her.

"Well, Tom here and Lynne pulled their weight," Samantha reminded Marty. "I couldn't have done it alone, not this well."

"Sure you could, and did," Tom countered. "The important things were yours, Sam. You're a hit."

Marty glanced at his watch, then nervously glanced at it again.

"And I'd better get going," Tom said, "or I'll be a flop."

"Oh no," Marty told him. "I was just checking the time. The evening's young. Stay awhile."

He must be joking, Samantha thought. It was 11:24.

"No, I'm really tired," Tom said, letting out a large, unsocial yawn. "I just felt I wanted to be the last man. Gives me a sense of inflated importance." With some difficulty, he lifted himself out of his chair. "I've got a client coming in at nine tomorrow morning. One of those IBM executives being transferred to New York. Wait'll he sees the prices on the apartments I'm showing him."

"Where's he from?" Marty asked.

"Denver. He should've stayed. Well, folks, this was a memorable one. You've got a nightful of gifts to open. If you don't like mine, give it to me. I like it."

"I'll love it," Marty said.

Tom kissed Samantha. "I don't care if I make him jealous," he said. "The hostess always gets a kiss from me. What else is there?"

"Tom, take care getting home," Samantha said.

"Maybe some tennis this weekend?" Marty added.

"Yeah, why not?" Marty opened the front door and Tom slid through. "Saturday," he said.

"Fine," Marty replied.

Tom walked to the elevator, which came almost immediately, and he was gone.

Now Samantha was alone with the man she loved, the man she feared.

In the apartment down the hall, Cross-Wade and his men gathered tensely around a small black speaker that was broadcasting the sounds from the Shaw apartment. A phone connection kept Cross-Wade in touch with the visual observers across the park, their long lenses aimed at Marty and Samantha, but he knew their reports would soon cease as curtains were drawn.

For a few moments after closing the door behind Tom, neither Marty nor Samantha said a thing. Marty just gazed around the apartment, looking almost nostalgic for the good times that had just ended. Samantha watched his every move, his every glance, searching for some sign, some gesture, that the moment of hell had come. There was none.

She couldn't know it, but he still hadn't decided. It was 11:31, and he still hadn't chosen between the roles of father and executioner.

Suddenly, he rushed toward Samantha. For an instant she felt scared, but realized there was a warm, mellow smile on his face, and tears in his eyes. He embraced her, then stepped away, looking at her as he had on the day they were married.

"What can I say?" he asked. "How can I thank you?"

"Marty, you don't have to thank me."

"Oh yes I do. Sam, I never had anything like this. I never had anyone to *give* me anything like this."

"Now you do," Samantha answered.

"I sure do. And I'm gonna hang on to you, too," Marty said. "There aren't too many people in this world who have happy marriages, and I happen to be one of them."

It was never-ending, Samantha thought. He'd play it to the last moment.

"I want to take that trip," Marty went on, "if it's safe for you. I mean..."

"I'm sure it's safe, but I'll ask the doctor."

"I hope it's a girl."

"Why?"

"Because she'll be like you."

"And if it's a boy—like you—is that so bad?"

"Not as good as the first choice," Marty replied. He still had that moisture in his eyes. "Boy, what a surprise! What a night! Hey, I'm gonna have to take that course—you know, the one where the fathers learn how to help with the delivery."

"Yup. I've got all the information," Samantha said.

Then Marty turned suddenly melancholy. "I wish I had a family to share this with," he said. "That's the one thing I miss."

Samantha walked slowly to him, placing her arms around his neck. "I understand," she whispered. "But at least we'll build a close family...right here." She couldn't believe she was mouthing the words. Why did Marty insist on going on like this? Was it part of some required ritual, an acting out that had to take place before the murder?

"That's right," he answered. "We'll build our own family. Maybe Saturday, after I play tennis with Tom, we can shop for carriages and strollers, and stuff like that."

"A little early."

"For *my* kid?"

"We'll shop," Samantha agreed.

11:35.

"I think Daddy better get some sleep," Marty said, once again glancing at his watch. "A big day in the office tomorrow."

"I'll just put away a few things," Samantha said.

Marty walked into the bedroom, his mind still in turmoil. He liked talking about the baby, but he liked vengeance as well. *Decide*, he ordered himself. *Decide*. But it was hell to decide. He glanced under the bed to make sure the attaché case was still there. That didn't help him decide.

11:38. Automatically, he started getting undressed, laying his clothes down neatly on a chair. Then, just as automatically, he got into his pajamas and waited for Samantha to come in.

She came in a minute later, startled to see Marty ready for bed. Was this, too, part of the ritual? "You must *really* be tired," she said. "I'd guessed that you'd have so much adrenaline you'd be up most of the night."

"I've got the adrenaline," Marty answered. "I may not be able to sleep."

"You want some warm milk? That'll do it."

"No, it's no way to end a party."

Suddenly, Samantha saw Marty walk over to the bed and bend down. It was then that she noticed that the attaché case was under the bed. Her heart began to pound as she saw Marty going for it. Slowly, he slid it out, then started unzippering the top flap.

He reached inside.

Samantha was ready to say the words that would bring Cross-Wade crashing into the apartment. She looked around. If this were the moment, she'd grab the brass lamp on top of the bureau and hold it out to protect herself, or reach for the Mace.

Marty felt around inside the case. Samantha heard the rustling of papers and clips.

Then, his hand started coming out slowly.

Samantha saw a flash of black.

Marty took out his comb.

"I can't find the comb I keep in the bathroom," he explained. "I've looked everywhere."

Samantha let out a deep, agonized breath of relief... temporary relief, but still relief.

"What's wrong?" Marty asked.

"Oh, nothing, I'm just feeling the effects of all the excitement."

"Sam, sit down. Please. You're in a delicate condition."

And Samantha did walk over to the bed and sit. It was 11:44. In sixteen minutes, she knew, it would all be over. What was he waiting for?

He slid the case back under the bed.

"I haven't seen the other comb," Samantha volunteered. "You might have slipped it into a jacket pocket by mistake."

"Yeah, that's probably right," Marty answered, as he stood before a mirror and combed back a few stray hairs. Then he turned around. "My birthday will be over soon," he said, almost like a little boy who'd never grown up.

"I know," Samantha answered.

"I really don't want it to end. It's so important to me."

Here it comes, Samantha thought. Instinctively, she got up from the bed and walked nonchalantly over to the table lamp.

"Why are you walking over there?" Marty asked. There was a nervous edge to his voice.

"Just walking," Samantha answered. He was going over the line. She felt it.

"Why don't you come and sit next to me?"

What do you say? Think fast. "Marty, my leg fell asleep. I just want to shake it off."

"Your leg never fell asleep before."

"Maybe it's the baby. This condition does strange things."

"All right."

He seemed pacified, but there was a strangely hostile look coming over him. Now the fear welled up inside Samantha once more. The next time he reached into that case, she knew, it wouldn't be for a comb. She glanced up at the air vent, where the microphone was. Cross-Wade was listening. He *had* to know that Marty's tone was beginning to change.

11:46.

"Your leg feel better?" Marty asked.

"A little."

"That's good. That's very good."

"All right," Cross-Wade said to his crew, "let's get ready to charge." One of his men walked to the door of their apartment and opened it slightly. Cross-Wade and Loggins felt for their shoulder holsters and loosened their pistols, which they prayed they wouldn't have to use.

"Jesus," Cross-Wade muttered. "She hasn't opened the lock. I told her to do that. Their apartment is still locked." He had the key, but knew that precious seconds could be lost unless he could burst in. He was worried, even panicked. He'd made a solemn pledge to protect Samantha, and something had already gone wrong. Now *he* had to decide: Wait until Marty strikes, or get in now and prevent a crime, but miss the incriminating caught-in-the-act evidence he needed. For a few more moments, he listened to the speaker.

"I feel much better now," Samantha said, still trying to act, still wondering how close to the end Marty wanted to stretch this.

"I want you to take care of yourself," Marty replied. "You're carrying some valuable cargo."

"That I know."

"Come sit down."

What could she say now?

11:47.

She walked slowly toward the bed. And then, as if her thoughts were linked with Cross-Wade's, she remembered. "Wait a second. I didn't lock the door."

"I locked it," Marty said.

"You sure?"

"Sure I'm sure. After Tom left."

"I'd better check."

"Sam, I *told* you, I locked it."

"Marty, you were all excited. Did you hear what happened today?"

"No."

"I didn't want to tell you, not right before the party. You know, Mrs. Klein, on the next floor?"

"Sure."

"Someone got into her apartment. Robbery. They beat her up." Samantha sighed as any good actress would. "She'd left the lock open."

"So I'll check," Marty said.

"Marty, don't treat me like an invalid!"

It was the perfect line, and Marty was startled, startled

enough so Samantha could begin walking out of the room before he could respond. She looked back with a warm smile, to soothe him. "I'm only pregnant," she said softly.

He did nothing. Samantha walked to the front door, jiggled the lock as Cross-Wade had instructed her to, and left it open.

To Cross-Wade, listening intently, she'd just become something of a saint.

11:48.

Samantha walked back into the bedroom and sat down next to Marty. It was a risk, but she felt a sense of control. With the door unlocked, Cross-Wade was only seconds away. Marty seemed lost in thought, as in fact he was. The decision had still not been made.

"Penny for your thoughts," Samantha said.

"I'm thinking of names," Marty replied, lying.

"It's a little soon," Samantha said.

"But it's so much fun."

"Yeah. Well, if it's a boy, it's Martin Everett, Junior," Samantha said. "That I insist on."

"I'd like that," Marty replied. "At least I could start a family tradition."

"And if it's a girl?" Samantha asked.

"I don't know."

"No ideas?"

"Not really. Not yet."

"What about your mother's name?" Samantha suggested. Marty seemed to tighten. "No," he said. "Not my mother's name. I never liked her name."

It was another sign, Samantha thought. Marty's fixation with his real mother had slipped out. It was coming. He *was* over the line. It was a matter of minutes, or seconds.

Cross-Wade thought the same thing. At 11:49 he, Loggins, and a third man eased out into the hallway, moved down to Samantha's door and stood outside, ready to barge in. They now listened to the conversation on small earphone receivers.

"How about *my* mother's name?" Samantha asked.

Marty shrugged. A sudden moodiness came over him. "Why does it have to be *any* mother's name?"

"It doesn't have to be."

"How about Ruth Lenore?"

"That's very nice," Samantha said. "Did you just think of it?"

"My father liked that name. He once told me that if I had a sister, that would be her name. Ruth Lenore. I like that."

"So do I. If it's a girl, Marty, that'll be her name."

"You sure?"

"I'm sure."

"Dad would have been happy."

It was the truth. Dad *would* have been happy. He *had* wanted a little girl, and always spoke of naming her Ruth Lenore.

For Samantha, it was still one more sign. Now Marty was the little boy who'd adored his father.

11:51.

"It's unfair," Marty went on. "Dad should have had his little girl."

"It's too bad he died so young," Samantha lamented.

"He would have been very good to that little girl," Marty said. He seemed to stare into space, to slip into a different world. Although he was sure Samantha didn't know it, he was talking about his *real* father, Frankie Nelson's father, not the father he had invented in the fables he'd told Samantha and everyone else. "I'll bet she would've been the best-behaved little girl in town," he continued. "Dad would've made sure of that."

Samantha became increasingly frightened by the stare on Marty's face, by his morbid monologue. She felt for the Mace to be certain it was still there. Then she eased herself up and walked once again to the table lamp. This time he hardly noticed. It was 11:52.

In the hallway, Cross-Wade was sure the moment had virtually arrived. "Get ready," he whispered to Loggins and the other detective.

"He would've brought her dresses and ribbons," Marty intoned. "Great Dad. He was always so good to me."

"I'm sure," Samantha replied. She knew enough from Cross-Wade's theories about Marty's condition to ploy along skillfully.

"Did I ever tell you about the time he carried me piggy back through a kiddy park?"

"No."

"He did. And he had a bad back too. But he wanted to give me a good time. Mom wasn't along. She never went to kiddy parks. Dad liked all those things. Like electric trains. He liked electric trains. It was tough to afford them. Y'know, times weren't great."

"You told me."

11:53.

"He got me the trains, though. Just like the ones I got. The very best. Dad always liked the best things for me. He wanted me to grow up and go to college. I'm sorry he couldn't see me graduate."

He stopped. He looked at his watch. Then, he looked at it again, as if studying the time. "Come here," he said.

Samantha didn't move.

"Come on over here."

Cross-Wade heard, and placed his hand on the doorknob, turning it slightly.

Still, Samantha didn't move.

"You afraid of me?" Marty asked. Without waiting for an answer, he got up slowly and started walking toward Samantha.

She glanced back at the table lamp.

Marty approached her. He placed his arms around her.

11:54.

He held her for a full minute, not saying a word.

11:55.

"Dad would want to see our baby," he finally said. "No doubt about it." He turned around and walked into the bathroom. He closed the door. Samantha heard the water running for a short time. Then Marty came out. He walked over to the bed. Samantha could see that he was looking downward, toward his attaché case. She was ready to utter the words that would bring Cross-Wade.

11:58.

Marty smiled at Samantha, and blew her a kiss. "Thanks for a wonderful evening," he said, "and a wonderful baby."

11:59.

Without a word, he got into bed. He closed his eyes.

Samantha couldn't believe what she was seeing.

December fifth passed into history.

Martin Everett Shaw had decided.

19

Samantha kept staring at Marty.

Then she looked at the clock on the bureau. It was 12:01 A.M. It was over. It *was* over.

She felt every muscle in her body fall into repose. She felt as if half the weight had evaporated from her bones. And she felt complete again. The vague hopes that had sustained her during the horror she had lived through had been answered. Marty was no murderer. She still didn't know who he was, but he wasn't the grown-up version of that pathetic little boy from Omaha. Spencer Cross-Wade, sent the wrong medical records, had apparently been misled somewhere else as well. Yes, there was all that evidence—the similarity between the room in Omaha and this bedroom—but evidence is often misleading, Samantha knew. Cross-Wade had told her so. In the chaos of this moment she couldn't explain all the contradictions, all the signs pointing to Marty. She only knew that he lay there, harmless, on the morning of December sixth, an innocent man looking forward to becoming a father.

Cross-Wade still stood outside the front door with Loggins and another detective. Now Sergeant Yang, who'd been waiting in "their" apartment, joined him. For the police, there was only bafflement. Cross-Wade felt for Samantha, cheered for her, but he recognized that the calendar schizophrenic may have eluded him.

"I don't understand," he whispered to his detectives, all of them feeling foolish standing outside the door of the innocent man. "Everything pointed to him."

"Everything was wrong," Yang lamented.

"Maybe," Cross-Wade replied. "Maybe not. He may just have decided to stop killing, or to skip a year, or whatever."

"Or maybe it isn't him," Loggins said.

"Or maybe it isn't him," Cross-Wade agreed. "In that case, somewhere, a young woman has died tonight. And *I* am responsible."

"Not true," Yang said.

"It is," Cross-Wade insisted. "Accountability, Sergeant. Accountability. And tomorrow, we must start all over again. Back at square one."

Cross-Wade was interrupted by the clicking of the doorknob. The officers watched as the knob turned, slowly, hesitantly. It reached the limit of its turning radius, then the door opened.

Samantha stood there. She was not surprised to see that the officers had huddled right outside her door. She *was* surprised to see Yang.

"I didn't know..." she began to say, looking at Yang.

"I wanted to be here," Yang replied.

Then Samantha shifted her eyes to Cross-Wade.

"I have no answers," Cross-Wade told her, whispering so as not to awaken Marty.

"Neither do I," Samantha whispered back. Then she went to throw her arms around Cross-Wade, an embrace that reflected the ordeal they'd just been through. She just stayed there, her head on his shoulder, as he placed his arms about her.

"I feel I've served you poorly," Cross-Wade said. "You have my profound apologies."

The other officers stepped away, not wanting to interfere with this private moment.

"I know you did your best," Samantha replied. "Who knows what's in Marty's mind."

"How do you feel?" Cross-Wade asked.

"I don't know," Samantha told him. "I'm relieved, enormously relieved. Obviously. But I still don't know who my husband is. And we're going to have a baby."

"I have a feeling all the answers will come out," Cross-Wade said. "I hope they make you happy."

"Thank you."

"We'll be leaving now. We are, as I've always told you, at your service. I have this case to solve... still. I'll be working on that."

"Good luck," Samantha said. She removed the Mace from inside her gown and handed it back to Cross-Wade without comment.

"And good luck to you, madam. I'll be watching for your birth announcement."

"You don't have to watch," Samantha answered. "You'll be the first one I'll call."

"I'm gratified, Mrs. Shaw."

Samantha said her farewells to Loggins, Sergeant Yang, and the fourth man, whom she'd never met. She felt a tug toward them, an emotional connection that the victim always feels toward those involved in her case. She lingered in the hallway a few moments, then slipped back inside.

Samantha gazed around the darkened apartment, wishing she'd known at the start of the party what she knew now. She would have had a much better time. She would have felt the original fullness of her bond with Marty, the sense of completeness in being with him. Even with his mysterious past, the knowledge that he was not about to try to kill her would have been the greatest relief.

Now she walked back into the darkened bedroom. Lights from the hallway let her look once more at Marty's face, so content, so pleased, so relaxed. His breathing was regular, his body still. Was he dreaming? Probably, Samantha thought. Marty had always been a heavy dreamer. And if he *was* dreaming, it was probably about the baby, about walks through Central Park, about the swings and sandboxes in the Adventure Playground, about the first day in school and the meetings with teachers. Marty would relish all of that. It would give him that feeling of family that he'd always missed. Samantha easily drifted back to the belief that Marty's past was noble, if secret, and that it would all be made clear in some grand moment with his child on his knee.

She got undressed and put on a light blue nightgown, Marty's favorite. She was ready to get into bed, but then thought of something, a gesture, that she thought Marty would like. Samantha went over to his desk, sat down, and took out a blank piece of note paper. On it she wrote, "Both of us love you." Then she took the note and placed it on Marty's night table. He was sure to see it when he woke up.

Samantha got into bed. Instantly, she felt Marty's warmth beside her. She knew she'd have trouble falling asleep, her mind still filled with the rushing events of the evening, but that warmth comforted her, gave her security.

"Good night," she whispered to him, obviously expecting no reply, but feeling the need to say it nonetheless.

She could hear the city quieting down outside, the traffic thinning, the strollers retiring. She thought about Spencer, Cross-Wade and Sergeant Yang, no doubt disappointed that they didn't get their man, and she thought about the mystery of the calendar killer still at large. But, inevitably, her mind returned to Marty's exoneration, and to all it meant for the future.

It was 12:16 A.M.

Samantha rolled over and rested.

20

At 12:35 A.M., Martin Shaw opened his eyes.

He hadn't been asleep. He'd been fully awake.

Waiting.

Waiting for the precise moment.

Martin Shaw *had* decided. And now he would carry out his decision.

Slowly, deliberately, he got out of bed. He started walking out of the room.

Samantha, unable to sleep, heard him and opened one eye. She watched Marty, assuming he was going to the kitchen for one of his midnight snacks. She decided not to join him. Give the man a chance to be alone with his thoughts and joys. She heard him walk down the hall, then was sure she heard him enter the living room.

Marty walked to the closet where the electric trains were stored. He started taking them out. Quickly, he set up a simple layout in the living room, only an oval of track about five feet long. He placed the trains on the track and turned on the power.

Samantha heard the trains. What was the matter with the guy? Or was *anything* the matter with him? Maybe he, too, couldn't sleep and decided to play with his trains, just as other men would take out a book, a stamp collection, or watch television. It was strange, but not entirely alarming. In fact, she concluded that this was a good sign: Marty was enjoying himself. Maybe the trains reminded him of the baby. Trains and children got along very, very well.

As the trains were running, Marty stared at them intently. "Do you like my trains, Dad?" he whispered, too low for Samantha to hear. "Am I doing a good job for you?"

He walked back into the bedroom, slowly. He looked at Samantha to make sure she was asleep. Samantha didn't move. She didn't want Marty to know she was awake, still believing that these moments alone were good for him. Marty reached under the bed and took out the attaché case. He withdrew the videotape of the Douglas Edwards news show. Samantha opened one eye and saw him do it. But he often bought videotapes. So what?

Marty walked back to the living room with the videotape. Samantha heard him moving furniture. She could not see that he was moving the old Model 30 TV set back from the corner, where it had been pushed. The set was mounted in a cabinet that also held the Shaws' videotape machine. Samantha recognized the sound of the machine's tape door clicking open. Still she was not suspicious. Marty watched videotapes all the time. Then she heard the door close. There were several more clicks as Marty turned on the power for the video machine and the television set itself. The old tube set began to warm and the sound started fading in about thirty seconds later.

It would be a movie, Samantha thought.

It wasn't.

She heard a man's voice. He was delivering the news. She recognized the voice, but couldn't quite place it, although it sounded like one she'd heard long ago.

Douglas Edwards. That was it. She remembered. She remembered how he'd had this news program on CBS in the 1950s, sponsored by Oldsmobile. She used to see glimpses of it on the old black-and-white Dumont that her parents had in their living room.

But why was Marty watching an old Doug Edwards tape? He wasn't a nostalgia buff, and history definitely wasn't his fetish. He was a bit of a TV hound, though, and maybe he'd simply acquired an old TV tape to remind himself of the early days of the medium. Or maybe he was doing research for some public-relations project. What did it matter?

But why was he watching a tape while the trains were running?

Still, Samantha was tired and Marty was probably overflowing with happiness, so what was the difference?

Marty watched the tape, mesmerized. He remembered how Doug Edwards had sounded that horrible night. He remembered the calm, even tones, the undramatic delivery, the straightforward manner.

Everything was ready.

The trains were running.

Doug Edwards was on the Model 30.

Marty looked around. Was there anything out of order? He focused on the portrait of Samantha that Len Ross had gushingly given to him on behalf of the staff. Who needed *that* in the living room? He took it and placed it in the kitchen, out of the way, out of sight.

He was ready for the last great ritual before the act. It was 12:48 A.M.

Marty slowly walked back into the bedroom. Again, Samantha pretended to be asleep. Marty went to her side of the bed. He reached down and grasped a small alarm clock on her night table.

Samantha sensed his presence and barely opened an eye to see what he was doing.

Marty picked up the alarm clock.

He started turning it back.

Back exactly one hour.

Back to 11:48.

Back to December fifth.

Now a spike of fear so sharp it seemed to slice her in half shot up Samantha's spine.

Marty walked to the clock on his desk. He turned it back. It had a calendar. Samantha watched with one eye as the "6" became "5."

Why?

What was going through the mind of the father-to-be?

Frozen with fear, Samantha listened as Marty left the room and walked around the apartment. She heard him stop several times. The direction of the sound told the story.

He was stopping at wall clocks.

He was turning back the time.

He was turning back the date.

December fifth...again.

No, Samantha thought, it couldn't be true. He wasn't actually going to do anything. That was foolish. Stupid. This was just some little fetish, something she didn't understand, maybe something immature and boyish. That's all it possibly could be, and yet she remained in bed, still paralyzed with fright. So many strange things had happened recently.

Marty stood in the living room, observing what he'd done and finding it good. It was so much like that night in 1952. It was more like it than the nights of the other murders, which often had to be done outside. This was ideal. This was the way it should be.

"I hope you're proud of me, Dad," he said. He did not whisper. Samantha heard him. What was *this*? "I've done everything I could, Dad. You hear the Doug Edwards program, don't you? Sure you do. And listen to those trains. The same ones you got me, Dad. I've got them set up right, the way you did."

Samantha could stand the suspense no longer. She

lurched out of bed and started walking slowly toward the living room to see for herself.

"Everything is the same, Dad," Marty went on. "That's what I've tried to do."

Samantha reached the edge of the living room and gazed in. Marty immediately saw her. "What's going on?" she asked.

He did not answer. He just stared at her.

"Tell me," she insisted.

Marty glanced at a wall clock. It said 11:53. After staring at Samantha a few more seconds, he started moving his lips, but no words came out. A quaint, questioning look appeared on his face. Then the sound of his voice came, soft, kind, almost reverent.

"I'll get a job," he said.

"Marty, you *have* a job," Samantha answered. "You run a company." What's happened to him? What's gone wrong?

"I just wanted him to have these trains," Marty went on. "He's always wanted them."

"Who, Marty?"

"Not in front of the children, Alice!"

"Alice?" Samantha asked. "Who's Alice? Marty, what are you talking about?"

"Frankie loves the trains."

"Frankie?" And then Samantha remembered. Frankie Nelson was the name of the boy in Omaha, the boy who, Cross-Wade had said, grew up to be the calendar killer.

Oh my God, it's true! Samantha realized it. No doubt. There could be absolutely no doubt. Frankie *was* Marty. *This* was Frankie, drowning in his own past, his mind a prisoner of December 5, 1952.

He'd turned back the clocks and date.

It *was* December fifth.

He was going to kill. Samantha knew it. And there were no police. There was no protection. There was nothing. She was alone with him.

"I'm not a bum," Marty said. "I need a break."

"Of course you're not a bum," Samantha answered. What could she say? Humor him. Maybe he'd stop.

"Not in front of the children, Alice!"

"Of course not."

Maybe she should scream. But that would panic Marty and, by the time someone responded, it could all be over. Run for the door? He'd surely catch her. No, the only chance was pure, agonized self-defense. Samantha was trapped and she knew it.

"Maybe they'll find out about you!" Marty blurted out. "Where'd you spend the night, Alice?"

"Marty, what are you saying?"

"Where'd you spend the *night*?"

"Here, Marty, here."

"Not in front of the children, Alice!"

"Never, Marty."

Suddenly, Marty started stalking back into the bedroom. He stopped. "Come with me!" he ordered.

"Why?"

"Come with me!"

Samantha eyed the front door. Marty stood in her way. He'd never let her by. She walked with him into the bedroom. "I'll find the money for the trains somewhere," he said.

"Of course you will."

The attaché case was no longer under the bed, Marty having taken it out to get the tape. It was leaning against a night table. Now Marty lunged for it. In a flash, he pulled out the hammer and chain.

"Oh my God!" Samantha screamed.

The sight of the weapons was the ultimate confirmation of her deepest fears. She saw an opening, a clear path to the front door. She bolted.

Marty was faster.

He stopped her, tripped her. She rolled over and over. "Don't do that!" he ordered. "I want you here, Mom!"

Samantha sprung to her feet. "I'm not Mom! I'm Samantha, Marty. I'm not her!"

Marty didn't answer.

He charged at her.

He raised the hammer.

Samantha screamed, then grabbed a lamp, hurling it at Marty. It hit him, a metal point puncturing his arm. He stared at the blood. "You're not nice, Mom. A nice mom doesn't hurt her Frankie. You were never nice."

He came at her again. She snaked around furniture, finally grabbing an alarm clock and trying desperately to turn the hours ahead once more. "December sixth, Marty. December sixth."

But Marty swung the hammer at her, knocking the clock from her hands. It smashed to the floor before she could change it.

She saw another opening. She shot past Marty. He caught up with her. She broke away. He blocked her path to the front door. She bolted for the kitchen. There were knives there. *Knives.*

He trapped her in the kitchen.

"Not in front of the children, Alice!"

He said it over and over.

"It's too late, Marty," Samantha pleaded. "It's December sixth. Nothing will change that, Marty. Turning back the clocks won't change it. You're too late. You can't kill me. It's not part of the game."

"Not in front of the children, Alice!"

Samantha went for the silverware drawer, throwing it open. She thrust out her hand to grab a knife.

She was stunned.

There were no knives.

They had all been used for the party and were in the dishwasher...next to Marty.

Samantha had nothing. She had given back the Mace.

It was all over. She was sure of that.

Marty walked slowly toward her. She backed against the counter, too frightened to scream.

Marty's face broke out in a strange, mystical grin. "Dad,"

he said, "this is for you." He lifted the hammer above his head.

Suddenly there was an enormous thud behind him.

The apartment's main door swung open.

Samantha saw only a blur, then a flash. Her ears rang from the sharp report.

She heard a horrid, choking groan.

Marty's grin turned to shocked surprise.

He collapsed to the floor.

"It's finished," Spencer Cross-Wade said, holding his service revolver and looking compassionately at Samantha. "I'm sorry it ended this way."

Samantha hardly heard. Her ears were still deafened from the sound of the gunfire. Shock overwhelmed her body, her senses. She barely saw Cross-Wade standing before her. But in a few moments she felt his supporting arm around her shoulders, leading her out of this room of horrors. As he did, she glanced down and saw her portrait, now splattered with Marty's blood, oozing across her face, staining the auburn hair that had symbolized Marty's obsession.

"Sit down," Cross-Wade said to her as they reached a couch in the living room. "Try to be calm. You're safe now. There is no more danger."

Samantha closed her eyes, trying to rebound from the convulsion that had struck her world. Cross-Wade looked around and saw the electric trains still running, the tape of Douglas Edwards still beaming forth, in its 1950s grainy glory, from the old Model 30. He stopped the trains. He snapped off the tape machine. The remnants of Marty's past were suddenly quiet.

"How did you know?" Samantha softly asked the man who had just saved her life.

"One might call it the detective's instinct," Cross-Wade answered. "I was riding home and I looked at my watch. It suddenly occurred to me: It had turned December sixth here, but it was still December fifth in the one place that mattered...Omaha, Nebraska. They are an hour behind.

Marty may have lived here, but on this one day his mind slipped back to Omaha time."

"He turned back the clocks," Samantha whispered.

"Yes...to Omaha time. Your husband wanted perfect vengeance. He tried to duplicate, as exactly as he could, his night of nightmares in 1952."

"It wasn't Marty who tried to kill me tonight," Samantha insisted, still speaking in a whisper. "It was Frankie."

"Precisely."

"I will always love Marty," Samantha said.

"I hope you will," Cross-Wade replied. He got up, walked to the phone, and put through a call to the coroner's office.

It *was* over. The terror of the calendar schizophrenic had come to an end.

Epilogue

Marty was buried four days later. Samantha had never thought about his death, and he had left no instructions or preferences. But now Samantha knew who he really was, and how he really felt. So she flew his body back to Omaha and had him buried in the little cemetery he had visited often... beside Dad. He was buried under his real name, Frank Nelson, which would appear on the headstone. And Samantha made sure that Dad's grave was neatened, and the stone set straight.

She had invited Marty's friends to come to Omaha with her, but understood that the cost, and the scandal surrounding his death, would keep the number low. In fact, only one friend came—Tom Edwards, forever Samantha's rock, the man she knew she could depend on. He made all the arrangements with a funeral home in Omaha, secured the legal papers, even ordered flowers. Most of the people he dealt with assumed he was one of Samantha's close relatives.

In the months following Marty's death, some of Samantha's friends drifted away, believing Samantha somehow tainted by the calendar schizophrenic saga, which was reported in detail in all the papers. Lynne, at her husband's insistence, was correct but not close. But Tom was thoroughly devoted, caring, giving of himself. He started visiting Samantha every day, taking her to dinner, sometimes to a movie or a Broadway play. He even drove her to the doctor's as the baby grew nearer to term.

Tom and Samantha became close, and Samantha developed a deep feeling for him. He was becoming so much like Marty, the Marty before Frankie took over. Maybe he was emulating Marty, maybe he'd idolized him. Samantha liked that, for she still clung to the side of Marty she always wanted to remember.

The baby, a boy, was born on schedule. Samantha asked Tom for his advice on a name. Tom had only one answer: Martin Everett Shaw, Jr. And so Marty Jr. came into the world.

Tom and Samantha grew even closer after the birth, with Tom coming over and taking Samantha and Marty Jr. out for strolls three or four times a week. It was inevitable: Fourteen months after Marty's death, Tom and Samantha were engaged.

Just before the small wedding, Tom told Samantha he wanted to visit Marty's grave. He wanted to go alone, he said, to pay his respects to his closest friend, perhaps to say a few words silently.

Samantha was so moved. It made her love Tom more. She respected his privacy, and so he flew back to Omaha and went to the cemetery.

It was an icy, miserable day as he entered the cemetery's gates.

He approached Marty's grave and stood over it.

And he did say a few words:

"I think of you every single day. No one knows what we were to each other. No one suspects. I'll marry her soon, and carry on for you. I'll do what you wanted to do...for you, and for Dad. This I solemnly pledge to you. December fifth will come. She doesn't know this time. She won't get away. Rest well, my brother."

He left the gravesite.

Two weeks later Samantha Shaw joined Thomas Edwards in a chapel, and became his lawful wedded wife.

The next day, Tom took a train to Queens and bought a hammer and chain.